Creaking Floorboards

COLBOURNE MILLER

Synopsis

Ian Wills has already lived a fully rounded life. His background was privileged. He's travelled the world and worked some peculiar jobs. A good-looking guy, somewhat of a misfit, never having reached his full potential, he's struggling with his current predicament...

'We're all full of tears but only
the bravest let them flow...'

'When you're doing what you
want nothing else matters...'

'From the misfit is
born a genius...'

Colbourne Miller

Colbourne Miller's

Creaking Floorboards

A Clement Ivan Publication

First published in Great Britain by *Clement Ivan*, 2015
www.clementivan.com
Copyright © Colbourne Miller 2015
Cover © Colbourne Miller 2015

www.colbournemiller.com

Paperback ISBN 978-1-910973-00-4
eBook .Mobi ISBN 978-1-910973-01-1
eBook .ePub ISBN 978-1-910973-02-8

For Mum and Dad, to all my friends and family, the people in my life, past and present, and all the loving animals who helped me through each day.

Friday 19th September 2008

Seven years. No, seven and a third years! Bloody hell, that's how I just turned forty-one. It's true what they say, 'blink and you'll miss it'. Sometimes I wish I had missed the last seven, not forgetting the third... seven and a third years! 'Life begins at forty', 'You're as old as you feel', 'Everyday is a new day', 'One door closes and another one opens'. A complete pile of old humbug! Bullshit! Wishful thinking! At this age one door closes and the next one slams straight in your face.

I have spent the last month glued to the *Beijing Olympics* and *Paralympics*. It's a funny thing to watch, in an odd sense I mean. It stirred up lots of emotions and has turned me into a pathetic quivering wreck as I have, on a painfully daily basis, compared my troubled life to the truly amazing feats of these *superheroes*. To any right-minded person this is, clearly, a rather stupid and extreme exercise, doomed to failure... I feel like I have gone through the menopause, twice. Not that I am an informed expert on the menopausal process. However, when I recall the behaviour of some of my friends' mothers' whilst in my late teens I can now appreciate that the erratic and somewhat extreme character transformations were undoubtedly manifestations of the aforementioned condition...

Mind you, when you're a moody hormonal teenager who never stops *wanking* and has recently found a small damp hole down some spotty girl's knickers you think every adult is a frigging old *psycho*... Invariably, anyone over the tender age of twenty five is deemed *boring*, as they are at the beginning of the lifelong poverty and commitment trap and you are at the starting gates of sexual experimentation and liberation... Rather ironically the over twenty fives now find themselves committed and inexorably tied to all those things that they themselves rebelled against just a few short years ago. They are doomed to a life of false hopes, property value highs and lows, nepotism, jealousy and 'keeping up with the Joneses'. Like generations before they will go through all this suffering and thankless sacrifice in order to feel *normal*. To breed, carry on the lineage. To produce ungrateful *sprogs*, who, sooner rather than later, never cease to insult and undermine you. They bleed you dry, age you, your fresh-faced looks rapidly turn into a washed-out skeleton covered in a layer of ever thinning skin, where day by long-suffering day your veins become more like an embossed road map and your hair disappears from where it is aesthetically pleasing, only to prominently reappear in the most unpleasant and difficult-to-maintain regions of your increasingly saggy body.

The thing with children is that they are great to start with, when all is new and exciting. The first bloodstained appearance of the *little angel*, who is genetically predetermined to turn into a replica of one of the parents or, worse still, a combination of the pair of you; the first smile, first tear, first noise, first word it utters, first full head of hair, first tooth, etc. Gradually, as time passes, old friends that you grew up with and were an integral part of your youth slowly fade away. They have kids, you do or don't, but we all move around and your life keeps being reborn. As a man you invariably end up with a few old friends, if you are lucky, or indeed allowed any! Certainly any female friends, even the ones you haven't slept with, are no go areas, totally off-limits... Your social circle begins to revolve around the school gate, the parents of children your wife/partner has selected and, for reasons unbeknown to you, deemed appropriate company. Their motives might be due to a real fondness for the person or persons concerned but, more than likely, the rationale would have more to do with social standing, increasing your market value through association with the appropriate company. Whatever the reasons, you end up with these *bloody people* being foisted upon you, and that's that! They probably loathe you with equally large bucketloads of venom, but through mutual convenience you are now inextricably bonded by a foul-smelling and hard-to-prize-apart long-lasting adhesive.

On the rare occasion you are allowed to actually meet up with old friends you either click straight back into the 'good old days' or you have absolutely nothing in common as they have had their personality suitably removed by their partner, whom you always detested. This can happen to an old male or female friend. With an old female friend, the one who was always the life and soul, up for anything, free-spirited and everybody wanted to shag, but no one did, for unfortunately the one thing she wasn't was a slut, it is particularly distressing to witness. On first appearance there she is, just the same, although older of course; however, it soon becomes apparent that she is horribly trapped and is now a shadow of her former self, she looks totally lost, dazed and soulless, and the husband/partner is normally the most pompous twat you have ever, and I mean ever, met.

Anyway, I thought the *Olympics* were amazing... What I wouldn't give or do to have an *Olympic medal!* Bronze, silver, any colour would do, although gold would be bound to make one's head swell to alien proportions. People would be throwing themselves at your feet, queuing around the block to give your sanctified body a free *Blow Job* just for the privilege of momentarily touching it.

Remember them, *Blow Jobs?* As a teenager I can distinctly remember my first *Blow Job* and it bloody hurt. 'The Biter' we used to call her. Not very original I know, but that's what she did, hence she ended up with that rather unfortunate nickname. However, there was a plus point to having your young and tender *cock* chewed to kingdom come! Bloody amazing actually, for a man of any age! She was famous for her open-mindedness: prudes would consider her notorious! Due to other teenager fumbles I subsequently learnt that she was the only girl who didn't gag. She even let you come in her mouth, and swallowed the lot too! She was absolutely amazing. An ecstatic head rush more than made up for the soreness of a chewed manhood... How much more thrilling could a naïve country teenager's life become, I remember rhetorically declaring to myself soon after the event... Added to which it didn't matter that I was devoid of tissue paper! Mind you, had the initiation taken place in my bedroom rather than a dark wood, and had she been unwilling to clean up, this would not have been an issue for small balls of stuck-together loo roll would have obligingly appeared from under my pillow, bed, desk draw or countless other nooks and crannies of my sperm smelling digs!

I am sure this scenario was and still is played out in bedrooms of adolescents throughout the land: Places where mothers tread carefully, venture in at their peril, so wait until we are at school or out doing things we shouldn't. Then in they dash, holding their breath in the vain hope that they won't suffer the misfortune of inhaling that clammy teenage aroma of sperm mixed with out-of-control hormones. *En route* to the window, which they are determined to open so the overpowering smell can escape to the outside world, they stumble over plates of half-eaten food, glasses partially full with various coloured liquids that have been there so long that they have formed their own mould-encrusted tops, a mixture of dirty and clean clothes, an assortment of half-opened books, laptops and other gadgets that they don't understand, then last but by no means least they come face to face with our crusty *semen rags...* They know what we are up to, after all they quite probably live with our father and he has a *cock*! Regular sex between them more than likely evaporated long ago so she probably comes across his *semen rags* too, so to speak... Regardless of their obvious knowledge of our regular meat-beating, the subject of masturbation is never ventured into. A great taboo is masturbation, between mothers and sons at least, although this is not a subject you really want to discuss with your mother, or indeed your father, so the *quid pro quo* suits all parties equally... However, in this in-your-face world I am sure there are parents out there who positively relish such conversations with their unassuming little creations. We can all remember getting erections, fiddling with ourselves for the first time, fiddling with it constantly, and then quite naturally rubbing it up and down, literally to kingdom come. So the bloody *Do-Gooders* can rest assured that their little intellectual *Johnny* knows exactly how to do it and where to put it to make a baby too. So leave the poor *Johnnies* alone, I say... Not that this will ever stop these nosey, interfering, sanctimonious, hypocritical, loathsome people who, unfortunately, appear to be everywhere in the modern world.

Life is something that we all have to endure, so complaining rarely makes any sodding difference; an *orgasm*, on the other hand, seems to help you forget about almost everything. It's just for that split second though, for me anyway, as during the build-up I often focus on things I have to do, things I'd like to do, things I'd like to do to someone in particular, then *POW* you're right back there again with that person. If that feels comfortable, then I suppose you've found your one: the one most suited to be in a bed with, to share your fragile life. Nevertheless, that nagging 'what if' feeling still tends to haunt the peripheries of even the most furtive minds. However, the first half of your life is over and this is where you are, in the here and now. You can't go back to the naïve idealistic world of youth, with all its fantastical aspirations and the time to philosophise your future away… No, time stands still for no man. Which sounds rather crass, but is a definitive fact. 'Yes Sir. You fucked up. I fucked up, ninety nine per cent of us fucked up…'

Saturday 20th September

It's bloody hot today. Not that I'm complaining, especially after the rubbish August weather. I love it! I am happily sprawled out on my hardwood *Steamer Chair*, in the lovely little oasis that is my suburban garden.

There was a time when it was *de rigueur* to possess a *Steamer Chair*, which is quite understandable as, unlike inferior softwood, they do not rot. They last for bloody years and require very little maintenance. Though, nowadays, in order to preserve the rainforest they are being shunned in favour of metal and moulded plastics. Of course no one wants to destroy the rainforest, but is polluting oil-based plastic production and smelting minerals at high temperatures the best alternative? Recently, I have noticed some sustainable hardwood outdoor furniture in my local Garden Centre! Which was a welcome find, if not a little questionable! Are these people really going to wait fifty years or more for the teak to grow big enough to, at the very best, carve out a child's foot-stall? Maybe far fewer people on the planet would be a better way of preserving the rainforest! Failing that, we could all have an everlasting hardwood *Steamer Chair* that could be passed down the generations, the only condition being that a hardwood tree is planted every spring when you bring your faithful *Old Steamer* out of winter hibernation.

I'm sure that astronomically overpriced *teak oil* they sell in minuscule cans is a total con! What's wrong with cheap bog-standard *olive oil* to preserve this *colonially English* essential? I'm definitely going to try that this winter. In fact, this will be the first time I've oiled it at all, which is very naughty of me, but as a consequence my *Steamer* possesses a rather distinguished weathered look, with just the right number of surface cracks to give it charm and mystery in equal measure.

To lie, near-naked, on my reclined *Steamer* with the warm sun penetrating my bronzing torso slowly draws me into a state of drowsiness, where my mind wanders at leisure. I imagine myself back in India, at *The Rambagh Palace Hotel*, without a modern day tourist in sight. I am an *English Civil Servant* relaxing with a ubiquitous gin and tonic, the quinine doing wonders for my state of health, especially my libido! I am just returned from my district on the Rajasthan plains for a weekend in the *Pink City...* Tonight, after cocktails and some considerable feasting, I shall have my pleasures fulfilled by two local women in a brothel within the city walls. Sexually placated, I shall return to the hotel and happily proceed to dance the night away. Several hours before dusk, at the coolest time in the twenty-four-hour cycle, I shall accompany a young colonel and his wife to their rooms. His wife has recently arrived from England to join him, as he has been posted back to the *Pink City* to pacify the Maharajas. She is an actress, well known for her dalliances with theatrical contemporaries, men and women alike. She is truly liberated in the *Bloomsbury* way, and we all engage in the most wonderful coitus. At one point, to steady the quivering ship, the Colonel and I engulf her from both sides, clasping one another in a high five. The vessel we are eagerly steering duly erupts with multiple tremors which filter up from deep within the wild and treacherous confines of the sea bed. Our anchors remain steadfast and solid, inserted in the moist, slippery holes at either end of the rocking ship. Eventually they become increasingly jilted by the ever-ferocious storm, slipping further outwards from wetter and wetter receptacles only to plunge back in, further and deeper than before. The storm rages on and on, wailing low-pitched grunts and high-octane shrills become more and more exaggerated, the inclement weather is nearing its climax, the swell of the ocean is enormous, nothing can stop its progress now. An almighty explosion consumes the battered ship, she is rapidly filling and sinking with the weight of tons of white-crested sea water, the bruised anchors unable to hold her a moment longer; then, without warning, the anchors begin to soften, their metal melts away and within moments they are gone, without a trace... Breakfast is a quiet and blissfully happy affair. All three of us have been to heaven and back; we are young, virile experimentalists with the world at our feet. Afterwards, brimming with contentment, we part with our celestial memories intact: useful tools in coping with our old age!

It's the heat. I find it is, anyway. Along with a decent amount of chest hair! I'm sure I'm correct in assuming that men with definitively hirsute chests are far more sexually liberated, and altogether hornier than the more smooth-skinned among us. Apologies in advance to *Smoothies*: I have to admit, I've always been rather envious of *Smoothies*... As a younger man I desperately wanted to be one, often shaving down my body hair. In fact I once shaved off all my pubes, bum and sack hair: nearly completing a forerunner to the modern-day 'back, sack and crack'. If only I had known, I would have already made my fortune. I have to say it did look rather odd, as my hairiness was considerably disproportionate. However, I'm sure that I'm not the only man, or woman, who in a brief moment of self-titillated excitement, or just plain old boredom, has exemplified this look. If you have tried, or are now seriously thinking of trying this, my top tip is to leave at least three millimetres of hair unshaved. Go for the designer-stubble effect; it looks cooler, makes your genitalia appear acutely larger, but best of all it doesn't itch like buggery when it starts its inevitably rapid re-growth. I realise that some women may not want their genitalia to look acutely larger, so if you fall into this category please don't try this at home!

The other night I was watching a programme, God only knows why as I hate telly at the best of times, where all these women were desperate to have their *'flaps'* sliced off so they would appear more *petite!* Quite mad, if you ask me: what's wrong with ladies' *flaps*? They're a kin to an entrance sign… Next door's pussy has just jumped over the fence! I love it. It's blue/grey in colour, like one of those Weimaraner dogs. It has stunningly enticing amber eyes with complementing jet-black pupils and fur like silk, which I am desperate to stroke. The feline tease has been playing with me for over two weeks now, ever since the neighbours left and took their moggy with them. Moggy and I were the best of friends, but now she has gone this thoroughbred beauty has incorporated my garden into her patch. However, in order to have any chance of stroking her I shall quite simply have to bide my time, and wait until she stops playing with me. It's such a very small thing to crave and sounds completely mental, but in my little world it's something akin to a sexual challenge, the thrill of the chase and all… Once I have stroked this thoroughbred, which will happen, I shall be thinking about the next encounter and then the subsequent ones, until it all becomes very familiar, and we all know what that breeds..! Cats, unlike us mere mortals, seem to be masters of contempt, without the need for familiarity at all; which, to women, more than likely sounds like the description of a man, their husbands even. The male of the species is not so far removed from the cat family, for we also have the ability to compartmentalise our lives. Sex is sex, sport is sport, food is food, work is shit and love is sex. Simple!

Returning to the subject of heat! Heat from the sun I mean, not stifling central heating, which I abhor. A few years ago I had a German girlfriend who loved the central heating on full blast. It was bloody awful, like living in a sauna. A friend of mine is still married to one, and she's just the same. They try and cook you! It's like slow torture (dodgy ground, I know) and it's probably done purposely, to get rid of you with little fuss…. Pussy just came back, she was within three feet of a stroke, but quickly did an about-turn and jumped back over the fence. She's either a stroppy female or a bloke doing a bunk…. Well, it worked; the unbearable central heating, I mean. She was stunning: five feet ten inches tall, a natural blonde with legs up to her armpits. Alas, it subsequently transpired that she was a barking-mad control freak, and as it is patently unsafe to have two *nutters* living under one roof there was no way I was going to move in with her. A lucky escape on both our parts, I suspect.

We English love heat, and we just don't care what shade of red we turn. Even when I am drowning in Factor 25, it still happens. Everywhere goes brown, barring my face. Oh, and my *willy*, of course. They both end up looking like the pinkest parts of a well-cooked lobster. Still, I suppose a red *willy* is the price you pay for the primeval urge to sunbathe naked. On the other hand, eating whilst sunbathing in the *buff* is tricky, and best avoided! Particularly biscuits, cake or sandwiches, for they always tend to crumble, and invariably end up nestled all over your pubic bush. Advantage the *shavers!*

Foreign language lessons have started up next door.

Initially I thought it was Russian but I think it's more likely to be Lithuanian or Polish. I believe Lithuania was once part of Poland, so I'm sure the languages have some similarities. They're rather unfriendly and sullen-looking at the best of times, listening to their overly loud vocals and harsh downbeat tones quite an affront to the ears of a softer-spoken Englishman. However, all these irritations pale into insignificance when they decide to turn on the CD player and blare out their awful *Europop Rave Infused* noise! It's horrendous. Multiply the worst song in the *Eurovision Song Contest* by ten and you are just about at the right level of irritation. The weekends are the worst. Saturday night has gone on until five a.m. before now. Another favourite is to constantly block my car in! Even though I politely ask them to refrain from this selfish activity, they just grunt at me, then repeat the scenario a few days later. I put the attitude problem down to decades of subjugation. Their minds now battling against their conformist communist psyche, still not completely able to cope with a newfound environment of excessive freedoms!

Fortunately, this problem usually only rears its ugly head at the weekend, for during the week they are too busy undercutting our tradesmen, who seem to be leaving for Australia by the dozen. But when the noise, which they pass off as music, does go on, it is always pumped up to the max. Consequently, every part of my body, house and garden vibrates to the irritating, mind-numbing beat. Last night I reached my optimum tolerance level and had a little neighbourly chat with one of the insidious protagonists. He was slightly apologetic, but I wait with bated breath!!

Back to *undercutting...* It only lasts a while, until the newcomers become aware of the going rates, and the expense of this country becomes apparent then they soon want a pay rise. However, it sadly appears that our *Child Suited Masters* don't get it, couldn't care less, or are just plain stupid. Take your pick..!! A family man with a mortgage and bills to pay needs a fair rate of pay. Five Eastern Europeans renting rooms in a similar property can undercut him and send loads of cash home to boot, where the money is worth considerably more and can set them up for life!

When we've been displaced from our low-paid jobs (check unemployment rates before *Tony Blair* allowed them open access to our labour markets) and the economy falters as they're sucking money out the country and putting little back in, they can either return home with wads of cash or join our burgeoning benefits bonanza. In fact, I believe this is already happening. *Quelle surprise..!* Only Sweden, Ireland and the good old UK have allowed this free-for-all. Other Western European nations, being far less obsequious towards the *'Bullies of Brussels'*, pragmatic, and altogether more circumspect, have sensibly implemented a seven-year restriction on *open access* to their labour markets (since 2004), in order to allow a degree of economic convergence. Still, our 'wiser' leaders have a propensity to keep the indigenous people at the bottom of the pile. If you dare to confront them on this lunacy you're in danger of finding yourself in very hot water, a lot of bother even. At the very least you'll have your name detrimentally touted around by these loathsome self-righteous, self-promoting, champagne-swilling liberals; and if that doesn't shut you up they, aided and abetted by the partisan BBC, can ultimately destroy your reputation in a flash by publicly branding you a fascist, racist pig! Seems quite reasonable, really...

Monday 22nd September

Night has fallen. It is just before eight p.m. and it is pitch black. Now we can all complain incessantly that the evenings are drawing in, it'll soon be Christmas, how time flies, we never had a summer this year, we cannot afford to turn the heating on, and there are Christmas decorations in our local garden centre and it's only September! Unfortunately all the above are true… It was a very observant family member who informed me of the *Christmas decorations* situation. Apparently they've nearly finished building the grotto in readiness for the throngs of snotty-nosed, totally spoilt, tattoo-bearing, *X Factor-Wannabe*, anaemic-looking kids. After all, their wish list of imported Chinese goods becomes longer and longer as prices for non-biodegradable crap goes into freefall, so it seems perfectly prudent to start a little earlier each year.

Alas, prudence belongs to a bygone age: as 'The Credit Crunch', or 'Greedy Fat Bastards Failure Crunch', has all too painfully reminded us when *The Masters of the Universe*, those ever-so-talented, articulate and oversized claret-swilling baboons that gamble with our futures came tumbling back to earth. Unsurprisingly, when the frenzy of greediness turns into a competition as to who can ride a tightrope the longest whilst simultaneously balancing the country's savings on the tip of their nose, they fuck up. However, the longer they can master this insane balancing act the bigger the bounty, perhaps another shiny new car, a yacht or more property for their portfolio, at some ridiculously inflated price of course! It's a win-win situation, as even when the cards inevitably start to tumble, along come the *Great British Public* in the form of our pathetic *Prime Minister* and, hey presto, they are instantly re-indulged with more of our hard-earned cash to replace the billions they have already gambled down some mid-Atlantic toilet!

If only I knew how the system worked when I was starting out! But, regrettably, I was brought up in a family business environment with little knowledge or insight into the dark and murky world of *Merchant Wankers*... Over the years, I have had the unfortunate pleasure of rubbing the expensive *Savile Row* shoulders of some of these creatures, by and large finding them to be as repugnant, greedy, egotistical and shallow as I imagined. However, one can at least say that they are consistent, rather akin to that famous wood stain which does exactly what it says on the tin.

My cynicism could come across as *sour grapes*, which is more than likely true! Who wouldn't enjoy the fat pay cheque, fine dining, fast cars and countless freebies? My problems would start with my refusal to conform and lick the right arses. This would inevitably lead to conflict, with me telling my boss to 'piss off, you arrogant, stupid, brown-nosed little cretin,' or words to that effect! Hence I have been accepted as a *Local Delivery Agent!* Not for the *Russian Mafia*, nor a *Multi Level Marketing Company* or even a *TV Debt Recovery Firm*. I have gone through an arduous internet sifting system, been spewed out to an *HR Call Centre* in Manchester, sent and received megabytes of emails, had a preliminary interview and thorough assessment to become a *Local Delivery Agent* for a leading supermarket chain... The irony is that I am highly likely to be distributing my fair share of the aforementioned *Christmas Decorations*, as well as considerable amounts of totally unnecessary packaging. Still, 'every little helps', 'try something new today', and so forth. *'Whatever!'* I think I might need to nail the catchphrase before the all-important induction weekend. I'm actually quite excited: a full weekend of activities; this *Local Delivery Agent* malarkey could be the making of me! Roll on Saturday, nine a.m.

If whizzing around suburbia in a company delivery van doesn't set my world alight and pull in the beautiful people, then I have 'Plan B' up my sleeve! Geography and History were my most successful subjects at school so it seems perfectly feasible that I could pursue a career in the media, television preferably. I have always loved travel and had an interest in other cultures. I sound like some *Drag Queen* at an over-aged *Beauty Pageant!* Anyway, this brainwave has nothing to do with the fact that I have just watched *Bruce Parry* swanning down the Amazon meeting indigenous tribes whilst partaking in all sorts of weird and wonderful rituals..! What's wrong with a *mid-life crisis?* I bet everyone who passes the age of forty is having, will have or has had one…

Perhaps a *mid-life crisis* can be deemed to be finally over when you don't feel the need to say *cunt* simply to shock or embarrass people for no apparent reason! I rather suspect that my crisis is and will be perpetual, as I could never envisage dropping the use of this vulgar, inane, insulting word. A crude one I know, however it is a wonderful conversation-stopper and has the ability to encompass all your intended meaning without the need for a rant or diatribe. Nowadays, its connotation is more than an ugly description of the *vagina* and therefore not a derogatory term aimed solely at women. Its power is far greater and, as with other swear words, is now part of the current mainstream vernacular.

My gin and tonic has really kicked in now. That's the beauty of being, what I consider, a casual drinker; you only need one stiff drink and you're off. However, in order to stave off alcoholism and succeed as a *casual drinker* you simply have to abide by the rules of the game. Never have a routine!

Tuesday 23rd September

The ability for one's mood to change is quite incredible... Every morning I wake up to the extremely annoying alarm tone on my mobile phone. The tune is now so familiar that I hum to the beat and fall asleep between the repeats, only to wake again on cue for the next round. After three or four repeats it becomes intermittent white noise and I just stare at my bedroom ceiling, feeling morose and not wanting to ever surface. Wouldn't it be better to sleep the day away? This I have tried, though it's quite a hard task to master as you invariably become wider and wider awake, so much so that in the end you are far too conscious to conquer the art of self-enforced sleep. By now the time is fast approaching eleven o'clock, you've wasted the morning, you're a bear with a sore head, all that's left to do is smash your intrusive mobile phone into tiny pieces, then randomly attack your hideously egotistical neighbours.

Every morning follows the same ritual, my stomach churning and grumbling until the first loo session is over: a comforting long wee. My stomach then settles slightly, but my mind starts to run wild, which immediately sets it off again. I momentarily ponder, pace, stare, sit, then off I dash back to the loo for the inevitable main event! These are but a few of the trials and tribulations of being an HSP, a *Highly Sensitive Person* no less! I read it in some crazy self-help book, but I have to say it defines me to within a millimetre of a perfectly fitting glove. Anyway, by now I'm ready for a cup of tea and slice of thickly buttered toast: half plain buttered, and the other spread with thin-cut marmalade. Approximately one hour later, after turning the telly on and off, opening post, titivating the garden, emptying bins, staring into cupboards, writing large cheques to utility companies, and trying not to think too much, my body is ready for a cup of cafetière coffee and a further slice of fattening toast to accompany a much-needed second caffeine fix of the day. This time, half the toast plain buttered, as before, with the remaining fifty per cent covered in a thin layer of deliciously salty marmite. Heavenly!

Another trip to the loo soon follows, I procrastinate further and my mind slowly wanders, throwing up images of a new life under the olive groves of southern Italy. Every day is quite naturally perfect; the sun always shines, the people adore me, especially the olive-skinned women to whom I am a *Quintessential English Gentleman...* My residence is a beautiful little villa nestled in a sun-drenched hillside, with a westward-facing swimming pool. I never tire of the nightly sunsets, sipping *Limoncello*, legs dangling, my bronzed feet submerged in the cooling aquamarine water. *Che paradiso!* My dogs are beautiful too. One is an excitable *Welsh Border Collie*, the other a rather wilful *Chocolate Labrador* who is intent on hoovering up every spare crumb of food and windfall from my abundant fruit and olive trees, my final canine friend being a small sand-coloured *Pug* with the cutest crumpled black face you have ever seen. I'm not normally one for little dogs, usually finding them too yappy and bossy; certain small men come to mind! However, I once did some dog-sitting and that's when my love affair with the little breed began in earnest. *George* was his name, which I did find rather odd at first; nevertheless we became the best of friends, and calling his name out in public gradually ceased to embarrass me. *George* and I were simply inseparable, and everywhere I went *George* dutifully followed. Indeed, I have many photos of *George* and would love one of his little namesakes following me around one day.

I haven't made that cup of tea yet and my stomach is still a bit iffy. See, I've broken my own routine, which can happen if I'm feeling rather more anxious than usual. We all know the feeling of being over-anxious: for me this invariably occurs with regards to family affairs. Families, I am sure, are a constant roller coaster for the vast majority of the human race, so my condition is quite probably perfectly normal and therefore not a condition at all. This is how it is. Predetermined by a higher power, out of our control...

Will my mother telephone this morning? Should I call her now, later, or should I wait for her to call me! You now how it is, especially for sons: you must perform your duties as expected, natural order should always prevail. If you're telephoned you must have the appropriate amount of time to listen and speak as required, or to accompany your mother to luncheon at the stated date and time, there's no room for manoeuvre, at least not on your part anyway! When you dare to decline, stating that you can't speak now as you are at work or rushing out the door and that you'll call her later, this is not well received! You instantly realise that you have overstepped the mark, gone too far, teetered on being disrespectful, and are in for a hard, bumpy ride where you will have to conjure up all of your well-tried and tested diplomatic skills to extricate yourself from this frequently visited 'black hole'! In fact, when you dutifully call the following evening and your mother can't speak because she is, as usual, slaving over an extremely hot martyr's stove, you immediately feel guilty, selfish even. Despite your remorse she instantly regains the power in the relationship by abruptly cutting you off, whilst simultaneously managing to curse your useless father. Only mothers are blessed with such genius!

Should I phone this morning, or later? Am I being punished for the first misdemeanour, or am I becoming paranoid and creating my own HSP story? Perhaps your mother is simply busy and will phone you another time. Who knows? Mother does! However, mums are very important to sons, even though the relationship can be rather erratic and stormy at the best of times... Time for tea!

I now feel totally relaxed. Well, as relaxed as a *Highly Sensitive Person* can ever be. Tea in hand, I've just soaked away my troubles in a long hot bath: a pleasure I haven't afforded myself for around a fortnight. Showers, unfortunately, seem to be all the rage in this day and age: more ghastly continental mediocrity. Admittedly, they are quick and convenient, though in my humble opinion a bath is far superior. Granted, you soak in your own ablutions, but your muscles become more relaxed, the pores open, and as long as you clean yourself thoroughly with a well-lathered bar of *Imperial Leather* (forget all those cream soaps, they make your skin itch to buggery and beyond) the results are far longer-lasting than a quick gush of water from above. Finally, to avoid ingraining bath scum into your freshly cleansed body with your favourite fluffy towel it is imperative to first rinse one's body with the bath/shower mixer attachment. So, for a successful bathe that knocks the socks off any form of electric-power-spray or jet-propelled showering system, simply ask your *Man Friday* to draw you one. It's a far superior way to start the day!

The relaxed demeanour of the post-bath state can last for varying amounts of time. If you have children, as you will surely know, this can evaporate at the blink of an eye and it's more than likely that you will have had a quick shower instead, the whole bathing ritual consigned to a fading memory from the near or distant past: a time before *sprogs* when your partner adorned the bathroom with a ridiculous number of scented candles, bath foam rising like phoenix from the ashes, and a glass of your favourite tipple seemingly floating on a small mound of rose petals scattered around the periphery of the tub. Though, even such an unadulterated loving gesture is not without peril, as when you venture into *Cleopatra's* cauldron you inevitably kick in half of the aforementioned accoutrements with you, slip, and nearly choke yourself to death on the synthetic foamy water, then on the return journey you crack a tooth or two on the bath because there's no room to swing a cat, as this supposedly romantic crap is all over the floor as well! A damn good argument usually ensues, probably with the main protagonist being one or the other's mother. You then opt to take a shower instead and do your own thing for the rest of the evening..! Wasn't that a sign? Have I made a serious misjudgement, or am I simply deluding myself? After all, they said they would *change*, i.e. do things my way with a smile on their face... Time goes on regardless and your life continues in a vacuous and miserable time warp or you part company, throwing up different obstinate hurdles for you to contend with.

Anyone who has gone through a trauma, however severe or mild, will know that in order to maintain a modicum of sanity when you begin to come out the other side you need to keep yourself as busy as possible, so I fill any spare moment with activities. This afternoon's activity being swimming, I pedalled a mile through suburban traffic and caught the last forty minutes of the adult only swimming session at my local pool.

Once I have warmed up with a few practice lengths I'm off and away, in training for the *London Olympics*. My stomach becoming increasingly taut and muscly as I fly up and down, whizzing past the older men in *Speedos* and the sudden influx of dozens of senior ladies with sensible grey haircuts. The session is due to end soon and the men in *Speedos*, who, despite their advancing years, all posses that instantly recognisable swimmer's build, gradually disappear one by distinguished one. The local pool is not arduously long, 25 metres, quite *bijou*, which helps with the length count, sustaining morale, and exponentially increases the sense of achievement.

By now I'm in a minority, the only man left in fact. I have become pinned to the side as the misshapen mass of *Grey Ladies* fill the pool and begin to swim in a myriad of purposeless directions. Not content with invading my space they insist on swimming at the slowest speed that is physically possible without drowning! Their talents are seemingly endless, for they are able to hold full-blown conversations at the same time as idling aimlessly around the pool; not only in twos either: this they can manage in a group of three, or even as many as five! I am witnessing *multi-tasking* at a supreme level. However, I am not one to be intimidated so I continue to swim. I maintain my course, only leaving at the very last permissible moment before their *Water Aerobics Class* begins.

Upon my moment of departure I leave the pool with my head held high, whilst simultaneously inhaling and holding my breath, determined to reduce the appearance of *middle-aged spread*. Some *Grey Ladies* turn their heads to stop and stare. Who can blame them, for I am the *400 metre Freestyle Olympic Champion* in the *over-forty* category... Nevertheless, all they are interested in is my muscle-clad torso and the perfectly filled front of my funky trunks. They couldn't give a damn about my commitment, God-given ability, personal sacrifice, or arduous training regime. All they want to do is follow me into the male changing area. They dream of watching me slowly peel off my *maillot de bain* to reveal my firm butt cheeks, *perving* at me as I bend over, my manhood hanging, to step out of my water-soaked swimming trunks and slowly wring them out over the tiled floor where the smelly chlorinated liquid gradually disappears on its long journey down the soak-away to the drains beyond; peeking as I place the damp trunks on a metal hook above the slatted changing-room benches then turn to grab my towel from the adjacent hook, where momentarily I am fully exposed before wrapping it around my athletically toned body and making my way to the male shower rooms.

Whilst I'm showering a multitude of hands appear. They begin by gently caressing my body, then delight in massaging me with my favourite lathered soap! A few daring *Grey Ladies* have taken a chance and followed their lustful hearts. At first I am rather shocked, surprised, a tad tentative even; however, they quickly succeed in arousing me in a way I never imagined possible, so naturally I relent! In due course we become a rhythmic amoeba of erotic lustfulness, skipping, carefree, along the road to perdition in a frenzied sexual amalgam that finally explodes into an all-enveloping climax of gargantuan proportions... Now I have something to look forward to in life: *Retirement!*

Wednesday 24th September

Morden station, for the uninitiated, is the end of the *Northern Line Underground.* The advantage of living near the end, or beginning, whichever way you look at it, is that you are guaranteed a seat. Then, when you return from whatever you were up to in town you can simply fall asleep and wait for the public address system, or guard, to wake you up when you hit the buffers.

We are now between *Tooting Broadway* and *Tooting Bec*…. My dad's company used to supply tea to the 'loony bin' at *Tooting Bec.* At least, that's how *Cockney George*, his warehouse foreman, quite unashamedly referred to the asylum. Obviously, this wouldn't be acceptable terminology today; however, back in the 70s people didn't buy into political correctness, and he wouldn't have meant anything derogatory by it. He was just a charming Cockney geezer with Brylcreemed jet-black hair, whom everyone adored, and was one of the last men who dared to 'call a spade a spade'.

There was a big black man called *Carl* who delivered tea all over London, from 'loony bins' to regular hospitals, restaurants, hotels, offices and good old working men's cafes.

----- *Clapham Common* -----

The tube is full now, every creed and colour catered for. Upon our reaching the *Claphams* (*South, Common and North*), on climb the mainly young English professionals, not so many now though, what with the *credit crunch* and looming recession, which by all accounts is already here.

Anyway, *George* and *Carl* had the most marvellous relationship. *Carl* originally hailed from the West Indies. He came over with his parents in the 1950s, one of the *Windrush* generation. *George*, on the other hand, was one of a dying breed of working-class 'Pie and Mash Londoners', salt of the earth types.

George called *Carl* all the names under the sun, always spoken in true Cockney style with the classic roll of the shoulders, the head movements of a semi-professional boxer, a wide-eared grin and a twinkle in his eye. The more he insulted *Carl* the louder *Carl* chuckled, until, unable to contain himself any longer, the *Frank Bruno* look-alike would roar like a lion. *Carl* always gave as good as he got, heightening the atmosphere to fever pitch:

'You useless black bastard, I told you to deliver Di Paolo's first thing,' *George* would heckle.

'They was closed man so I decided to go back later... You see what I am saying, George?' *Carl* vainly responded in his mild Caribbean accent.

'You're fuckin' useless you are…. What are you?' *George* loudly remonstrated, with a wry smile.

Carl replied, 'I'm a fuckin' useless, George, fuckin' useless.'

'That's right, fuckin' useless. Now go and put the kettle on!' *George* barked, with an ever-endearing grin.

All towering six foot four inches would then gaze down at *George*: 'Yeah man, chill your bryl, I'm gonna make your honkey tea.'

Completely unacceptable now, but commonplace banter in the 1970s. Today this would be a top race case: just mention anybody's pigmentation and that's your life over! *George's* funeral was packed. *Carl* and his large family attended, as did well over a hundred mourners of all creeds and colours. He was someone whom people warmed to. Yes, a completely politically incorrect man, a racist by modern standards. Despite all this he was a uniting force. People respected his honesty, hard-work ethic and no-nonsense kind of straight talking. Everyone knew where they stood with *George*: his razor-sharp Cockney wit and fire-footed humour let him get away with murder. *George* was an old-school patriarch: he would tell anyone, no matter whom they were or where they came from, that they were, in his words, *fuckin' useless!* He obviously didn't offend as much as a twenty-first century *Pseudo-Leather-Sandal-Wearing-Do-Gooder* would have us believe, otherwise nobody would have turned up at his funeral!

----- *Kennington* -----

Shit, this is my stop... I have to change platforms here....

I've just managed to catapult myself through the closing doors without being chopped in half. I've left the suits behind, hurtling towards the *City* via the *Bank* branch of the Northern Line. I'm now among a throng of media types, art students and budding actors heading towards Embankment, Leicester Square, Tottenham Court Road and beyond. The mix is eclectic, exciting, colourful, fascinating, altogether far less repressed than the insipid men and women in suits. The only downside to the parting of the suits is the lack of expensive perfume and aftershave to sweeten the airless carriage.... But wait a moment, my nose is sensing something, an odour is definitely filling the air. Yuk! BO, body odour! It's probably one of the unwashed art students. 'Not that I'm one to stereotype,' as *George* would often say!!

Thursday 25th September

Yes, I'm back on the Underground... The lady to my right is munching on *Hula Hoops*. The smell is tolerable as they are ready-salted and not one of those ghastly synthetic flavoured varieties. It reminds me of the 70s all over again, and a childhood spent largely out of doors, whiling away endlessly hot summer days on my *Chopper Bike*, *Space Hopper* and *Skateboard*... Funny how a single smell can evoke such strong memories, and so quickly (just spotted a shocking shiny mauve tracksuit with multi-coloured orange, yellow and lime-green sleeves, inhabited by a very red-blooded-looking male) throw one back in time. Of course, then, life was much more exciting, simpler. One was a child after all, naïve and full of the carefree joys associated with a metaphorically eternal spring. It never ever rained, every summer was long and hot, all you did was play until you were physically exhausted, then, the next day you did it all over again; perfect bliss! My poor mother spent the entire summer holidays running around clearing up our mess, endlessly catering for me and my siblings, not to mention cousins and copious amounts of friends. 'Thanks Mum.'

I'm sat waiting for the train to depart. Three stops to *Charing Cross*.... We're finally off. It's lunch time. So travel conditions are bearable. Airport scanner that could read your mind! is the headline on the free paper that a South American-looking woman sitting opposite is reading. I bloody well hope not. The last thing anybody wants is for people, or even worse the state, to know what we are really thinking! We *English* would be thrown into a *Politically*

Correct Correctional Facility, forced to eat *halal* meat, our thoughts strictly overseen and monitored by an unholy alliance of *Taliban Sympathisers* and the *Do-Gooders of Islington...*

----- *Embankment* -----

Gerald Depardieu has just sat down next to me…! Why did they bother with *Charing Cross* and *Embankment* when they are only seconds apart? Thinking about it, the *Northern line* might have been built prior to all the interchanges at *Embankment*. If so, why didn't they go through *Charing Cross*, or wasn't it there then! Did they build it afterwards? Was there a 'chicken and egg' situation going on? Perhaps it was logistically easier to interchange through *Embankment*. Maybe *Charing Cross* was built solely for the overground railway connection, so people didn't have to walk the slight incline to reach it from *Embankment*. Well, I really am puzzled: something to research later.

-----*Charing Cross*-----

Told you! Here in two shakes of a lamb's tail... *Ciao* for now.....

Just got in; it's after midnight. I checked the tube map on my A-Z. *Charing Cross* has interchanges too. I don't know what's going on!

Friday 26th September

Last day of freedom before my *Induction Weekend*… It's a scorcher for the end of September. I'm back on my *Steamer Chair*, taking in the rays, with Factor 25 massaged into every crevice of my beautiful body. The washing machine cycle has just finished and that annoying intermittent *bleep* is doing its thing. *Highly Sensitive People* everywhere will know how unbearable a high-pitched recurring noise becomes. So, without further ado, this *Muscle Machine* is going to have to levitate itself and sort it out……

All done, washing hung out too. It's a perfect outdoor drying day, hot with a light breeze. Scorcher, hot, roasting, whatever you like to call it, it's about time! Summer has arrived very late this year, in true Indian style. Too many grey days in a row can turn one's thoughts in a dark and dangerous direction and may lead to the onset of *Seasonal Adjustment Disorder*, so I am very grateful the sun has decided to come out in time to save me from this condition. Being an HSP is quite enough for one lifetime, thank you!

Sunshine definitely releases endorphins, lifts the spirits and expels the grumpy gene, for a while at least. However, if it shone constantly, I'm sure it would lose its allure. People in warm sunny climes can still suffer from depression. As a matter of fact they quite often crave the weather we are over-indulged with. A Malaysian friend of mine nearly spontaneously combusted with pure unadulterated joy when she saw snow falling for the first time! Some foreigners I have spoken to love the rain and a more temperate climate, along with all the government *freebies* one would imagine! Well, if you're brought up in the equivalent of a fan oven, the only escape being awful air conditioning, which is great at spreading germs and causing colds, then I suppose our mild and damp climate must seem rather appealing. After all, if you're cold you can always put on another layer, a very abstemious English thing to do; but quite proper and now positively *de rigueur*, what with global warming and all.

Before modern heating systems and the discovery of the plastic manufacturing process we must have been a very green society. I know we were burning fossil fuels as rapidly as funeral pyres are lit in the sub-continent, but we didn't buy *shit* every five minutes. Stuff lasted a lifetime in those days. Unlike today, 'Made in England' was a byword for excellence. We recycled everything, without nanny councils' interference; packaging was limited and far more likely to be biodegradable. The Golden Years definitely belonged to my grandparents' era. My grandmother's generation had, and still do have, compost heaps, milk bottles and fizzy drink bottles were all reused, vegetables were grown in your garden or bought loose, meat was sourced locally and purchased from a High Street butcher, without being encased in the packaging version of the 'Krypton Factor'. Shopping from a grocer's shop, the civilised forerunner to the modern-day supermarket, was habitually carried away in your own lifelong bag, a cardboard box, a brown recyclable paper bag, in a hand-held wicker basket or in a basket attached to the front of your bicycle made for one, sometimes two. How times have changed!

The modern-day supermarket requires a route map and several aspirin to deal with the excessive choice on offer... Eventually you find the mayonnaise, which is probably hiding on a shelf above the frozen-food freezers. On picking it up you realise that you needed it for *Egg Mayonnaise*; a hunt for eggs ensues and some minutes later you locate them, adjacent to the marmalade, but nowhere near flour! This reminds you that you have forgotten the cress to put on top of the *Egg Mayonnaise*, so off you march, bashing several day dreamers with your trolley *en route*, back to the store entrance and the vegetable section.… Bread! You have also forgotten bread, which you need thinly cut and buttered to surround the *Egg Mayonnaise*. Bread-hunting follows. Do you want 'in-store bakery bread' or pre-manufactured 'off the shelf bread', you ask your now numbed little brain? After some time traipsing around aimlessly with your disobediently directional trolley you stumble across the bread area: which turns out to be located in the middle of the store and you have, therefore, passed this aisle at least a dozen times already on your quick shopping trip..! Still recovering from the shock of the prices, you peruse the selection. You have already discounted bread baked 'in store' as that will complicate matters too far, besides, you are likely to end up buying a massive amount of strategically placed cheap doughnuts that will only make you fatter and more angry. You also discount the 'thinly sliced value bread', as, even though you are on a tighter and tighter budget, you have already tried it and it was an indigestible failure. So you draw the line here and move along the aisle, close your eyes, and pick up something edible. The price is extortionate, but you justify it on health grounds, wishing you had bitten the bullet and headed for the 'in-store bakery' section instead… Whilst negotiating the route to the check out you grab a couple of those ever-so-cheap *T-shirts*. You can't believe the clothing prices: you see some *jeans* that are cheaper than a pack of *pork chops* but look perfectly well made, and fling them into your already overladen trolley for good measure.

Several hours later, when you eventually return home,

your 'bags for life' jump out at you as if to say, 'Why didn't you take us with you on your shopping bonanza? After all, that's what we're here for! Stupid!' Then, the guilt of the dozen or so plastic carriers you are wrestling with suddenly consumes your body, which triggers yet more guilt-ridden emotions as you realise that a small *Indian child* must have sown on the intricate pattern of shiny sequins that frivolously adorn the pockets of your *£5 jeans*. A few deep breaths later you proceed to put the shopping away and begin to hum a tune to distract your thoughts, any tune that comes into your head. It's probably a song that you overheard another on-the-edge-of-reason-person humming in the supermarket earlier.

You are now in a trance-like state but soon become distracted by the dog, your screaming kid, a knock on the door, or all three together. Your head is spinning and you are only just managing to keep it together. However, it all becomes too much as you are still worrying about the fact that you are supporting *Third World child labour*. Consequently you stumble on one of your burgeoning plastic carrier bags, which takes a thousand years to biodegrade, and the free-range eggs slip from your grasp and explode like bouncing bombs. The whole kitchen is covered. It's a white-out situation. You take in several deep breaths and your eyelids naturally close in unison… Moments later, suppressing the urge to scream uncontrollably, you gradually open your eyes again. The mess is greater than you originally thought but your dog is already at hand helping with the clear-up, enthusiastically licking the egg volcano. Your *toddler* is sat contentedly in the middle of it all, smothered in *scrambled egg* and trying, determinedly, to put an index finger up the dog's anal cavity. To cap it all, the telephone rings. It's your mother! Uncontrollable sobbing and wailing ensues.

That same evening you dress up in your new clothes... The *black T-shirt* suddenly seems too tight and has a very shiny appearance, and the *jeans* are extremely blue and have the propensity to slide off your backside, thus revealing your builder's bum to the whole wide world... When your husband, partner, etc. returns home from work they ask you if you are auditioning for a TV talent show, like *Grease is the word*. You ignore them, and by the end of the night the slimming *black T-shirt*, which was supposedly 100 per cent cotton, is soaked with *sweat marks* where it is tightly hugging your stomach, breasts and armpits. The *jeans* just refuse to stay up, even with a belt; so in the end you relent, walk around the living room stark naked, and hope for a *bunk-up* instead... If this fails you grind up some glass in a mortar and pestle and sprinkle it over the bloody *Egg Mayonnaise*, which you stupidly decided to make for your partner, seeing how it is their absolute favourite dish!!

Monday 29th September

I think the mini Indian summer is waving goodbye. Cloud is bubbling up and the westerly wind is fighting a losing battle with a south-easterly one. Consequently, I have retreated to the garden shed where I have a rather comfortable bedroom chair to park my backside upon. I like looking back towards my neighbours' houses and wondering if their lives are as dreary and frustrating as the rest of the human race's?

The *Pole* who owns the house next door is selling up. The sign has just gone up. He owns another house over the road, which is also up for sale. Now the economy is ruined he's probably decided to head home. Lucky him, he can escape with money in his pocket; meanwhile the mad social experiment our foolish masters have presided over is falling down around our feet. Still, we are the *Great British Public*: all we have to do now is tighten our belts, and *Grand Master Brown* will guide us through this ludicrous mess he unwittingly created. So, nobody need panic, just eat 'Value Baked Beans', throw on another jumper, and make sure your bills are paid on time! After all, the hierarchy have to eat....

Further *diktats* will be published by *Brown's Politburo* as and when the *Great Leader* and his *mignons* see fit. ----- See published press for details ----- All further *diktats* must be followed to the letter and enacted within ten minutes of their release, and failure to comply will result in the state nationalising your house and any business you may own. Your savings and any tangible assets will be given to foreign companies to liquidate as they see fit. Your vast mortgage, along with any debts, will become the domain of the British state, paid for by you, then, if you default, tax payers will have to chip in until your death, whereupon your children or other relatives will inherit any outstanding debts as a burden to their future slavery.

People from any country in the world, apart from Britain, will have the ultimate right to enter this country and occupy these repossessed houses. They must merely prove that they have come from a region of the world, or any planet in the solar system and beyond, where a war or any form of oppression is in operation. To prove this fact, when entering Britain, or any subsequent time that is more convenient to the aforementioned entrant, they simply have to say 'Yes' when a *Wishy-Washy Official* asks the question: 'Have you come from a region where a war, or any oppression or human rights abuses, have ever occurred?' If they do not speak English or fail to reply through fear of answering 'No', the official will answer 'Yes' for them. Everyone will receive an aforementioned state-repossessed property, free language lessons, and a twenty-four-hour translation service and *Ikea* and *Tesco* vouchers will be mandatory. 'Every little helps!'

The homeless Britons will be dealt with very severely..! Their passports confiscated in case they try to abscond to a 'life in the sun' in the booming penal colony of Australia. They will be held in holding camps in the English countryside and set to work in the fields in order to replace the exodus of Eastern Europeans returning for a better life back home. Lastly, but by no means least, they will be forever known as *'White Trash'* and forced to wear baseball caps at off-centre angles, only be allowed to wear *Burberry*, and be forever covered in chunky *Bling!!*

My Malaysian Chinese neighbours, on the left-hand side, have been busy slashing their garden to pieces. They have certainly succeeded, as they now totally overlook me.

I knew this was on the cards, but seeing the effects of their labours is quite horrific! It's true environmental sabotage. No tree, shrub, or modicum of green foliage has escaped the barbarous onslaught.

A couple of months ago, when they first moved in, the woman of the house gleefully informed me of her expansive horticultural intentions and even tried to advise me on how I might improve my lovely garden, by wielding the axe on it myself..! Her beautiful *sumac*, which turns stunning shades of red every autumn, was to go as according to madam it is a 'weed'. She then proceeded to point out that my own *sumac* tree needed to be destroyed as well..! Having gardened all my life, had a professional landscaping company and grown up around horticulture, and my own mother, like so many English people, being a passionate gardener, I found her somewhat trying. Nevertheless, I politely let the extremely tiny woman, no more than four feet ten inches in height, ramble on with her bountiful 'expert' gardening tips. When she had finished I advised her that my *sumac* was a seedling from her bigger tree, then delighted in informing her that I was deliberately leaving it, allowing it to establish itself, as I had an awful inkling that the new owners (i.e. her) would chop the beautiful mother tree back down to earth. Her husband and daughter smiled nervously, but the matriarch remained as cool as a cucumber, a consummate ice queen.... I just about managed to contain the overpowering urge of my vocal cords, silently mumbling to myself 'Fuck off and stop trying to teach an Englishman about gardening.' After all, if there is one subject we English know the most about it is more than likely to be gardening! However, I am not unduly worried. Come next year my eclectic mix of camellias, ceanothus, buddleias, lilacs, laurels, bamboo and, of course, the beautiful *sumac*, will be popping their joyful heads above the fence on their march northwards. I can only imagine her horror as she witnesses the mass horticultural advance of this contrasting green army, powerless to stop its certain dominance of our border. One nil to *Blighty!*

I nearly forgot, the Induction Weekend is all done and dusted and I am soon to start my career as a *Local Delivery Agent...*

Inductions seems to be a way of slowly trying to *brainwash* you into thinking that this company that you are about to give up half your life for is really an exciting and challenging place to work! Indeed, you already have the company slogans and buzz words imprinted on your long- and short-term memory. If required, you will strip naked and masturbate in front of your *Line Manager*. You are a *Company Man* now, somebody who would rather keep their uniform on than risk the exposure of civilian clothes. You will never purchase a product from a rival supermarket, the mere mention of a competitor's name sending shivers down your robotic spine. You obsessively idolise your *Store Manager*, as far as you are concerned he is a demigod, the nearest a low-level *mignon* such as yourself is ever likely to be to the true *leader,* at least until the final day of *judgement.*

When *Judgement Day* does arrive you will have reached the end of a long human conveyer belt. Your bar code will be scanned at the burgundy and orange gates and your history will be qualified and quantified. Your *final assessment* will be overseen by the *greatest fattest cat of all leaders.* Smugly sipping on extra-thick buffalo cream, he will determine your rebirth to a higher corporate power or, more probably, freefall into a pit of packaged waste as you are far past your *sell-by date...* You are knackered, a useless washed-up corpse, too many years of low-paid manual slavery leaving you beyond redemption. You will not 'try something new today', not this day, nor ever. You did 'spend a little' during your life but you had no choice in the matter, as after paying your mortgage and inflated bills you were too indebted to eat. 'Live'. This happened, but 'Live a lot', definitely not. Oh well, at least you benefited from being part of a 'team', being screwed over together and all!

Newsnight.... I don't know why I bother to watch it! Another bank has been nationalised in Britain, two in Europe, and the American House of Representatives have rejected the '70-Billion-Dollar White House Bail-out Plan'. Come tomorrow, I'm sure this will be old news and more banks will have mega-merged, or been rescued by the taxpayer to stave off bankruptcy. If I hear the phrase 'American sub-prime Mortgages' or 'Buy to let' mentioned one more time I think I'll quite possibly self-combust. One thing is for certain, the *Greedy Wanker Bankers* who presided over this huge gamble will not be offering to return their inflated 'bonuses for failure'. Meanwhile, we have the unadulterated pleasure of watching our house values rapidly head southwards, along with our equity and dreams of escaping to a more simple 'life in the sun'. There's no chance of selling your house now; mortgages and buyers are non-existent... Millions of us stoical *Brits* are extras in the same hideous narrative: having bought into the property hype we jumped onto yet another sinking ship of Titanic proportions, naïvely believing the propaganda that prices would keep on rising due to ever-increasing demand, smugly thinking we were sailing off into some far-flung utopian paradise. Oh well, that's what happens in this age of 'casino capitalism': 'You win some, you lose some!' Back to *boom and bust!*

To cope with the dawn of the 'age of austerity', I expect people will just opt for more *sex* and *binge-drinking*, just cheaper brands, that's all! So, if you're lucky enough to have any cash left, buying shares in condom manufacturers and brewing companies would seem to be a dead cert: they're sure to rise! Act fast and buy into the bubble early, though. Buy low, sell high; but remember to text me before the peak, so at least I can jump ship in time, this time. *Good night….*

Tuesday 30th September

I was up early today and walked into *Morden* town centre, which is not the most inspiring of walks, in fact that is probably one of the biggest understatements known to man. Even with the sun shining the suburb of *Morden*, which is actually just in the county of *Surrey*, although it is officially part of the *London Borough of Merton*, is a rather drab and uninspiring place. Although, to be fair, they have tried to inject some degree of character, having now block-paved the pavements, and the London plane trees do soften the 1930s shop fronts, when in leaf at least. A large 60s tower block which houses the council offices is the somewhat unfortunate focal point of the town; then, on the road out of the centre towards North Cheam, there is a construction of sheer *Herculean* proportions, dwarfing all around it. This enormous edifice is the *Mega Mosque*.

The *Mega Mosque* was built several years ago, though not without controversy. According to my previous neighbour, a quite charming *Anglo-Indian* man in his early sixties, there was a huge outcry by the local community, and several petitions against the intended size of the *mosque*. Unsurprisingly, majority opinions were ignored, and overridden by central government, who were terrified that a refusal would seem like prejudice against the *Muslim* faith as a whole. Thus, with the help of an *Arab Billionaire*, the largest mosque in Western Europe, at the time, was constructed in unassuming little Morden: population 1,000 in 1927!

One of the *mosque's* minarets is clearly visible from my landing window and, as it faces a westerly direction, it looks quite spectacular when enveloped by an explosive sunset. Nevertheless, spectacular sunset or not, I do feel as if the land of my birth is being changed at a furiously fast pace with scant regard to the wishes of *Indigenous Britons*... Our so-called leaders repeatedly ignore the majority, rubber-stamp and fast-track all their nonsensical policies, riding roughshod over thousands of years of our heritage and traditions. If you dare to question the logic of a policy of *self-destruction*, in other words the madness of *open-door immigration*, you are branded a *fascist*, insulted, bullied into submission, and told 'Britain is a nation of immigrants...' In other words, 'Lump it, like it, or leave..!' This must surely be the only country in the world where *charity* doesn't begin at home.... *Quelle surprise..!*

So the oppression of the *Ancient Britons*, who have lived on these islands for over four thousand years, is still alive and flourishing today... From the Romans, Saxons, Vikings, and Normans, to the world invasion of the last sixty years, the ancient indigenous people are routinely trampled on and now find themselves an ethnic minority in their own land. We are the much-ridiculed *Aboriginal Britons* who, being liberal minded, have welcomed and tolerated newcomers for centuries. Our generous attitude is our ultimate downfall; for the clutches of power are fast-moving, already transferring to people from other tribes and beliefs. Our national sovereignty is quickly evaporating, only to be consumed by the French, Germans, Chinese, Indians, Middle Easterners, Eastern Europeans and anyone else with a few spare *ducats* who wishes to *hoover up*, with our idiotic masters' encouragement, our few remaining natural resources and blue-chip companies.

Up the hill, a couple of minutes' walk past the *mosque*, is *Merton College*; then, a few hundred yards further on sits a lovely old *church* which has been partially rebuilt but still retains its ancient charm. The *church* is open to people of all or no faith; anyone can freely stroll around the churchyard, look up through the horse chestnut trees at the old bell tower, then enter through the lovely oak doors into a place of serene sanctuary. I'm not particularly religious, more spiritual to be precise. I find most organised religions quite terrifying, as it seems to me that tolerance of difference is rarely accepted. If it is, it's due more to a patronising pity towards someone's lifestyle or lack of belief, rather than an unbiased affirmation. The ubiquitous hand of friendship may be offered, but only for their own salvation: adhering to the new principled way of life that their benefactor has prescribed for them being the key to their continued inclusion. Hallelujah!

I shall never accept the concept of *heaven and hell*. *Jesus* was a man who purportedly reached out to everyone, including non-believers, the poor and afflicted. Over time, his message has been totally misrepresented, a sort of religious *Chinese Whispers..!* As the *Son of God*, if there is indeed 'One True God', he was bound to spread kindness, and promote harmony and inclusion, not division. But, so I believe, in both *Christianity* and *Islam* there is a day of final judgement. If you are a non-believer or infidel, then that is just too bad: you are going down, not up to *heaven!* You are deemed beyond *salvation* as you have stubbornly refused any attempt at last-minute conversion. Would this bizarre twist on the Christians being thrown to the lions really be the message that *God* wanted *Jesus*, the man who sacrificed his life for us all, to spread far and wide around our small planet?!

Organised religion, as we sadly know, can be used as a powerful tool to recruit disaffected and normally quite rational people. It's like advertising; repeat something often enough and some people believe it. It has the potential to consume one, eventually becoming your entire being. Anyway, the point I was trying to make was that this is supposedly still a Christian country and the local *church* is small, quaint and welcoming to all. The *mosque*, on the other hand, is quite enormous, and somewhat intimidating! It must be the length of at least two football pitches, and has a huge dome and towering minarets, along with high fencing and a manned electric security gate at its entrance! To the non-Muslim, whether intentional or not, this can only appear like a successful attempt at deliberate separation from wider society. A place where the *goings-on* are secret and mysterious, outsiders are not welcome nor wanted, therefore fuelling a symptomatically toxic combination of resentment, fear, and suspicion.

It is quite ironic, in a disturbing way, how the *mosque* in Britain is security-bound! I keep hearing that some *Muslims* feel 'under siege' in this country. Well, the *London Bombings* were not carried out by *Christians, Hindus, or Buddhists* and as an *Ancient Briton* I feel discriminated against and under 'permanent siege' in my own backyard. I can pass a whole day hardly hearing *English* spoken, any language but to be precise! Every time I hop on a bus, tube, or train, or walk out of my front door, I am in the minority.

Face-covering is another *bugbear*… With regard to the wearing of *burkas*, I and many people I have spoken with, especially Western women, find it extremely insulting that we are considered too lowly to view another person's face. How can you possibly engage with someone you can't even see? How would you recall them again? They could be anyone! The only people it suits are the men who are often subjugating them.

A few weeks ago a '*White-Trash*' friend of mine was in the local job centre and was asked to remove his baseball cap! He questioned the security guard as to his reasoning, for he wouldn't have objected on the grounds of manners. However, he was told it was for security. He had to remove it in order to be identifiable! My '*White-Trash*' mate then politely asked if this 'rule' would apply to someone wearing a burka? The answer was, 'It's a religious symbol...' My mate went on to state that wearing his baseball cap was a 'religious symbol' to him! The security guard smiled, wryly, but he was still discriminated against and obliged to remove his cap. Need I say more..! We all know how ridiculous this country has become. If you want to 'buck the system', just start a *religion* and make sure you recruit enough followers to legitimise it, then you can think, say, and behave how you like under its veil of intolerance and superiority.

I think I might choose *sweets* as my god. Roll myself around in pink candyfloss with giant liquorice shoelaces for eyes then pound around the streets with attitude! If I am stopped and questioned by the authorities or looked at in a slightly odd way by any mortal soul I shall, along with my followers, sue the government, claiming discrimination under the auspices of the *Human Rights Act*...

That's quite enough of this talk for one day; I'm starting to do my own head in... If only it were puerile nonsense... Anyway, I'm definitely rubbing myself up the wrong way. Maybe I'll head for the swimming pool. This HSP needs some reinvigoration on such a grey, cool, drizzly day.

Later:

I have just devoured two slices of bread smothered in

thick, full-fat mayonnaise. Swimming certainly gives you an appetite, especially for carbohydrates and fat, leaving all your hard work quickly undone. However, on the positive side, it was accompanied by a healthy plate of Cos lettuce, blood-red tomatoes and beetroot; despite them being generously tossed in a lovely creamy Caesar salad dressing from my nearest 'Try Something New Today' store. All the above was satisfyingly washed down with piping hot tea, served in a thin porcelain mug… It is imperative to use this type of mug as the tea keeps hotter for longer, and the sanctity of the flavoursome *brew* is not in any way bastardised. For those who have not tried tea this way, I urge you to give it a go. Thick clay mugs don't cut the mustard! Keep them for serving freshly brewed coffee, for which purpose they are far superior to a porcelain mug, for a fine porcelain mug can equally ruin the coffee-drinking experience… Remember the golden rule, 'Thin for tea and thick for coffee'. After all, coffee is a thicker, richer, more rounded drink, and tea thinner in texture and very delicate in flavour, so this all makes perfect sense.

As you get older tiredness comes and goes, but early afternoon is a crucial moment. If you're lucky enough to be a child, teenager, or generally without responsibility at this hour of the day, there is usually an uncontrollable temptation to have a *nap*, take *forty winks*, indulge in a *siesta*, and so forth. Whichever term we use, invariably that *comfy sofa* absorbs our body for a short while, as we soon fall into a slumber, our stresses and strains temporarily exorcised… After what appears an eternity one normally awakes in a mad panic, all your stresses and strains immediately jumping back on board. They soon start to play havoc with your crooked middle-aged back, throwing one leg into a gigantic spasm.

Then, as you awkwardly rise from the *comfy sofa* your lower back locks, whereupon the remaining culprits leap into action to tense up the few dormant nerve endings in the outer reaches of your ailing body. You imagine hours have passed since you 'nodded off', you now have bucket-loads of *saliva* running out of all four corners of your mouth, you are red in complexion and your hair, if you have any left, is glued to your cheek by said saliva while the remaining dried-out strands have formed their own ridiculous parting halfway down one side of your head. Slowly but surely, you are turning into one of your grandparents or, worse still, parents, with the *combover* to match!! Life is, indeed, one big cycle. Birth to child to adult to older adult and back to child again, before inevitable death, and then who knows what!

The *swimming pool* was empty at lunchtime. I mean *empty*. At 1.20 p.m. I was the only person in that pool. It was fantastic. I couldn't believe my luck. I was master of all I pervade. I set to work on my lengths; one breaststroke, then the next front crawl, and so forth. Progress was being made and I was soon flying through the breakwater that my increasingly athletic body was creating. I was on fire, a true 'champion' in the making. My body was toning up with every stroke, my rippling muscles ever enlarging as any excess sinew disappeared and finally retreated altogether... Upon my final exit from the pool of magic I would possess the body of a true *Greek Adonis*. Throngs of people from *Multi-Cultural London* would line the streets on my bicycle journey back to Morden, gasping and sighing in amazement at my beautifully defined triceps and biceps, the adoring masses elevating me to the status of a living *deity*. At a stroke, I should become the greatest, undisputed pinnacle of perfection that had ever graced this revolving planet!

Alas, after fifteen minutes of solitude, wild thoughts and fantasies, peace and tranquillity were no more. Yes, they were back: the *Grey Ladies* had returned! This 'Seniors Water Aerobics Class' must be a regular lunchtime affair, so I shall have to arrive a little earlier in future..! I don't want to be too disingenuous: after all, they have as much right as I do to be there, the only difference being that I actually swim in the swimming pool and the majority of them seem to think it is a 'drop-in centre' where it's obligatory to hold multiple conversations whilst slowly motoring all over the place warming up for the main event.

Smell is a very powerful sense! As more and more of them indulged in the water it gave off an increasingly toxic aroma of perfume. Along the length of the pool there were three of four main huddles of conversation, the loose cannons proving as annoying as the last time I graced the waters. One lady soon took it upon herself to swim painfully slow widths of the pool, on several occasions causing me to swerve severely. She eventually ceased this activity, but not to be outdone her friend and co-worker in 'fucking up my lengths' decided to swim at me, *kamikaze* style. I swerved and let out an almighty 'Tut'. She was undeterred, so on her next suicide mission I elected to swim underneath her. There was no way she would attempt to lower herself to try and trap me on the floor of the pool, for she certainly wouldn't dare wet her oversized *perm!* The plan worked, I had outmanoeuvred her and swum a very long way underwater in the process. She appeared quite surprised, and never crossed my path again… I was rather pleased with myself, reinvigorated, and carried on swimming for ages with a newfound, seemingly endless, youthful energy… There's still plenty more life in this middle-aged sea dog, I wryly muttered to myself as I ate up the lengths. One nil to a *Highly Sensitive Ancient Briton!!*

Later Still:

I have just had the delight of enduring one of those annoyingly useless service calls from my *mobile phone* provider, the one that is named after a *colour!* What a futile waste of time! Bloody customer service, support, liaison, registration, it's all bonkers. If these trained *Zombies* think they're contributing to the economy and enhancing your mobile phone experience the world has gone mad....

The human race managed to survive perfectly well for millennia without these intrusive devices. For years I resisted purchasing one, joining the *lemming-like* flow, finally succumbing when I was self-employed, and thought it would be good for business. However, this turned out not to be the case, although I can hardly blame the phone for that: my malaise and general lack of enthusiasm for the project was ninety-nine per cent to blame. All I ever really wanted was to be a 'star of stage and screen', not a bloody Landscape Gardener/Carpet Cleaner Combo. So in my delusional little world keeping my underused mobile phone for the 'two-for-one cinema nights' was the next best thing to stardom... Big mistake!

I just can't see any upside to these bloody things, all they've done is deny us our anonymity! You can be pinpointed to within a millimetre of anywhere on the planet, your movements traced by GCHQ, passed onto MI5, MI6 or who bloody ever, not to mention your partner or an overbearing relative being able to track your every philandering minute..! Then there is god-awful *texting* and the demise of our spoken language. We now have a generation of people under the age of thirty who are obsessive 'texters', spell 'r u' and think it's correct! 'GR8..!' No doubt the Oxford English Dictionary will soon decree it to be so... People appear incapable of communicating verbally any more, conversation, social techniques and etiquette dead in the water... After arranging to meet up with their 'friends!' via *text* or that other curse *email*, or worse still *Facebook*, they find it easier to get 'pissed', vomit and undress in public rather than philosophise. Really, they have very little in common, certainly no way of expressing themselves, for they're hardly acquainted. They are consumed by a meaningless, superficial, virtual and selfish world! When they leave school with nine 'A Stars', but without an ounce of common sense or interpersonal skills, they are more than likely going to end up as another faceless representative of a *Mega Bank*, *Insurance Company*, or the *Mobile Phone Company* named after a *colour*... Hence, as a result of this intrusive fielded call my *blood pressure* has increased tenfold....

It started with my standard reply to any unsolicited telephony:

'I am rather busy at the moment.'

The usual response was forthcoming:

'I'll call back another time.'

You don't want them to call you back another time, for you never asked them to call you in the first place, so you reluctantly agree to talk quickly now as some faceless person on the next shift will call you again whether you like it or not! They've had the green light, so before you can change your mind they're off like an impatient bullet from an overheated gun. They hook you in at speed. They can't reel the script off quick enough, for they hate this shit just as much as you do...

'Please can you tell me the first two letters of your password?' The *Zombie* asks…

I rack my brains, sifting through the endless number of possible answers; was it an anagram of my name, my mother's maiden name, the name of a friend or relative, a film title, or a political party!? All of which I have used in the past for the ever-increasing array of companies that now require you to jump over these ridiculously high security hurdles. Eventually I come up with an answer and to my great surprise, and relief, I am spot-on first time… He continues with his scripted customer follow-up bullshit, the soothing tones of his deep *Geordie* accent making it just about bearable:

'You requested a paper bill and this costs one pound fifty a month… Would you like to upgrade to a non-paper bill, an online bill?'

In other words, log on to their website, which will inevitably waste hours of your life as it crashes at the opportune moment. Besides which your already fragile identity and dwindling bank balance are likely to be stolen! I reply:

'I've always had a paper bill. I have been with your company for five years. I certainly never asked to start paying one pound fifty for the privilege of knowing how much I owe you each month!'

'Ay, but the system changed several months back now and you would 'av been notified on ye paper bill in any case.'

What he meant was that somewhere on that overcomplicated mish-mash of excessive printing this fact was ambiguously and surreptitiously declared to me!

'But why should I pay you to send me a bill when I am a paying customer?' I replied with a certain degree of annoyance.

'The system has changed, sir. We don't wannna use more paper than is necessary.' I was politely advised in more homely tones.

'Well, incessantly phoning me up and forcing me to use copious amounts of electricity to view my overpriced bill is hardly the way forward, is it?' My tolerance level was now reaching its optimum for this type of extortion by stealth. Poor chap…!

'Okay, sir, would ye rather continue to pay one pound fifty and stay with ye paper bill? the Geordie replied in a somewhat sarcastic tone, though with wry humour lingering in the background.

'No… No, I would certainly not. Thank you… I was not aware of this extortionate change, and certainly do not wish to pay to see how much I owe you each month… Added to that, I demand a refund for the months you have taken already and I do not expect to see this charge on my bill next month,' I responded like an angry drug-fuelled madman who had run out of money for his next fix.

'Okay, sir, ye gonna have to have an online bill if ye donna want to pay the one pound fifty charge… Like I explained previous, the system has changed, sir. We are trying to become a greener company, sir. We don't wanna see global warming get out of control and we wanna bring our valued customers along on the journey with us. "Green us, green you, green phone." That is the official motto and mission statement that we wanna take forward in this new cent'arie.'

'Well that sounds absolutely wonderful, but I'm not paying the one pound fifty…' I said slowly and sarcastically.

'I am sorry, but if ye donna go for an 'online bill' ye

gonna be charged one pound fifty,' he retorted.

'I haven't any more time to waste on this stupid charade. I want to speak to your manager.'

'I'm sorry, but there is no manager available just now and he will only tell ye the same as me. This is the new system now, sir,' he declared once again.

'Well, fiddly dee! What an unsurprising surprise. Let's all be cocksure and arrogant while we hide behind the telephone, shall we. "Customer Service" my arse! I want to speak to your spotty little manager right now!' I demanded, hands trembling, face twitching with soon-to-be-uncontrollable anger.

'There is no need to speak to me like that, sir! Ye are obviously upset by the change of system and the new "motto and mission statement"', the Geordie was slowly and menacingly telling me as I cut him off in mid-sentence.

'Ha ha ha, you stupid little boy, I hope you're stuck in your job for the whole bloody century... Fuck you, fuck your company, fuck your manager and stick the "motto and mission statement" right up your tight little arse... Thank you and goodnight,' I shouted insanely as I gyrated around the living room like a muscle-jellied lunatic on the cusp of perpetrating a major random atrocity.

I shouldn't imagine I shall be hearing from the mobile phone company named after a *colour* and owned by French, Germans or whichever foreign firm has taken them over most recently, not for a while at least!

Thursday 2nd October

Hello… Our train has just left *Morden Station*. The time is 9.20 a.m. I am one of two English people out of sixteen passengers in our carriage.

----- *South Wimbledon* -----

What will happen to the demographic here….? English percentages are down again! A rather stunning South Asian Lady has just hopped on. Seventeen to two now, quite possibly seventeen to one for my compatriot may be of Huguenot, Roman or Viking descent, to name but a few of our continental marauders. I could quite easily be the only true *Ancient Tribal Briton* aboard!

----- *Colliers Wood* -----

Already..! Two elderly Chinese Ladies and an Eastern European with the complexion of 'Little Red Riding Hood' have joined the horde, twenty to one. Maybe this is a metaphor for that game show '15 to 1!' Although, rather than being subtly covert, they may as well have just called it 'Outnumbered' and be done with it! Whichever way you count it, fifteen, twenty, ten, fifty, I am still the 'one'; in my own land as well!

I'm sitting on the end seat, next to one of those vertical glass panels and an upright yellow pole! Funny really, as a Polish-looking teenager alighted at *Tooting Broadway* and her bum is currently squashed right up against the clear glass, just inches from my face! She is pushing so hard that her bum cheeks look like they're going to split into two. Her jeans are stretched to capacity, practically morphing into her skin; her thick studded belt is gently swaying in unison with her curvaceous body and faint scratch marks are starting to appear on the glass… If she's not careful she's in danger of crashing through the lot and landing on my lap!!

We've had *Balham* and are now pulling out of *Clapham South*, where a smart-looking middle-aged English Lady has accompanied us on our journey up the *Northern Line*. She is probably around fifty-five, give or take a few years. Her black suit cut to perfection, fitting like a glove, her lips and nails painted in earthy red, her shoes expensive, matt-black leather, the *pièce de resistance* a most striking black, brown and red handbag. All in all she's a picture of understated sophistication. Senior ladies, and I mean 'Ladies', who are sadly few and far between in this dumbed-down scruffy world, do tend to possess an air of style which is often lacking in their younger counterparts.… I suppose they have had far more life experience, so they've already worked out what suits and what is a definite 'no no'. As one inevitably grows older one realises that wisdom comes as looks sadly go, with the occasional exception, as per the *Senior Lady* within.…

The older you become the more the next generation of spotty-faced youth gain society's attention. Gradually you yourself become invisible, a mind overflowing with accumulated knowledge that no one seems to have the time or will to listen to! Their loss..! If only they could see it, they could save themselves incalculable amounts of wasted time if they took just the slightest bit of notice: after all, you've already stumbled through most of the pitfalls encountered by a foolish know-all.… However, I'm probably expecting the impossible… We've all been through it! The years when we thought we knew absolutely everything about everything, showing total disregard for any authority on the particular subject in question, no, we knew best! It's only a few decades of wrinkles later that you realise what an arrogant moronic buffoon you were back in your own blinkered youth; by which time the people you wished you had listened to either can't be arsed with you any more, have died, or are suffering from memory loss!

----- *Clapham Common* -----

My head is spinning with the sound of harsh, abrupt, Eastern European tones. My ears just cannot tolerate it for much longer. I try to block it out, without success. It's far too loud and down beat, it makes guttural German sound like a language your mother could send you to sleep with whilst reading you a *Brothers Grimm* children's story... I'm sure they are Polish, which wouldn't be hard to guess as they are everywhere. But whoever they are, they're far too boisterous. It's just not 'cricket', very 'un-British' behaviour on a public transport system. The respectful sound of silence far more sociable all round!

I wish the little bastard next to me would stop invading my arm rest...! I was here first. But he has gradually and, to his way of thinking, subtly pushed me off it! He obviously thinks he is far superior or something, as he has a mathematical book sprawled across his lap for all to see... Now his bloody book is starting to encroach on my personal space! Selfish tosser...

'*Ancient Briton*, you are fucked...' If you're lucky you may eventually be granted a little patch of your homeland on an indigenous reserve on the Isle of Wight! Although the island will inevitably have to be renamed, as anything *white* will have been consigned to the bowels of ancient history... Fifty years from now the few of us who are left will be scratching out an existence toiling the soil on that little wind-swept isle. People like *Bruce Parry*, although he will undoubtedly have a far more exotic-sounding name and appearance, will come and interview us, curious about our funny ways, strange beliefs, and primitive Neanderthal rituals! They will want to see for themselves if we are still as savage as their ancestors portrayed us! Do we become uncontrollably, wild, aggressive, antisocial, near-naked after consuming grain-fermented beverages? Once intoxicated, are we still prone to mass projectile vomiting and notoriously lurid free-flowing sex parties…? Our relatively low birth rate, compared to the newcomers, shall be our ultimate downfall; along with an insatiable appetite for 'Binge-Drinking', 'Fast Food', and 'Frankenstein Ready Meals' that will probably render us sterile anyway… If we do manage to escape the *Island Reservation* we're just as likely to end up a rare species in zoos in all four corners of the *New World*. Failing that, an expensive gastronomic delicacy!

----- *Charing Cross* -----

Friday 3rd October

I have just switched on the telly to accompany my 'Weetabix and tea', whereupon a smug, supercilious, condescending arsehole leapt out at me! I'm sure every country has at least one trashy early-morning *Humiliation Show!* We have *Jeremy*, who seems to be a demigod within the bowels of Daytime TV. Masquerading as *Mr Streetwise* he unashamedly attempts to roughen up his middle-class accent in order to suit the demographic of his show. He also possesses the most important quality to front one of these awful excuses for entertainment, squeaky-clean perfection! *Jeremy* is so perfect that he hasn't made a single misjudgement throughout his relatively short, saintly life! Therefore he assumes the divine right to judge, insult, critique, moralise and generally defame whomever he pleases.

The current topic is *Stop ignoring your Daughter, I'll prove you're the Dad..!* More live DNA results, one should imagine. Followed by a barrage of never-ending expletives and the chance of a good old-fashioned fight! …. Here we go. *Mr Gobby* is off:

'Amazing… at nineteen years old, you are an amazing lady.' Perfect *Jeremy* then turns to her part-time sex buddy, 'But you're just scum… You're a disgrace… If you don't step up to the plate, mate, I'm going to encourage this Amazing Lady to never let you have contact with these children you say are yours… If they are..! You look really, really happy… Don't you?! What are you here for??'

The *Scumbag Male* replies:

'I don't know if I want to be a father!'

Jeremy shouts back, angrily, with pure unadulterated authority:

'You what... Go away from here... You know what?! This is the first time I've ever said this on MY show.... Get up off that chair and leave.....Just gooooooo!!'

Time for a pooh, I think…………..

That's better... At least I've lightened my load... However, this compulsive crap is still booming out of the telly, there are now two nineteen-year-old 'losers' on set. They are an item, and she is pregnant with the delinquent's baby. Hence this segment's title:

We're having a baby….. Should we even be together?

Jeremy is off again:

'Why were you laughing?'

'At you,' replied the shell-suited ugly little crew-cut bloke.

Well, that was like a red rag to a bull. *Jeremy's* mouth leapt into action, his squaring-up posture ironically and paradoxically mimicking the yob's nonchalant stance. He continued with irritation in his voice:

'If you're going to take me on at least sit up straight. Take your hand away from your mouth and pull your shell suit up…' The *cocky little urchin* tried to come back at him: 'Shut your mouth.' *Jeremy* quickly interjected.

'What are you going to do about it? You can't touch me…'

'You're a boy!' *Jeremy* screeched back.

'You're a muppet…!' This retort really got to *Jeremy!* After all, the show has his name all over it, and people are expected to kowtow to him, not challenge him! His jaw dropped so wide you could practically see his tonsils. His face was a picture of utter disbelief. He lowered his whole body and stooped over the sloppily seated *oik*, manically shouting:

'You're a tax-sucking bum.......'

Unshaken, the *yob* went on, his smirk now transformed into a wall-to-wall grin:

'What you going to do, you can't do nothin' about it, can you....? If I wanna drink all day and you pay for it, I will.'

Jeremy is done with him now, and turns to the *trashy girlfriend* instead:

'How much does he drink?'

She mumbles back:

'Well, not much... On payday he drinks more but when he 'aint got no money he don't drink much... innit.'

Profoundly observant of her, what a blight on our education system! She really does believe that *payday* is the correct term for 'benefit or free-lunch windfall day'. God help us! If I ever reach retirement day, morons like her are quite incapable of working to keep us going in our twilight years... Food bank here I come!

Realising that she is as much of a lost cause as the ugly yobbish boyfriend, he turns once more to ask him:

'We know you think you're hard mate, but do you even care about your unborn child... Do you?'

The grinning *oik* replies coolly and arrogantly, in a deliberately slow tempo:

'Course I'm bothered about me baby... What's it to you anyway?'

The silly pregnant *bimbo* smirks and *Jeremy* is now well and truly done. Fortunately for him, and sane people everywhere, time has caught up with the dire but admittedly entertaining spectacle of general ignorance, and the credits start to roll... At a push, one could even feel a little sorry for *Jeremy*. The *Mockney Cockney* has well and truly met his match, for those *'White Trash'* definitely had the measure of him, and weren't going to play ball... The poor man does have his self-righteous hands rather full, as he has taken it upon himself to educate such people, install responsibility, and turn them into morally model citizens! And all in a matter of minutes! A 'tall order', to say the least, but I do feel that a calmer person who has mastered the art of communicating without shouting might fare considerably better! Just a thought..!

The next programme was all about *Dubai*, which must be an interesting place to visit, though the over-the-top opulence was absolutely mind-boggling! One minute they were showing you around a '7* Hotel', then you were in the middle of a gold market, then on that ridiculous man-made island where *Posh and Becks, Rod Stewart,* and a whole host of 'A-Listers' have sinking holiday homes. Finally, we were being whisked around an enormous shopping centre full of designer boutiques, fast food restaurants, and a ski slope..! The hotel was quite awful: yellow gold dripping off every available nook and cranny, the entire joint covered in thick purple carpet, huge mirrors bolted to bedroom ceilings so, whether you liked it or not, save for titillation during 'kinky sex', you would be subjected to a permanent aerial view of your ever-receding hairline...! The whole feel of the place was tacky, glitzy, nouveau glamour; brash and in-your-face. Yuk...! Good understated taste and subtle elegance all but vanished since the sun set on the *British Empire!*

All I want is a little villa in the *Italian Hills* so I can escape this exponential profusion of modern vulgarity. £200K would do. Is that really too much to ask? Why can't one of those vacuous money-laden celebrities foot the bill for 'People of Taste' to escape the shitty grey suburbs?! After all, they would only have to forgo a couple of nights in that hideous '7* Hotel!'

I'm quite glad this 'cultural morning' has come to an end: the prospect of a grotty tube journey to town now holds a certain allure... 'I'm living in the real world! The raw grimy city is good for my soul. It humanises me......!' Very idealistic, quaint even. But I'd still rather have an 'A Lister's' cash. Who wouldn't...? It's just so unfair. Why do these dreadfully pushy and egotistical people always end up holding the purse strings?! Maybe if I turn my back on *Paganism* I shall arrive at the gates of riches and freedom! *Tony Blair* converted to Catholicism and he is simply raking it in. That's what I'm lacking: *Divine Intervention!*

Morden Tube:

I've just avoided being *spat at* by a very grand-looking *African Lady* in traditional dress! Despite her finery it was not the most welcoming of receptions as I entered the station foyer! And to think I was looking forward to my journey to town today, after the opulence of *Dubai* and all... Talk about extremes, they certainly are right in-your-face in good old *Morden*. I can feel the allure fading as I speak. I wonder if 'Please do not retch, then gob out the contents of your throat' is part of the ridiculous charade of a *Citizenship Test* that this increasingly desperate *Labour Government* is planning to roll out to pacify the critics of their *Open-Door Immigration Policy!*

It is about '35 to 5'. I'm not sure if that's better or worse odds than yesterday, but I'm feeling decidedly *pink* today... We've just reached *Balham*. A few more *Pink-Skinned Britons* have joined the party on the world's most multicultural tube line. …We're all very well behaved and extremely quiet, unlike the *'trash'* on the television this morning!

It's amazing what you notice about people whilst commuting..! On the whole, fair-skinned folk usually have lovely glowing skin until the age of thirty-something. After which everything tends to deteriorate. Unless you're lucky enough to have inherited youthful genes, this is the age where your skin starts to sag, begins to lose elasticity, and wrinkles gradually become permanent lines. Your former flawless body is now in cruel decline as you slowly transform into a person you neither know, or wish to recognise! I'm beginning to sound like a television commercial for some miracle anti-ageing cream….. People with darker skin seem to be far more fortunate, the aging process invariably kicking in much later in life. However, I've just noticed that the only place they seem to age is on their hands; at least this is the case with the man sitting to my right…. Do I qualify as a racist for discussing the effects of the ageing process on skin colour? If I am to be dragged over the coals by a *Stasi*-style zealot I could at least base my defence on the grounds of promoting the merits of darker skin over milkier tones…. This bland and uninspiring modern world a terrible consequence of the disproportionate power of suffocating *Do-Gooders*, a far too vocal minority that successive governments never cease pandering to! Despite their moral superiority and successfully gagging free speech, until now, much to their annoyance, they are still unable to control our minds! How long this will last is anyone's guess..! Our faculty of consciousness is somewhat of a rarity in the human body, for it is one of the few organs that hardly ages..! As far as I'm concerned I still feel like an unblemished, sex-crazed teenager. Until I look in the mirror that is… A pastime I now, quite sensibly, tend to avoid like the plague…

I am not entirely sure why I did come up to town today….! I have a pounding headache, sore throat, diarrhoea, need the loo, desperately, and feel like I am about to vomit profusely. All this in the inhospitable confines of a public place! Nearly at *Charing Cross* now, there should be a public convenience here; or perhaps I might frequent the facilities of the hotel next to the station, as I'm sure it will be cleaner, warmer, far more tastefully decorated! Anyway, the public loo is more than likely full of men massaging their *inflated cocks* whilst pretending to pee into the urinals. So the hotel cloakroom wins hands-down: a far more civilised and appropriate place to be violently sick!! Although I'm pretty sure neither the guests nor hotel staff will thank me for the visit when the essence of my stomach fluids begins to permeate the pristine corridors of *The Charing Cross Hotel!!*

7.30pm:

I have just returned home to be greeted by yet another letter for *Mr Mineev!* Yesterday I had one for his sidekick, *Miss Lavrouchina!* She sounds like a competitor at Wimbledon: 'Miss Lavrouchina leads by three games to love, final set….' All I seem to do lately is return unpaid bills to sender, with explanatory notes stating that these people no longer own the house and do not live here any more... These *Debt Collectors* are certainly not very clever; it has been a year and three months since I bought the house, at an extortionate price, and they still don't get it! Boy, are they stupid dumb-asses. *Mr Mineev* and *Miss Lavrouchina* have clearly done a 'bunk'. They have either returned to *Eastern Europe* or, more probably, are living around the corner under their real names! Their debts are in *Blighty* to stay, so the only way the bank will recoup their easy-come, easy-go lending losses is by hiking up charges to the long-suffering *Great British Public*. However, we should be honoured to help out: after all, we're all European now…!

After sifting through the post for the eastern side of Europe, I opened my dreaded *Credit Card Statement*. The amount outstanding was stated to be £5,000, which did take me aback somewhat as I was convinced that I had decreased it to £4,500. I went through it all in my head, backwards and forwards, retracing my steps over the last few weeks to make sure that I wasn't going completely mad….. Several minutes later, having concluded that I was still sane, partially anyway, I grabbed my phone, took a deep breath, and started to dial the dreaded *Call Centre*, when, just to the left of the *Helpline Number*, I spotted the error. No surprise there! It was none other than my dear friend *Mr Mineev…!* I had inadvertently opened an Eastern Europe side letter. Talk about adding salt to the wound! I'm sure he's smiling away, just up the road no doubt, knowing he has got away with it. Arsehole!

That sounded like a *Didgeridoo…!* I've heard one being played in Australia, but the Lithuanians next door?! *Quelle surprise!* We have definitely become a 'global village' now. Before we know it, *Eskimos* will be *Morris Dancing* and I shall have to go and buy myself some *Lederhosen*. Mind you, I have always been partial to the 'Birdie Song', and the thought of bare flesh on leather is rather erotic. Let alone all that liberal thigh-slapping and spanking!! The thought of it rather makes up for today's trials and tribulations, even being sick in the public toilet at *Charing Cross..!* It turned out that the hotel one was 'out of service', for cleaning!

Sunday 5th October

On the way back from posting a letter I was treated to a very distinctive and memorable sight! Not the glimpse of a rare song bird, nor a fleeting glance of the elusive badger, but a *black and white striped female!* This female was of the human species. There are indeed many varieties of 'Homo Sapiens', but this one definitely made a lasting impression, and not for romantic reasons either....

The legs were thin, covered in black Lycra, with matching black thigh-length boots. The synthetic knitted sweater was big and baggy, gathered in at what should have been her waist by a large black belt. The huge horizontal stripes exaggerated the heavily pregnant stomach and the pallid facial complexion matched the hair, which was severely scraped back and scrunched up into a neat ball on top of her head... I know this is a very popular look nowadays, especially in our eclectic urban areas, so what gives 'middle-aged hormonal men' like me the right to criticise? Nothing in the slightest, I have no right to moralise... However, when she re-emerged from the take-away munching on one of the largest *Donor Kebabs* I have ever seen, proceeded to light a 'fag', and at the same time took a call on her mobile phone, my jaw dropped in total disbelief, raw mesmerised amusement. A consummate multi-tasker, she duly began screeching to her mate on the opposite side of the street:

'Alright, Carla...? This is the most "meat" I've 'ad all weekend!'

Carla engaged her loudly:

'Yeah, that's 'coz I've 'ad your share, mate... Ask Mehmet for one of 'em long saveloys!'

The Black and White striped one replied:

'Good idea mate, I fancy a bit of 'im…… c.u. latersssss Carla.'

See how exciting the mere task of posting a letter can be! There's never a dull moment around here….

Sunday Night:

I am engrossed in *Tess of the D'Urbervilles*, another great BBC costume drama. Tonight is the last episode and I am enjoying the first class acting, beautiful rolling scenery and fine English stone houses of Thomas Hardy country, although it definitely looks like the Cotswolds rather than Dorset! Regardless of geography, it makes for splendid viewing after a dull and wet Sunday. My only criticism the sight of *Angel*, *Tess's* husband, gallivanting across the English countryside, searching for *Tess*, while the seasons keep changing before my very eyes! One minute the trees are positively verdant, the next full of autumnal hues, then seconds letter they are completely devoid of foliage, and all in an afternoon's ride!

Poor old *Tess* doesn't have much luck with the opposite sex… She is raped by her first suitor, abused by almost everybody, after which she has to endure the shame of a non-Christian burial for her illegitimate child! To add insult to injury her husband is unable to forgive her for being 'taken' against her will, hardly her fault one would have to conclude, so he does a runner to Brazil, of all places! *Tess*, though shunned and abandoned without hope as a subjugated woman of her time, dutifully waits for him to return one day! She hands over the 'guilt money' that he has left her to her obligingly large family, then sets to work in the fields for years of hard labour on less than the minimum wage.

A horrid distant relative, who is on the moneyed side of the family and is only too aware of her plight, keeps popping up to dangle a 'Get out of jail free' card in front of her. But, despite the awful conditions she now finds herself in, she resists the temptation, for this is the *brute* that violated her and ruined her life in the first place! 'Tosser...' Ultimately, however, she is tricked into a union with this *vile creature* and once again, forever loyal, she puts her family first so as to save them from destitution.... After his long self-imposed absence *Angel* eventually 'gets over himself' and decides to return home to reacquaint with *Tess*, a presumption of the time! Meanwhile *Tess* kills her abuser in a struggle. Reunited, she then has a few days' happiness with her beloved *Angel* (God only knows why she even bothers with him after his cowardly behaviour! Mind you, there weren't any Hostels for Battered Women in those days, nor 'Benefits' for that matter!), before Officers of the Law quickly track the pair of them down and she, who else, pays for her troubles with her young life!

This is how she is repaid for her altruism, obsequiousness, kind-heartedness, and high morals..! In this day and age she would be considered an absolute *saint!* Though she would quite probably still be ostracised, but, perversely, for being too puritanical. People would give her a wide birth precisely because she tried to maintain her dignity. There would more likely than not be a 'fly-on-the-wall documentary' pertaining to her strange habit of sexual abstinence, her ability to survive in such austere conditions (no satellite TV, takeaways or mobiles), and the madness of achieving all this on the minimum wage, without a social security payment in sight....!

Just as it was true several hundred years ago, even today

her conscience and good character would prove her ultimate downfall… So we really have not progressed much! After all, cheats, liars, and the downright lazy still, as they always have done, nick the front row seats on the first-class carriage of the *gravy train!!*

Wednesday 8th October

A bright blue sky today.... The autumn leaves are picture-perfect, a patchwork of gold, ochre, yellow, amber and bronze. An *autumnal rainbow*…

Emigration is totally off the radar on a day like this. The sheer beauty of a perfect autumn day is utterly breathtaking: something magical to be savoured, nostalgically remembered on a long dark winter's evening. The Weather Man has promised us two more days the same, which would make three cloudless days in a row, quite a record in England. But let's not get too carried away as a good old-fashioned *British Gale* is due to arrive in time for the weekend, so families everywhere will soon have to start putting Plan B into action – 'Indoor Barbecue anyone?!'

The White-Suited Yob next to me has just lobbed a sweet wrapper over his head, and it is now displayed for all to admire on the ledge above his seat – Charming!

I'm on the tube again, as you've probably realised… I seem to spend half my life on here lately, so surely I must be entitled to some form of fare reduction! Anyway, reverting back to the awful 'Yob', it's amazing how other humans' vile habits can change one's mood in an instant. I thought *Guardian readers* would be more conscious of the environment! But it just goes to show that the old adage is quite true, 'You can't judge a book by its cover.' This repulsive and selfish *pasty pig* is probably one of those 'right-on metrosexual socialists', from a leafy middle-class background, who jumps on any old 'liberal-minded bandwagon' but, contrary to his supposed credentials, behaves like a 'cheap-suited football hooligan…' He's so confused and contrary. He thinks he is 'Mr Green'! He has a season ticket to Chelsea, a Second Home, a badly paid foreign *Au Pair*, Private School Fees to find, or Coaching Fees to pay to help his perfect 'Little Dears' gain entrance to the nearest 'Grammar School', etc. etc. and so on and bloody on and on and on and on... This **'Gross Pig'**, being such a *Contrary Minded Do-Gooder*, probably snorts *cocaine* by the bucket-load; thus contributing to the rapid destruction of the planet he thinks he wants to save! For, unbeknown to him, they have to keep on cutting down more and more of his beloved Amazonian Rain Forest to grow the bloody stuff in the first place!! God, I loathe him….

He's now pushed my arm off the arm rest! 'Filthy Smell Bag….' His legs are so wide apart, in that ridiculously classic *Alpha Male Pose*, that if he were naked we would all be subjected to a revolting 'full-frontal' view of his ever-so-small 'willy!' I bet he drives a *Sports Car* too... Dickhead….

----- *Kennington* -----

I've changed trains, thankfully escaping the 'A1 Twat'.

----- *Waterloo* -----

The time is 10.14 a.m. The carriage is full, though not unpleasant, for, during daylight hours at least, a better class of person usually alights here… They come up from the Home Counties. On the whole they speak properly, have manners, and do not read the juvenile and patronising *Guardian!!!!*

----- *Embankment* -----

I now have a free hour and a half to kill, so I'm going to chill out and soak up a few rays… I recommend *Embankment* to anyone with time to spare. Take a stroll across the amazing footbridges that have been constructed either side of the *Hungerford Bridge*, which carries rolling stock to and from *Charing Cross*. Their official title eludes me, something to do with the *Millennium* I think; or is that the one further up the river, near St Paul's?

Anyhow, firstly, facing the *Thames*, cross the bridge on the left hand side... Having traversed the river and taken in the magnificent view downstream towards the inspiring dome of *Sir Christopher Wren's* masterpiece, the one and only *St Paul's Cathedral*, treat yourself to an espresso, cappuccino or latte on the 'Southbank', preferably on the terrace of the *Royal Festival Hall...* Away from the drone of London traffic you can quietly sip your coffee whilst immersing yourself in the activity of artists and buskers below, the ancient muddy river providing a magical backdrop as it sweeps its way towards *Tower Bridge*, the tidal estuary, and out into the turbulent clutches of the *North Sea*. Alternatively, simply stare at the beauty all around you, especially at night, or while away your time 'people-watching'. After this therapeutic interlude explore the *Royal Festival Hall*, book a seat for a production at *The National Theatre* or nose around *The National Film Theatre*: your choices are endless.

Before you leave, spare some time to enjoy the wide array of street artists further upstream. Then, ascend the steps to the other bridge and marvel at the sight of *The Houses of Parliament, Big Ben*, and the *Millennium Wheel*, more commonly known as the 'London Eye...' Marvel at the view from the centre of this bridge: it sure is a sight to behold, one that increases in mysticism and beauty on every visit, but particularly at night when it transforms into a most magically inspiring wonderland.

More often than not a struggling artist is selling an oil or water colour of one of the iconic views. But, for me, the trip is only complete if, as I slowly pace across the bridge, the Romanian-looking band are playing their chillingly romantic folk music... The small guy who plays the accordion has the most piercing blue eyes. He always looks as if he is on cloud nine, ready to float away to a secretly cherished land full of sweet dreamy pleasures. I often intriguingly wonder why he always appears so blissfully happy! Does he hold the secrets to *Nirvana….!* Oh to be a Romanian Gypsy! Mind you, I've never heard him speak, so, for all I know he could be from Bolton!

When you again arrive on the north side of the river do not simply jump back on the tube but wander past the ferry and pleasure-boat terminal and soon you will be presented with the wonderful sight of the *Egyptian Obelisk,* one of three known collectively as *Cleopatra's Needles.* Which is actually a misnomer, as they were built around a thousand years before her lifetime; the twin to the London obelisk can be found in New York City, a third one, whose other half remains in Luxor, is erected somewhere in Paris… After marvelling at its antiquity and the fading hieroglyphs, take a good hard look as the Egyptians long for it to be returned. Then, cross the busy road to enter the relatively unknown jewel that is Embankment Gardens.

The Embankment Gardens stretch both sides of the footbridges and are a true paradise, a little oasis amongst the madness of city life. There are a myriad of bronze statues depicting various famous people, some paying tribute to our brave '*War Heroes*', towering 'London Plane Trees', small grass areas, stunningly exotic perennial and annual borders, an abundance of park benches, the little café where you can buy your obligatory 'espresso', and a quaint and active band stand: altogether making this, I feel, the best 'gardens' in London.

For me, what makes *Embankment Gardens* so special is knowing that as one unwinds, contemplates, and stares, you are actually sitting in the *Temese, Tamesas, Tamesis, Tamisiam, Tafwys, Thame, Thame-Isis*, now simply 'The Thames...' The land having been reclaimed from the mighty river itself, in fact just beyond the *Band Stand* there sits an original *Watergate* which must be at least two hundred yards from the present-day shoreline... The history lying beneath as you relax there on a warm, pleasant day is immense... My mind always starts to wander, conjuring up images of *Water Taxis* carrying unfortunate pitiful figures towards their grim fate at *The Tower of London*, rich Merchants to their *Riverside Mansions*, Royalty to *Hampton Court* or *Greenwich Palace*, Parliamentarians to *Westminster* and the buzz of ancient '*Frost Fairs*' that covered the river when it froze over for long periods during severe medieval winters. It truly is a magical and inspiring place which sits directly upon thousands of years of our *Great British History....*

I have just awoken from my slumber in this bijou *Garden of Eden*. My hour and a half is well and truly up. It's time to stop daydreaming and head off into the madding crowd. I'm sure one of the 'Buxom Office Girls' standing nearby will be more than delighted to take ownership of my idyllic bench seat, near the café, just to the right of the huge plane tree... If I was fifteen years younger she would probably already be here. Sat on my lap!

Friday 10th October

I am back on my faithful old *Steamer Chair*, courtesy of the depleted rainforest, enjoying another day of the resurgent Indian summer. The breeze is picking up, but the autumn sunshine still powerful enough to temper its effects.

Crispy Cos lettuce is the perfect partner to smooth duck paté… I like to spread it onto the curvaceous leaves, then squeeze over fresh lemon juice, followed by a few turns of coarsely ground black pepper; before finally indulging my salivated mouth with the crunchy, tangy, sweet-and-sour taste sensation... and no, this is not a voice-over for a well-known supermarket chain!

Eating outside, with the sun on your back, certainly heightens your taste buds and has the ability to transform even the simplest of snacks into a perfect feast..! The Melton Mowbray pork pie I cut into even quarters, one slice of thick buttered wholemeal toast with the crust attached I cut into soldiers, the supermarket finest hummus with roasted vegetables I carefully dollop onto one corner of the plate with a dessert spoon, my crispy Cos lettuce and smooth duck paté sensations I place to the side of the plate, and taking centre stage are three small vine ripened cherry tomatoes. Not being much of a drinker of alcohol, definitely never indulging too early on a weekday, my accompanying beverage is a piping hot cup of English tea. *Perfecto!*

After all this laziness and over-indulgence I now feel like a *'nap'*. I'm savouring these last few blissful hours before I, again, adorn myself with my polyester-enriched uniform. Yes, come four-thirty this afternoon, I shall be slowly dressing myself in irritatingly hot synthetic garments and duly departing for that *Retail God.* If you live in South-west London or Suburban Surrey and *shop online* with my fine company you stand a good chance of me delivering your groceries, in copious numbers of *orange plastic bags!* The time of my arrival will depend, wholeheartedly, on the *Satellite Navigational System* working and my ability to read house numbers in the pitch dark from my 'one-man van!'

On Tuesday evening I was let loose on my own! I was a solo *Local Delivery Agent* without the luxury of an 'onboard buddy' to steady the ship, as on the two previous occasions....! When *John*, the Online Manager, initially informed me what I was in for that evening I have to admit I was a little apprehensive, fearful even, of the adventure that was about to involve me. My concerns, it transpired, were not at all unfounded!

I loaded the delivery vehicle with my customers' ambient, chilled and frozen produce, carried out a 'Vehicle Safety Check', filled in a 'Damage Report Form', re-checked the customers' orders, filled in yet more pages of paperwork, then off I set following the softly spoken lady's automated voice through the dark streets of *30s Suburbia...* Everything seemed to be in order, my nerves settled, it was evening rush hour but the roads weren't too clogged-up, and as I arrived at my first customer I started to relax a little. I was fortunate: the street was quite wide and I was able to park directly outside the delivery address. Time was on my side. I only spent five minutes unloading the mountain of heavy bags. *Company Policy* dictates that you are allowed six minutes at each doorstep and not a second more, so, as I pulled away a minute ahead of schedule I thought I was well on the way, clearly successful at delivering their valuable goods on time. Early even!

'Piece of piss, this Online Delivery Agent lark,' I

mumbled as I punched the postcode into the 'Sat Nav' for the next victim of faceless modernity… Deliveries came and went. Everything was swimming along nicely until I tried to reach *Mrs Helle-Clarke*, a First-time Customer living in Oak Close! The entrance to Oak Close turned out to be off Greenhill Road, which was conveniently located behind a privet hedge! Yes, that's right, a 'bleedin'' hedge! Despite this the condescending monotone 'bitch' on the 'Sat Nav' delighted in repeatedly informing me that I was arriving at my destination:

'You are arriving at your destination… You are arriving at your destination…' Unfortunately, I did not believe her, as I wrongly assumed that Oak Close would have a road leading up to it..! How foolish of me! Ignoring 'Mrs Sat Nav' was extremely costly, as I spent the next ten minutes driving aimlessly around in ever-decreasing circles looking for elusive Oak Close. During this period of high tension the annoying voice from above delighted in continually informing me that I was off the planned route and that I should turn left here, right at the junction, take the second exit at the roundabout, in fifty yards go straight over, in one hundred yards turn sharp left, and so on; until she finally gave up on me completely…

'You are no longer on the planned route. Smart Nav is checking traffic conditions and renewing your route. If you require assistance please use the touch screen…'

Eventually, after winning the 'Greater London Swearing Finals', I had a stroke of genius..! I telephoned the 'Ruddy Customer', which, according to Online Policy, I should have done when I realised I was well up 'Shit Creek' without the proverbial paddle. After she explained to me that she did indeed live in a close behind a privet hedge it was a piece of cake! I went straight back to square one, although the nearest available parking space was a hundred yards away from her privet-disguised house. Forty carrier bags later her hall was piled high and deep with bashed-about shopping and she was in possession of a '£10 Voucher' for my tardiness. So at least she was a *Happy Bunny!!*

The last nightmare of the evening involved a New Build Housing Estate, which *'Mrs Sat Nav'* didn't know existed. So, by the time I returned to HQ, I had dispensed with two more '£10 Vouchers', become overly hot, smelly, glued to my *polyester uniform*, dehydrated, and ready to commit murder..! All in all, it was a very stressful evening; but surely worth it for a little over £7.50 an hour! Which, I believe is around the 'living', or more like 'just about surviving' wage for London… No wonder they always need *Drivers!!*

Monday 13th October

The *Indian Summer* has been whisked away in a bundle of milky white cloud. Gone are the vivid blue sky, heat, stillness and tranquillity; a breeze is mustering and it seems as if the temperature is dropping in preparation for the sun's long journey towards the depths of the southern hemisphere... Please don't leave us; you gave us more than three weeks of hope and, but for the odd day here and there, tempered consistency in our daily lives.

Weather is, undoubtedly, a cruel commodity. Just as you become accustomed to the pattern, crash-bang-wallop, off it goes again, in a totally different direction... Why is the weather so harsh on the *British Isles* in particular? I read somewhere that we are plumb in the middle of six weather patterns, which is why we have, quite possibly, the most changeable weather in the world! We were probably singled out for 'Extreme Weather Tolerance' precisely because of our incredible *national psyche*. Only the *British* could cope with sudden and unpredictable hourly changes in weather! After all is said and done we are the most apologetic nation on earth: 'sorry mate', occasionally, nowadays, 'sorry sir' or 'sorry madam', but generally just 'sorry'!

Though we are not nearly as polite and well-mannered as we once were, forever apologising is definitely our forte: even our *yobs* have the *sorry* gene stamped into their DNA. Hence the 'sorry mate', 'sorry luv', or after a public brawl with another pink, flabby-fleshed, tattoo-drenched, inebriated delinquent (male or female) the classic 'kiss-and-make-up sorry...' It doesn't matter if your trousers are halfway down your ass, your boob has flopped out of your synthetic singlet, the top of your pubic hair line is visible and your hair looks like it has just had an electric shock: after a punch-up *Lads and Ladettes* are, politely, 'sorry'. After which they are likely to down a few more convivial pints in the pub, followed by vodka chasers or some high-proof spirit laced with sweet juices... Inevitably, the *sap* begins to rise again, in turn creating yet more volatile reactions which are manifested either in another fight or a casual sexual encounter in the pub toilets, the local park, a bus shelter, or if it is *true love!* they may even wait until they return home to enjoy the novelty of *sex in a bed...!* Obviously we do not all behave in this manner! The quieter, more mature *Brit* tends to avoid town centres like the plague on Friday or Saturday nights, preferring to stay home to entertain friends and family or simply while away the evening in front of the mind-numbing schedule of 'Reality' and 'Z-list Celebrity TV Shows'. Control by Media or the Multi Billion Pound Drinks Industry... What a starkly depressing choice..!

Following *binge-drinking*, *queuing* comes a close second in the list of national obsessions. It is a practice peculiar to the English-speaking nations of the world, as we often find out, to our cost, whenever we venture abroad.... In *Blighty* queue-barging is an extremely dangerous pastime, unforgivable lowly behaviour, considered the height of rudeness... Should this repellent activity occur, the normally overly accommodating *Brit* will soon have his back up! Firstly, he or she is liable to tut their disapproval, which will soon be followed by a deep sigh, followed by a moan, groan, and then if the culprit still hasn't got the message they will actually engage a neighbour in the queue, a person they have stood next to for ten minutes without uttering a word, and loudly discuss the selfish and unacceptable behaviour of the aforementioned *queue-barger*... If public humiliation does not shame the perpetrator into joining the end of the *queue* a fellow, normally reserved, Briton will step in with a well-versed disapproving verbal onslaught. Generally, this is successful, it does the job, the *criminal* realising his misdemeanour reddening in colour and embarrassingly retreating to the rear of said *queue*. However, if he still won't budge, or pretends he hasn't got the message, the whole *queue* will slowly awake from its conformist slumber to engage in a series of group tuts. Several more people will then verbalise their disgust. Finally, if the *arsehole* is still in stubborn situ, a rare phenomenon strikes, our wartime spirit erupts, the *Brits* suddenly uniting, steadfast in their resolve, bonded together like superglue, inhibitions to the wind they will, in no uncertain terms, hurl deserved verbal abuse at the obdurate *tosser* in question...

We're forever saying 'sorry', 'giving way', promoting 'the underdog', believing unsubstantiated 'bleeding-heart stories' because we're not a nation of liars, giving charitably, allowing people second and third chances, giving people money and houses and generally pandering to their every pathetic need. Then when the ship is well and truly sinking, all seems to be lost and our backs are against the wall, we either emigrate or the fire within our belly reignites and we, finally, stand up to be counted. That is exactly how we won, on our own for a large part, two *World Wars*... Although the 'Politically Correct' would obviously dispute this point of view, any chance to rubbish our once great nation and away they go, as expeditious as shit off a shovel..!

The *P.C. Police* conveniently forget that it is the law-abiding majority who pay their inflated wages, affording them the time to propagate their narrow-minded, absurd and ironically intolerant mantra! *Freedom of speech* is their

'Divine Right' and it is our God-given duty to speak as they say but not act as they do, for only they have the luxury of conceited hypocrisy....! These moronic, overpaid 'Heads of State Supported Quangos' are our 'Unelected Masters', treacherous loathers of their own countrymen. To their ridiculously warped way of thinking the 'White British' must bear responsibility for all misdemeanours and injustices ever perpetrated throughout history (more overseas aid please!). If you are one step worse, in their narrow minds, than 'British', then you are quite possibly beyond reproach. Yes, 'English'! If you are unfortunate enough to be *English* and pale cream or crimson pink in skin tone, then you are expected to apologise for:

Slavery, Wars in any region of the world, any form of Privilege, Private Education, The Conservative Party, UKIP, The 'Racist' Police Force, your National Anthem, The Last Night of the Proms, Cricket on a village green, warm Real Ale, The Grand National, Hunting, Shooting, Elite Universities, love of all Animals, an obsession with Pets, being great Gardeners, keeping your Home and Garden in pristine condition, not paying enough Taxes, not learning enough Foreign Languages, taking polluting Foreign Holidays, Football, Yobs, English History, St George's Day, learning about your own Culture, trying to recreate our diluted English Identity, drinking too much Alcohol or Tea, and generally you must apologise for having any opinion about the state of a land that was once our Native Country!!

Even after apologising for this seemingly insurmountable list of atrocities your card is still indelibly marked! The 'scapegoating' has only just begun, and you have to be properly reformed.....! As an *Ancient Briton* all traces of your identity must be eradicated for the greater good of the new, superior, *Multicultural Society!* Unfortunately for you, there is no room for *Native* rituals and shenanigans: you must now immerse yourself in the culture and traditions of anyone but the *Britons*. Indeed, converting to any other religion, however intolerant, would be considered a success, a critical leap of real faith on the road to enlightenment. Finally, once your traditions and culture are but a blur in your new medieval mind and you are at ease mocking the ever dwindling 'host community' you will be deemed a triumph and awarded a shiny new '*P.C. Star......*' Hooray!

Welcome to the 'Disunited Kingdom' of the 21st century AD...... Sorry, that should be *AA.... After Allah!!*

Tuesday 14th October

I am back at *Supermarket Heaven* tonight, plying their wares around suburbia. I suppose I shouldn't complain! The last two days have been a satisfying interlude in my new journey up the slippery Retail Career Ladder.

Sunday was, all over the 'Disunited Kingdom', a perfect day of wall-to-wall sunshine. Absolutely still, not even the slightest puff of wind, the sky as vivid as in the Australian desert.

\----- The *Bluey-Grey Cat* is heading towards the house... He's crossed the patio and is curiously heading my way… Oh no! What a *cock-tease!* He's stopped, turned full circle and buggered off again, without me stroking him! How long is he going to carry on this 'cat and mouse game'? He must be a female: too many mixed signals! Nevertheless, I am a man of patience; I'll stroke the little minx eventually, however long it takes! \-----

Anyway, Sunday was perfect. I ventured to *Box Hill*, near Dorking, with my *Companion!* We had a very pleasant drive through suburbia, over the M25 and into the Surrey Countryside. Just after *Denbies Vineyard* we turned off the A24 and began our ascent of *Box Hill*. Stunning autumnal leaves, resplendent against a vivid green floor, soon gave way to slopes of dried yellowy grass, which, against the azure blue sky, transformed the landscape from the Surrey Downs to the wild planes of East Africa. Then, without warning, the sun was eclipsed, not by the moon, but by a thick and heavy hill fog. Undeterred, *Julie's* little white *Rover* climbed all the way to the top. We parked in the well-maintained car park and duly parted with our £3 for the privilege… Everything seems to be chargeable nowadays. Even nature is taxed!

The *fog* didn't seem to be shifting so we relieved ourselves in the cleaner-than-usual public toilets and perused 'The National Trust Gift Shop'. We left empty-handed, unwilling, indeed not needing, to purchase an oversized pencil for £4 or five pieces of chocolate chilli fudge for some equally exorbitant amount. Even with a 'Credit Crunch' in full flow prices are always sky-high in these sorts of places; although, to be fair, we were up a steep hill in the wilds of *Surrey*, far from civilisation; at least three miles south of the M25! So there were extra logistical costs involved in stocking the Gift Shop…! When we exited the retail hub, for the briefest of moments there was a glimmer of hope as we managed to identify the shape of the sun through the whiteness that surrounded us. However, it soon disappeared again, behind another tranche of swirling fog or mist. I have never been entirely sure of their differing definitions: is one on land and the other at sea?!

Our visibility may have been somewhat impaired, but it was soon re-awoken by the sight of throngs of cyclists, of all ages, bravely reaching the summit of *Box Hill*. They made quite an impact as they emerged from the milky cloud. Tight Lycra and cone-shaped helmets were the order of the day. They had all the latest gear and brand spanking new bikes. These were semi-professional or obsessive amateur cyclists! They were mainly men, apart from the odd female of the species; who were hard to recognise, for due to the fact that they were squashed back into their chests by tight black Lycra they seemed to have little in the way of bosoms at all: their *breasts* as hard to find as the *guys' crutches* were to ignore!

Lycra Shorts on men? This is definitely a very grey area..! Average height-men with a thick-set build can get away with this figure-hugging material, but the more lanky specimens, who were in the majority, did struggle to carry off the look; mainly because they were far more lily-white than the sprinkling of bronzed *Beefcakes*. However, the *Lanky Lily-whites* did posses a secret weapon! An ace card with the Ladies......! Yes, on full view, it was there for all to see, larger and longer than the *Beefcakes'* own kinetic heat-swollen centrepieces: 'The Lanky Man's Dick...!' My dropped jaw in the school shower was perfectly justified! Overly lanky guys do have Anacondas down their pants!

Having finished righting the wrongs of 'Lycra', off we rambled to the 'Viewing Point', the walk taking all of two minutes… As we vainly looked towards the hidden view we were soon joined by a host of families and loved-up couples with the same unrealistic intentions. There we stood, staring into the damp white abyss, laughing, chuckling and giggling like dirty-minded teenagers, still unable to erase 'Lycra' and *Sweaty Crutches* from our titillated minds! Eventually, our juvenility subsided long enough for us to decide to leave and return another day, when we could admire *Jane Austen's* legendary vista in all its beautiful glory.

Half an hour later we passed through a pair of magnificent black wrought-iron gates. Within moments our eyes met with the beauty of Red and Fallow Deer. This was my initiation to *Bushy Park*, opposite *Old Deer Park* and *Hampton Court Palace*. The park was resplendent, awash with autumn colours, all perfectly complemented by a resurgent vivid blue sky…. Driving down a tree-lined avenue you come to a huge circular pond with a divine sculpture at its centre. The road then carries on between an identical continuation of horse-chestnuts. Everywhere you glance the park is dotted with wonderfully majestic specimen tress, their drying leaves slowly turning into earthy hues with the help of a warm, southward-heading sun… Yes, *Bushy Park* comes highly recommended. Whatever the season, I'm sure it holds a special charm. And thanks to my mobile phone, which I normally regard as the biggest curse of the modern world, I have the most wonderful picture of a huge 'rusty-leaved oak' standing majestically, alone, against a cloudless blue sky.

When you are all 'parked out', leave your car in the car park, which is currently free! Walk out of the park through the gate on the *Teddington* side, turn left and soon turn right… These are wide residential streets with many varieties of broadleaf tress, and an incredible array of rather sumptuous detached Edwardian and Victorian houses: every one with its own character, charm and beautifully established gardens. Some have perfect picket fencing, others define their boundaries with iron railings or lovely London stock brick walls. The shrubs are as established as the trees that line the streets; viburnums, smoke bushes, sumacs on the turn from green to yellow to fiery red, Portuguese laurels, deep crimson hydrangea heads in the final throes of life before the onset of winter, pyracanthas laden with berries in red or orange, box and holly topiaries in the most beautiful shapes imaginable, even the occasional rhododendron in an unusual second flowering. Each front garden has its own unique charm. One had a little gravel courtyard surrounded by ground cover plants and heathers, but still with enough space for late perennial flowers to penetrate through, others had dahlias in all colours of the rainbow. Some houses had porches or walls smothered in Boston ivy or Virginia creeper in a stunning curtain-call of autumn colour. Old wisterias wrapped their way round black cast-iron drainpipes, across a wall, around a wooden sash window or the turned wooden posts of a grand entrance porch.

These streets deserve to be walked at leisure. On a perfect autumn afternoon they certainly lift one's spirits. *Multicultural Morden* seeming a million miles away….. After marvelling more and more, wishing we could afford to live in such an area, we were presented with 'The Adelaide', a quaint Victorian pub with a perfectly pleasant garden. Here we indulged ourselves in a good old 'English Sunday Roast' and a couple of 'Gin and Tonics' for good measure.

So there you have it, a fine way to spend a Sunday. I highly recommend it. The only downside was my 'Yorkshire Pudding', which wasn't a patch on my mother's highly risen home-made creations. These were hideous squashy individual portion-controlled offerings, obviously courtesy of *Auntie Betsy*, or whatever her name is!? I really should know, as I deliver copious amounts of them to the new breed of *Microwave Cooks* in mind-numbing suburbia. The same company sells frozen roast potatoes too, how lazy is that!!?

Wednesday 15th October

Around ten thirty last night, upon returning from my lowly-paid delivery shift, I flicked on the television, reclined into my two-seater sofa, sipped piping hot tea from a fine bone-china mug, stared, pondered and debated with myself the merits of taking on an extra driving shift at the supermarket!

Clapham South again, a lunchtime tube trip today, so there is plenty of space for everyone. A *Freemason* has just joined the train and has elected to sit opposite me. He is probably in his sixties, with a full head of hair (jammy git) swept back like *Elvis*, a rather translucent complexion, clean-cut finger nails, very few facial lines, a chiselled face and a square jaw. He is wearing Freemason's attire; the usual pinstriped trousers, a black single-breasted jacket, shiny black loafers with a small gold Dickensian buckle, a pristine white shirt, cufflinks, dark grey socks and a black tie with two thin diagonal red stripes and an emblem embroidered in between them. He is also in possession of a briefcase, which is burgundy rather than the usual black and is totally square in shape. All in all a very presentable surprise for a lunchtime tube journey up the *Northern Line*. I reckon he's *en route* to *The Grand Lodge*, near the Connaught Hotel in Great Queen Street.

----- *Kennington* -----

We have both changed trains and quite coincidentally end up sitting opposite one another for a second time… I'd stake money on him alighting at *Charing Cross* and walking to the 'Lodge' via the *Strand*. He certainly looks fit enough, so I can't see why he would bother to carry on to *Tottenham Court Road* to change trains for *Holborn*. Granted, it is a shorter walk to *Great Queen Street*. However, the time saved by walking from *Charing Cross* would enable him to already be there, in the thick of it! His crisp clothes stripped off, many a hand shaken in that odd but familiar manner, an ancient brotherhood dancing ritual in full flow!

How wrong one can be! I've just hopped onto the *Charing Cross* platform and he is sat firmly in his seat! Maybe he is taking the long route after all, or perhaps he isn't even a member of the 'Fraternity'! Moreover a Butler, Undertaker, or Struggling Actor! Maybe he's a secret 'porn star' heading for *Soho* to promote some filthy DVD!!

Anyway, last night my oldest friend, whom I rarely now see, jumped out of the television at me! This is the second time in ten years this has happened! On each occasion I had just returned home from my dead-end job. So, one naturally starts to question one's own situation and how it came to be the polar opposite of one's contemporary's, who is now a major celebrity! Well, maybe that's a little far-fetched. But he has certainly managed to forge ahead in the world of business, where I, on the other hand, have failed dismally! The first time this occurred I was married, in my early thirties, and my wife and I were running the country pad of a *super-rich couple.*

After we had catered a marathon weekend 'House Party' I collapsed onto the four-seater sofa that came with our furnished *Cotswold cottage* and flicked on the telly, only to be greeted by a very dapper-looking *Richard....! Richard* hailed from the same small *Surrey village* where I grew up. Up to the age of sixteen he attended *Oxted County School,* thereafter embarking upon his fledgling career in business... We lost touch with one another in our early twenties, which didn't surprise me as *Richard* was one of those people you were everything to for a while, before he inevitably moved on to fresher pastures. *Richard* was perfectly charming, funny, witty, laid-back, but extremely driven and therefore a social butterfly. All the girls took a shine to him, despite the fact he had rather small 'piggy' eyes and was far from classically handsome. When you were *Richard's* favoured friend he made you feel as if you were his sole priority in life; he was completely intoxicating and one instantaneously fell under his spell. Alas, it never lasted: he soon spread his wings and, if you were lucky, you were immediately downgraded to the status of casual acquaintance. Though none of this was done with any malice or intent, it was just the way he was. *Richard* never fell out with anybody, you simply enjoyed the time you were allowed; but he dictated its longevity, terms and conditions of friendship. I'm sure that is how, ultimately, he became so successful. He had bucketsful of manipulative charm that we all lapped up ad infinitum.

Anyway, *Richard* was in the process of being interviewed, albeit on a satellite channel, by a smart-suited presenter of a business affairs programme. This was a few months prior to the 'dot.com' bubble of 2,000, when the heads of the associated companies were being hailed as 'Masters of the Universe!' It sounds rather familiar, old ground being re-trodden, just by 'Merchant Wankers' this time. Mind you, the 'Merchant Wankers' are somewhat more fortunate as they are being bailed out by us 'Poor Tax Payers', trapped in our dreary dead-end jobs while they continue their vapour-trail around the world sipping *Dom Perignon* at our expense. That's modern-day capitalism for you, more akin to the medieval 'feudal' system. 'Twas ever thus...!

Back to *Richard*.... He had not changed a bit. Age had not withered him, the only difference being a fine Savile Row suit replacing his Comprehensive School uniform. Unlike

Richard I was fortunate enough to be sent to private school, which I now realise was a great privilege. Although *Richard's* family were by no means poor, his father was a bit of a whizz-kid: he had an insatiable appetite for fast, expensive, sporty cars.

Despite my good fortune, my private boarding school only succeeded in fostering and enhancing the independent, stubborn, anti-establishment gene that is prevalent on both sides of our family. As I have since discovered, to my cost, this means the world of business is not overly suited to me, or me to it. I have had flashes of success running my own enterprises but I soon become tired and thus begin to lose focus, then irritation and boredom set in, which usually turns to despair as I over-analyse the whole thing and end up wanting to run away from it completely... I love adventure, trying out knew things. The only 'consistency' I am interested in is with my friends, home and family... My biggest fear has always been committing myself to the wrong pursuit, the downside being that I can't commit a hundred per cent to anything. Consequently, this invariably leads to a life of permanent frustration as one never finds one's 'niche' or feels relaxed enough to 'plough on' regardless... This was not an issue for *Richard*, as he was always determined and focused. Hence the reason he is now a 'Telecommunications King' with his own successful 'Empire', living between Denver, Colorado and London! Puke...! I shouldn't be surprised if I next saw him on a business investment programme such as 'Dragons' Den'! Please God do not let me serve him 'canapes' at my next dead end job.....! Not that I have a problem with serving per se. In fact I quite enjoy the theatrics involved, but to serve a contemporary from the small village where you grew up would be a trifle embarrassing. Especially as he was the guy I went 'joy riding' with down my neighbour's half-mile drive, only to end up crashing my black and yellow 'Citroen Dyane' into their ornately over-the-top lion statue, where my little car became precariously wedged *à la The Italian Job!* That certainly took some explaining to the neighbours, and my parents! However, 'Richard's charm' did, as ever, considerably lighten the blow and reduce the gravity of the ensuing punishment.

Sean knew *Richard* too… They both lived in the village, whereas my family home was around a mile from the centre, in a bigger house surrounded by heath and woodland. *Sean* is a year younger than me and it is he who greeted me via television last night, the programme being about London's world-famous *Savile Row* and the handful of 'Bespoke Tailors' that still survive there to this day… Nestled behind *Regent's Street*, a stone's throw from the clubs of *St James* and the boutique shops of *Burlington Arcade*, this formed part of the traditional heart of London's 'West End', where 'City Gents' and 'Aristocrats' would mingle and spend their wealth on all manner of indulgences, some for wearing on the flesh, others solely for carnal fulfilment! World-renowned *Piccadilly Circus* and the neighbouring streets of *Soho* providing ample opportunity for many a 'red-blooded male', as comforting boys and girls were freely available in Victorian and Edwardian London… Women of means were also catered for, in whichever way they fancied, *Gay, Lesbian, Ménage à trois, Bisexual* etc... Come nightfall the genteel streetscape was rife with 'street prostitutes' carrying out *sexual acts* in carriages, dark alleyways, on park benches or, if you preferred, indoors in one of the numerous bars and brothel houses. For countless impoverished London families it was a far from uncommon way of supplementing their income. Many a young East End 'Nancy Boy' or 'Buxom Wench' would declare they were 'going up the Dilly'….

I'm digressing, back to *Sean*… Paris is the well-known queen of 'Ladies' Couture', but London has always been king with regard to 'Gentlemen's Attire…' The documentary was about the threat to *Savile Row* from an 'off-the-peg' retailer who had mimicked the history and prestige of the disparate group of tailors on the 'Row', then filled its shelves with clothes manufactured in *China!* They had cleverly mixed the old with the new, maintained a classic style, and even ventured into the sale of upmarket T-shirts sold at an appropriately exorbitant amount… Come launch day, muscle-laden young men in tight thigh-hugging shorts were unashamedly used to coax the throngs of young urban 'Wannabes' into store. Along with bucket-loads of aspirational marketing it worked a treat, as the Middle Classes entered in their droves to peruse the offerings of the latest fashionable 'House of Capitalism'. Some time later the 'clonish' throng dutifully re-emerged with branded designer bags hanging off their forearms, each one containing at least one £50 T-shirt lovingly wrapped in crisp tissue paper. Job done!

Sean's Father, looking very distinguished with his mounds of grey hair and claret-enhanced skin, was very philosophical, indeed he appeared rather amused by the entire stage-managed event; which rather flew in the face of the quiet, gentlemanly heritage of 'The Row…' His father proved an integral part of the programme, which is unsurprising as their firm is the oldest listed establishment on 'The Row'. The family claimed to be pioneers in establishing its reputation as the foremost 'Bespoke Tailors Street' in the world.

Sean came into view on several occasions but never

spoke… The poor 'Old Mucker' did look a little 'washed-up!' Mind you, with two young boys, a demanding European wife and a huge Clapham mortgage, it's no surprise he looked a little worse for wear than 'back in the day', when we were 'joy-riding', with *Richard*, in my hand-sprayed 'Citroen 2CV…!' I'll have to tune in next week to see if he's been upgraded from a 'walk-on' role. However, let's not feel too sorry for the 'guy!' For *Sean* has the joy of a family, lives in a desirable part of town and has an established business to run, albeit inherited. Then there is *Richard*, a successful 'International Businessman', and to rub more salt into my pathetic little wound they have both been on T.V! I, on the other hand, have failed in both. Marriage and business..! Despite my privileged background I have somehow ended up 'dumping' lazy people's shopping off! There must be a rational explanation! And being a *Highly Sensitive Person* I will not rest until I know the answer to my neurosis in suburbia!

The *Indian summer* is back…. The sky is clear blue again, the temperature has nevertheless dropped several degrees and we are now in the *Himalayan Foothills* rather than the heat of the *Northern Plains*. Oh, I nearly forgot, I finally touched the cat and its bluey-grey fur was as velvety soft as I had imagined, like pure luxuriant silk.

4pm already… I have demolished my 'cheese, bean and sausage melt' in just a few mouthfuls. I don't often indulge myself but when you are 'pissed off', as I appear to be most of the time lately, fat and protein wrapped in more fatty carbohydrates in the form of hot puff pastry scores a direct hit on the 'G-spot' of taste. This was dutifully followed by an extremely sugary jam doughnut, satisfyingly helped on its way down my digestive system by yet another cup of my standard piping hot brew. My previously rumbling stomach is now happily settled, and the forty-five minutes wasted in my local bank now seems but a distant memory.

Alas, *waiting* is standard practice in the *Morden branch* of my former *Building Society*. Which over twenty years ago decided to transform itself into a bank and then, more recently, was consumed by a large foreign operator who is heavily involved in 'F1 Motor Sport'. Unfortunately, the warm and sunny Mediterranean climate has so far failed to filter through into the cool arteries of its large UK arm…! I, along with a frail old lady, was a token *white blob* in a sea of people from around the globe. When I was eventually seen to - served would be too strong a word - the lasting impression was not one to be savoured in the slightest! The cashier, to be fair, thanked me for waiting, though her metronomic tone lacked conviction so, unable to contain myself, I replied with more than a tinge of sarcasm:

'Well that's what you do in here, isn't it?!'

Naturally she hardened slightly, as she hadn't anticipated dealing with such an awkward response. I must have been concealing my inner rage quite successfully, as she seemed totally unaware that she was face to face with an 'anti-everything-and-everybody maniac', or perhaps she was simply humouring me! Far more likely to be the latter I should say, for I am totally inept at polite pretence, and the smoke was literally bellowing out of my ears… The poor cow is probably close to a nervous breakdown herself, every day staring at endless people waiting 'in line', as the Americans would say, with only one other cashier, if she's lucky, to help her process the irritated horde… I don't think I could stick it, sitting there all day listening to the constant moaning and cynical jokes of the ever-increasing queue. After a while it must become very grating. I should imagine my customer service skills would be tested to the max and beyond! I'm quite sure it would be only a matter of time before I was relieved of my job after telling some pompous customer, not one like me of course, to 'fuck off….' Gone are the days when the customer was always right!

However, despite my ruffled feathers, the cashier remained professional and still tried to pacify me. She had probably overheard my earlier discontented mutterings towards her *Spivy Non-Cashier Colleague….* You know the type! They waddle around trying to look important, clipboard in hand, nose in the air, beyond approach. Then duly disappear through a side door or a glass-fronted office where you, *Plebs*, are strictly forbidden to venture… When said uninterested, pitiful little robot passed her disgruntled paying customers with more than total indifference was the moment my mouth automatically leapt into spontaneous observational action, declaring:

'If they moved any slower we would be going backwards!'

My on-the-edge sarcasm was loud enough for all to hear, but true to form the diminutive autocrat didn't flinch an inch as she marched past us and duly vanished into the aforementioned side door of never-ending coffee breaks. At least the young Indian guy next to me chuckled in agreement. In fact we struck up quite a rapport as we waited in line and discussed the merits of 'putting the kettle on!'

Anyway, the cashier was an old-school *West Indian Lady* with a deep and rounded 'Jamaican accent', which sadly, along with the great 'Cockney accent', is rapidly disappearing, only to be replaced by that awful new street talk that always has to end with 'Innit!'

She continued in her mission to placate me, saying:

'You normally have to queue in banks...'

I replied: 'Yes, that may be true! But in this particular bank we have to queue for far longer, and every time, without fail.'

She went on:

'I was in a bank around here the other day and I had to queue.'

Well, congratulations, I thought to myself. But it didn't change the fact that I had just spent forty-five minutes of my valuable life in her uninspiring establishment... I know it wasn't her bank, per se. However, why was she using a different bank? Obviously she didn't want to waste her time queuing in *el mio banco rubbisho* either!

'I have been in other local banks too, but this one definitely holds the world record for excessive queuing times!' I replied.

Our conversation was rapidly descending into polite edgy ping-pong; seeing as I am now over forty and trying to become mature, I decided I couldn't be bothered to fight her any more. Besides, I actually really liked her on a human level, especially her rich dulcet tones. So I saved my breath, then politely responded:

'Whatever...! I just want to pay this cash in now... It is what it is at the end of the day...!'

That's what this dreadful, unhelpful, stressed-out and unrewarding modern society has reduced us to! 'Whatever!!' We all walk around in our vacuous bubbles of fear, not sure what we are allowed to say or do any more; there are no longer natural boundaries or tiers of respect and, above all, no one is responsible for anything or anybody, come to that. Accountability is dead.

So what! Am I bothered! Whatever! There's nothing I can

do about it anyway! Get over yourself! Chill out man! etc. etc.

In the end we all seem to just give into the ideology of *dumbing down*, and slothfully slob our way through this selfish, self-indulgent life.

I definitely need to change my bank some time soon! Either that or pack my bags and leave for my pile of rubble in the *Italian hills*, before I kill someone and end up in prison with a load of feral sheep who have forgotten how to pronounce a sentence properly!

'*Innit Bruv!!!*'

Saturday 18th October

On my drive to work this morning for my marathon ten-hour shift I could not help but marvel at the fantastic turning of broadleaf trees, on what has been yet another lovely autumn day. I am totally obsessed with the leaves this year; only a complete heathen could fail to admire their overwhelming natural beauty. The combination of warm sunny days and cool nights has made them change with such intensity of colour that, before we know it, American tourists from New England will be showing up to check out the competition!

Just before I arrived at *Supermarket Heaven* I was pleasantly surprised to see a large group of *lads*, ranging from around the ages of eleven to thirteen, sprinting up the wide pavement in what looked like a friendly high-spirited race. Great team spirit, I thought, a breath of fresh air from the perpetual 'tabloid' demonizing of today's youngsters. These lads were up at a reasonable hour, on a Saturday too, defying stereotypes that we all associate with gangs of kids, not a knife-wielding *'Hoodie'* amongst them! They were consumed by the great outdoors, healthy and active, not sat in front of some violent computer game; *au contraire* these lads obviously wanted to succeed, to better themselves! They were not the type to abuse strangers in the street. Their gang was cohesive and civilized, with a mutual moral purpose to improve their status, through self-belief, respect and discipline! They wouldn't mug a granny, steal a mobile off another kid, 'Happy Slap' someone for the hell of it and upload it onto 'Facebook' or 'You Tube' as a badge of honour; no, these fine young men were probably in training for the *London Olympics!* Perhaps they were inspired by Britain's success and our fourth place on the Beijing Medal

Table, along with the phenomenal achievement of our *Paralympians*…

My general social cynicism had been proved wrong, my faith in humanity restored, or so I thought!! As I turned my car into *Supermarket Heaven* the magic was well and truly dispelled! The reason for their physical exuberance was not so high-minded after all…! *McDonalds* was their goal, and they couldn't get there quick enough. Even the dumpiest-looking one managed an impressive turn of foot. He was going hell-for-leather, anything to avoid the back of the queue, fearful they might run out of his favourite gastronomic delicacy! Come 2012 they will, more than likely, be clinically obese, not superstar athletes in the making. Still, that's the way they breed them nowadays. Send them all to *Boot Camp* I say, preferably in Siberia where their sedentary fat reserves will get eaten up more quickly. Having said that, there is probably a *McDonalds* there too!

Tuesday 21ˢᵗ October

Bhupinder is a very distinguished-looking *Sikh*, who wears a jet-black turban, has dark olive skin, a black trimmed beard, and dark brown eyes. He is the *James Bond* of *Bollywood* and on Sunday he was my buddy, shadowing me as I showed him the ropes. For after three whole weeks as a dependable *Local Delivery Agent* I have already graduated to the dizzy heights of an 'On-the-Job Trainer!'

Sunday, as its name suggests, was wall-to-wall sunshine. Though there was a slight chill in the air which reminded one of the proximity of winter and the inevitable long dark evenings. Deliveries were thin on the ground so we had a leisurely drive around suburbia, venturing to New Malden, Sutton, Morden, back to New Malden, Worcester Park, Cheam Village and then back to our beloved HQ… Tuesday and Thursday evenings seem to be very busy, sheer bedlam, so Sunday is definitely a good day to work, altogether it was verging on a pleasurable experience! Besides, I can't imagine that many people would want their shopping delivered on a Sunday! I certainly wouldn't. Added to which we are starting to close the month out, money becoming tighter as people try to survive to the next payday: if they are still fortunate enough to even have a job, what with the blind panic in the markets and the recession that is here now, whatever the politicians say... If the amount of 'value and own-label' products that I deliver is anything to go by 'The age of austerity' is definitely creeping back into vogue. Excessive over-consumption and bragging about the ever-increasing equity in your home has fallen out of favour like a lead balloon. We are all impoverished now. It is not so much 'keeping up with the Jones's', but rather 'hanging low with the Smith's' that is fast becoming the norm in today's economic car crash.

Ironic! Considering I am fed up with being a minority in my own backyard it is rather ironic that I'm always so easily able to engage with foreigners and people from ethnic minorities, though generally, people do tend to get on with one another on a one-to-one basis. I certainly have no issues with difference: I love to travel and I am extremely interested in other cultures and ancient civilisations. So, no, I am not a *racist*, as I and many *Ancient Britons* are forever being categorised by the out-of-touch *Wishy-Washy Divisive Do-Gooders!* I do not believe I am any better or worse than any other race. I just want to exercise my birthright to self-determination, like the *Scottish Nationalists* will be afforded any time soon!

The *P.C. Brigade* wilfully, verging on provocatively, refuse to accept that good community cohesion is wholly dependent on the *Indigenous Peoples* maintaining a significant majority in their own land... Look at any country where this is not so, and the locals slowly lose their identity as it becomes consumed by the rapid pace of change all around them. They become oppressed, disenfranchised, sold out by their duplicitous masters; which is very dangerous as violent civil unrest normally ensues, with resulting tragic and irreparable consequences, as has already happened to *Indigenous People* in the Amazon and many other parts of South America, to Native North Americans, Aboriginals in Australia, head hunters in Borneo and hill tribes in Burma, to name but a few... Anytime soon *Native Britons* are more than likely to end up in the same situation. The only unanswered question is, who will rule us? Will it be a combination of people from our old colonies, which would be a rather amusing full circle, or will the might of China conquer us entirely and have us all speaking Mandarin or Pekinese! Please God let it not be Polish or Lithuanian, as I can't abide the scary linguistic gutturalness, overbearing assertiveness, and altogether strident attitude.

All in all *Bhupinder* and I had a very pleasant day discussing a plethora of subjects. Having myself visited India, after my divorce, it was interesting to hear his opinions on his homeland… He has been in *Blighty* for some seven years now. The family home is in Kashmir but unfortunately over ten years ago he and his family had to flee for their lives, leaving much of their wealth behind them. However, it transpired that they owned other properties in the Punjab, the ancestral home of the *Sikhs*, so they were not completely desolate…! He came over to England with his parents and siblings, but they all returned as they found it difficult to settle in London. Too many 'Hoodies', one would imagine..! You can tell he is from a family of favourable circumstances: he exudes wealth. Besides, you rarely meet a poor Sikh. They are renowned for their business acumen; the 'Jews of India' is a common analogy used in the sub-continent… Wealthy parentage aside he came across as a completely calm, learned, controlled, caring and humble human being, quite saintly actually! If he unravelled his turban to reveal his long dark hair he would resemble a modern-day Jesus Christ!

'I love England,' he warmly declared. 'I haven't travelled extensively, but it is such a tolerant country and I want to help to keep it that way and give something back.'

More people like *Bhupinder*, please..! How refreshing it was to hear a young foreign man praise my country, and be grateful to be here as well! Rather than *Wishy-Washy Do-Gooders* encouraging people into 'hand outs' and the 'victim trap', or religious fanatics purposely stirring up hatred amongst some immigrants towards their adopted homeland in order to give weight to their own ludicrous and ill-judged crusade to change the very fabric of this country.

Bhupinder is a student in *Clapham*, hopefully not a *Sham College!* He is studying economics and sciences along with some A levels he is required to take as the exams he took in India do not match our curriculum! I'm sure his knowledge is far greater than ninety-five per cent of our own, supposedly brilliant, Graduates who don't appear to be capable of spelling or stringing a proper sentence together, myself included! English was never my strong point. Although compared with what you hear and read today I would have been on course for three 'A Stars' as you seem to be able to cheat at coursework, then on top of that they throw in lots of multiple-choice exams to give you even more of a chance of achieving high grades! It is more akin to a dumbed-down Quiz Show where nobody can lose. Everyone's a winner, regardless of their true aptitude! Anyway, I'm sure he will fly through, then after attaining these qualifications he intends to take a degree, and who knows what after that! His English is word-perfect, and for a young man he is such a gentleman, no more than twenty-five I would have thought. I hardly remember people's names any more as, usually, they fail to ignite my soul; but *Bhupinder* is made of different metal, one of those rare people you will never forget, his mark indelible… Since his family returned to India he is now alone in England, although that has clearly not diminished his resolve to succeed with pure unadulterated grace.

It was a delight to meet a fellow human being who was able to work whilst studying, as I did in my student days. The fashion amongst the vast majority of current students is to take out a huge loan; then, when they finish their, quite often useless, University Course they, from time to time, spent the last three years attending, complain bitterly about the huge debts they have accumulated! For the majority of them were too busy sleeping off their hangovers from the night before to fit in a 'part-time job'. Oh, sorry, silly me, that's all part of the modern-day creative process! Shame on them all! Not that I'm at all generalising; but there is, I'm sure you'll agree, some truth, 'innit!'

Before *Bhupinder* started working for the *Retail God* he was a minicab driver, and to make friends and help 'give back to society' he is a volunteer for *St John's Ambulance*. Which is another remarkable testament to his character and all the young people who give up their free time for the same noble cause, for as much as I decry today's visceral society I know there are still a few unsung saints among us... Why can't these inspiring young people be upheld as modern-day role models..? Why, because there is no money in it, 'innit!' You are obliged to give your time for free, which will hardly benefit you as inevitably it will interfere with your social life and diminish your chances of becoming a famous 'Untalented Celebrity'; which is, after all is said and done, the elixir of our age.

It's nearly one in the morning! I'm off to bed now for fear of becoming a *Grumpy Middle-Aged Cynic!*

Wednesday 22nd October

Yes, another wondrous autumnal day. 'I'm in heaven!' Just like *Irving Berlin* must have been when writing the unmistakable lyrics to 'Cheek to Cheek!'

Well, I digress a little, although it is truly another perfect day, weather-wise. Not that I can see it at present, as I am actually sat on the tube again… The carriage is quite full today as I left *Morden* at 9 a.m. Consequently I have become caught up with the flexi-time suits, part-time workers and a throng of impressionable young students… The beanpole standing directly in front of me has black drainpipe jeans hanging off his arse, as seems to be the current fashion. Most of his grey Lycra boxers are therefore on public show and the whole lot is precariously held up with a thick white patent-leather belt, so much so that you can practically see the top of his manhood! The *Middle-Aged Lady* standing next to him has deliberately turned her head in order to avert her gaze, to give the impression that she has no interest in his youthful man-sized bulge at all!

This tall, young, sleepy boy has an undistinguished-looking mini-rucksack, silver-effect studwork on his wide white belt, a black bomber jacket, a pale blue 'hoodie', and short-cut hair with a long *Soul Boy* quiff *à la* 1980s. He is a sort of modern-day sexualised *Punk Rocker* who is ready and willing to flash his huge cock at a moment's notice, judging by school showers that is! All the lankiest boys had 'biggies' and were only to keen to show them off..! If the statistics bear fruit he must have quite a phenomenal amount of 'wood' down there, a little too much for the *Middle-Aged Lady* to consume in one mouthful I would have thought! Although I'm sure she would love to give it a go, in fact I know she hankers for the chance as I have, once again, just caught her looking down longingly towards his snake pit..! I bet she's fantasising about prising open his 'lunch box', straddling the upstanding contents and slowly guiding it towards her hungry, moist receptacle! Or maybe she just wants him to treat her roughly and shag her from behind in a mad, frenzied animalistic onslaught of caveman-like lustfulness! Either way, she's gagging for it... As she finally, after a polite amount of time, raised her head back to its usual vertical position our gazes became locked, whereupon she slowly started to turn a darker shade of crimson! The *Young Lad* failed to notice her prying eyes as he seemed to be subtly staring towards a boy and teenage girl who were sat in the next block of seats. As he did so his tight jeans began to stretch a little further, which did not appear possible, for they were surely already at their limit of tolerance! But no, on they went, expanding even more. The shape of his crutch soon transformed from a large bulge into an outline of his 'weapon of mass destruction...' Who knows where he wanted to aim it! At the boy, the girl, or the woman! One thing's for certain, whoever received it would be in for a mouth-watering experience, if they lived to tell the tale!

----- *Victoria* -----

I changed trains at *Stockwell* today and I am heading for the *District/Circle Line* as I have to raid my 'C&G Isa!' Cashflow problems this month. Not that this particular month is so special in terms of monetary issues; like the majority of the human race I seem to be in a permanent 'Credit Crunch'.

11am:

I'm at *Temple Place*, enjoying the warm hazy sunshine whilst glancing over the *Thames*. This huge Victorian roof terrace, with plenty of Georgian-style park benches, the perfect spot to rest a weighty body… At this hour of day it is practically deserted, the only audible noise being the traffic travelling along the *Embankment* below. However, as you are higher up here your eyes naturally steer over the busy road towards *Temple Pier* and the docked 'Steamer Ships' which have been turned into fashionable bars for the pleasure of nearby office workers and tourists alike… The far side of the river is dotted with several 'Barges' that are piled high with rubbish and are slowly making their way eastwards to the landfill sites of the Thames estuary. There are also 'Pleasure Boats' packed with tourists heading westwards towards the *Houses of Parliament*, while others continue their journey in an easterly trajectory to take in the magnificent *St Paul's Cathedral*, the *Tower of London* and the iconic twin peaks of *Tower Bridge*. To my right, through the thinning leaves of the London Plane Trees I can see *Big Ben* and the wheel of the *London Eye*, offering me a new perspective to the view up river from the South Bank… After your eyes process the *Royal Festival Hall, National Theatre, Purcell Rooms* and the other 50s concrete structures of the *Southbank Centre*, the skyline and Plane Trees take over… Subsequently, if you turn your head forty-five degrees to the left, then immediately forty-five degrees to the right, you catch two medium-sized tower blocks which provide a perfect frame for your mental picture. Position your head back to mid-frame then slowly look up above the dappled light that penetrates the trees, squint into the faint autumn sunlight and let your body camera click to capture an everlasting surrealist photograph.

I'm taking my last sip of cold 'double espresso macchiato'

before I move to the left-hand side of my bench, so as to remain in line with the fast-moving sun and out of the direct path of the aforementioned trees. The coffee flavour just about wins through, but seeing as there is now quite a chill in the air it would be nice if it were hot!

The reason I found this little gem, for my coffee being cold and all, was down to my vigilance, which I rather shamefully did not share with the people about me at the time! However, if I had bothered to be more altruistic, a 'Good Samaritan', there is no doubt that in this 'P.C.-Mad Country' my face would have been all over the evening news. Not for good citizenship either, but for being a 'Xenophobic Indigenous Trouble-Maker!' Consequently, I thought to myself 'Fuck it, there is no such thing as society' and off I raced, at breakneck speed, down *Holborn*, whilst precariously balancing my takeaway coffee under my paper cup of free tap water…

By the time I reached *The Aldwych* my rucksack and sling bag were weighing heavily on my middle-aged left shoulder. But seeing as there was nowhere to rest I kept going, as I wasn't sure if I was out of range yet! I passed *Bush House*, home of the BBC World Service and the Australian and Indian High Commissions, by which time I was quite tired, but there was still nowhere to rest. However, I could now see the river from the top of *Surrey Street*, so down I marched past King's College Strand Campus until I reached the road's end where there was one of those green wooden cabins which are refreshment stops for 'London Cabbies' and act as a lasting reminder of an older, more cohesive London that belongs to a bygone age… My worries were now well and truly behind me, or so I thought…! I started to ascend the steps to *Temple Place* rather more calmly and with far less haste than my previous route march. Then, as I planted my right foot on the third riser, the paper cup of tap water destabilised and proceeded to fall, the contents duly ending up absorbed by my obliging trousers. My cup of coffee simultaneously launched its way southwards but, fortunately for me, and my trousers, the majority of my now tepid drink was retained by the white plastic lid. The water, alas, had no such cover, and moments later, when I had gathered my various belongings together, I realised that it must have looked as if I had been caught short in the hunt for a pubic convenience, for my linen trousers were well and truly drenched in the most embarrassing of areas, hence my need for full solar alignment... Wearing thin linen trousers was, as it transpired, a solid decision in the great scheme of things. They have responded to the sun's warmth and are now dried through, allowing me the chance to leave *Temple Place* with my dignity restored to its former pre-incident glory.

The Earlier Panic:

'Terrorist Alert...!' Was it a potential threat, or just my media-led fear taking over? Whichever way, my body's natural defence mechanism kicked in and I was out of there in a flash... Moments earlier, having found a sun-drenched table on the pavement outside the coffee bar chain and settled myself for the pleasurable ritual to follow, was the instant I caught the eyes of two *Somali-looking men.* One had a rucksack and was probably somewhere in his late twenties, the other was much older and was standing to the right of a Georgian red pillar box, looking rather uneasy, almost furtive. As I had fixed my eyes on the older man I couldn't be sure if the younger man was posting a genuine letter or not. Consequently, when my peripheral vision encountered the now anxious-looking younger man procrastinating in front of the post box was the moment I decided to flee…

Who knows if I was right or wrong? However, I wasn't about to wait and find out; 'bombs' and London having proved a lethal cocktail in the recent past. So, rapidly taking all into account, this was the moment I scarpered, for sanctity of human life is far more important than worrying if you have offended anyone as some poor soul scrapes up your body parts from a *High Holborn Pavement*.

I admit that I wasn't one hundred per cent sure; how can you be! Was I profiling them simply because of their appearance? Of course I was, but who could blame me? Self-preservation is the most basic of instincts. As our useless government, along with the *P.C. Brigade*, keep telling us, 'Be vigilant!' Just don't report anything suspicious unless she is an *old white granny in her mid-eighties!*

Thankfully, my worst fears were not realised. There were no explosions, and despite the fact that I hadn't raised the alarm, for fear of being arrested as a *Fascist*, my trousers were the only casualty of the whole international incident. Besides, if I hadn't encountered the *Somalis* I would never have discovered *Temple Place!!*

After Temple Place, J. D. Wetherspoons:

I'm now sat in the Holborn branch of this *English* enclave. If you want to meet up with fellow Britons or our Irish cousins then a pub is definitely one of the few places in this vast metropolis, or any of our other urban areas for that matter, where you can still have a mutual cultural experience with your kith and kin. It is a last bastion of 'Britishness...'

As the years pass by one tends to gravitate back towards one's own tribe; which is quite a rational phenomenon, something we are all, at some point in our lives, genetically predisposed to do. Listening to elders, grandparents and other members of the tribe is an important method of establishing rules, learning ancestral and family history, enforcing your common identity, respecting opposing communities, building confidence and creating general awareness of your roots and your rightful connection to your homeland. None of the above is in the 'P.C. Charter of Britain', unless you are from a 'Non-Indigenous Tribe'; then, unsurprisingly, you are encouraged, even funded, to celebrate your identity on a gargantuan scale. *Do-Gooders* in the media, town halls, local papers etc, all plunge in with uncontrollable vigour… We cannot avoid, even if we wanted to, the endless promotion of *other cultural traditions* that we are then unfavourably compared to. The over-represented *Do-Gooding Zealots* triumphantly conclude that they are far more meaningful than any celebration of the 'Great White Unwashed'!

So I was pleasantly surprised, shocked even, when the *British Olympic Teams* were hailed as heroes through the streets of London last week. They were even allowed to be cheered on in *Trafalgar Square*, which under the political stewardship of 'Red Ken' always used to be the sole preserve of 'Ethnic Majority Festivals'. If he could have got away with it dear 'Power-Crazed Ken' would have had 'Morris Men' shot on sight alongside the cull of the once famous Pigeons. Still, when *Sharia Law* is enforced as a final act of appeasement, culling will become '*de rigueur*'! Unfortunately, for naïve people like 'Ken', they are quite likely to be at the wrong end of the ensuing knife wielding. As the 'Non Indigenous Tribes' will soon forget that it was the likes of *'Ken'* who unwittingly engineered their rise to absolute power. History always repeats itself!

Paradoxically, however, it seems to have taken a fluffy blond of distant immigrant ancestry to, once more, make it just about acceptable to cheer and wave the English and Union flag in *Trafalgar Square*; without a doner kebab, Polish sausage or onion bhaji food stall in sight… Contrary to ignorant stereotypes we weren't all eating 'fish and chips' and swilling gallons of beer either… Our new London Mayor, who was elected thanks to an uprising against *Livingstone* in the suburbs, even dared to mention the 'Battle of Trafalgar' and our victory over the arrogant French and duplicitous Spanish. *Lord Horatio Nelson* must have been looking down with utter astonishment, for the day after *Trafalgar Day* the *English* had once again reclaimed his square, albeit over two hundred years late…! *Boris* having achieved the unthinkable! In just a few months he had made it almost acceptable for *'Indigenous White Trash'* to hang out in the *'Trafalgar hood'* again!!

Friday 24th October

We all know when we are disconnected from our solar plexus, floating aimlessly without purpose!

I have just returned from my friendly *Tamil corner shop* with a newspaper and a vacuum-packed bag of fresh coffee… The half pound of fresh ground coffee is now sitting in my cafetière, leaving barely an inch of space for hot water! Fortunately I didn't get that far, otherwise it would have been the strongest cup of coffee in history!

It has gone one o'clock and I am only just about to have breakfast! *Supermarket Heaven* begins at five, so I'll need to fit in lunch before I go too... This is fast turning into 'one of those days', which we all encounter from time to time. You haven't sat down, you've been from A to B to C at least fifty times, consequently your head is now circulating at the speed of a spinning top, yet you have achieved absolutely nothing. To add insult to mental injury you must soon leave the privacy of your own home for a shift of profit-making for your *Fat Cat Boss*; who, last financial year, stole £7.5 million in the name of *salary!*

I can only assume that this is all part of the great middle-aged treadmill; throw in the fact that you are a *middle child* and you are well and truly screwed, a misfit all round! I think I'll try that coffee after all! The resultant pounding head and insomnia should see me speedily through my driving shift: with a *head rush* like that I might even enjoy it!

Tuesday 28th October

A jet-black cat with white paws, chest and tail tip, and a white cross on his face, is currently precariously balanced on my garden fence… He has the most vivid green eyes: they look like fluorescent matchsticks and are staring straight at me. He spotted me at the kitchen door whilst I was making a cup of tea. He has been sniffing around on several prior occasions but until now my resident *Bluey-Grey Pedigree* has always charged him off. My little oasis has been turned into quite a feline battleground of late, the ultimate prize being the sun-drenched shed at the bottom of the garden where the victor can contentedly bathe on its warm felt roof.

Speaking of the devil, my pedigree conqueror has just appeared! He's busying himself scent-marking my fading perennials. Needless to say the black and white intruder has scarpered over the fence to Eastern Europe. He had best keep moving: what with recent reports of their kith and kin feasting on the *Queen's swans*, who knows which part of British wildlife is next on the menu…! Anyway, this *moggy* simply hasn't a hope in hell of seeing off *Mr Bluey-Grey*: he's far nimbler, especially on the feather-edged tips of my garden fence. He's built to the dimensions of a fine athlete at the peak of his career.

Speaking of *careers*, I know we all have to start somewhere but 'sales calls' really do hack me off… I was in fine fettle this morning, happily sipping my coffee, the sun was out, albeit with an accompanying chilly wind, and then off it goes, my dreaded mobile ringtone! As the years roll by the telephone tends to ring less and less, especially for men, which isn't altogether a bad thing as the ensuing conversation can often leave you feeling rather angsty. Anyway, upon answering, despite my hatred of unknown callers, any callers for that matter, I was still in a reasonably calm frame of mind. However, this soon changed when I was greeted by a young northern man from the price comparison website I had been trying out yesterday.

Shit, it's already 3.30 p.m..! *Supermarket Heaven* starts at four.

Well, I'm back…! The grind is over and I managed to whizz around the aisles after my shift, so the tiresome job of food shopping has been killed with the same laborious stone. After an evening shift the store is practically deserted, so it is a great time to shop. It's normally just me and a few kids, the odd 'wino' and the poor night shift workers who still have hours of unrewarding drudgery ahead of them.

What a night! It was bloody freezing and the *Northern Sales Boy* called incessantly… It even tried to snow at one point, although it finally turned into sleet… The shopping was piled so high that the tyres needed extra air to keep the whole caboodle afloat. Tuesday, Wednesday and Thursday are free delivery over £100, so people quite naturally spend just over the odds, stocking up with all the heaviest and bulkiest items imaginable: bottles upon bottles of water, endless bags of cat litter, tins galore, six months' supply of baby food, bulk packs of toilet roll, and enough nappies for an entire street of toddlers to fill…

Invariably, after you have delivered their forty or so bags of shopping, nearly tripped and severely injured yourself in the back of your overloaded van, sweated profusely, blocked a narrow street or, worse still, someone's driveway, and have been altogether far too obsequious, the customer simply smiles, falsely, as they close the door in your exhausted face whilst softly uttering a fake-sounding 'thanks' or 'thank you'. 'Any time, marvellous, it was a complete pleasure!', or words to that effect, you madly mutter to yourself as you return to your delivery vehicle and set off towards your next hideous encounter!

Reversing out of a cul-de-sac whilst steering a meandering path to avoid the plethora of stuck-out wing mirrors was quite a feat! Upon reaching the main road, having avoided any collateral damage, I prepared to turn out into the oncoming traffic when in shot a car to block my path. To heighten my predicament some *'tosser'* decided he wanted to leave the shitty cul-de-sac at the exact same time, appearing from nowhere to block my front end in too! I was stuffed, literally sandwiched! All of which was my own stupid fault, as I should have reversed into the narrow cul-de-sac in the first place, as the company van-driving course dictated! Alas, as it's only a shitty driving job that I don't intend to stay in for long anyway, I paid scant regard to the whole boring training rigmarole...

Despite all the aforementioned, I took a long deep breath, smiled like an emotionless robot and stayed calm, as is 'company policy...!': a calm and collected manner key to managing a difficult situation; though mine was really a cynical ploy to exude a civil exterior when all I really wanted to do was scream like a maniac, jump out of my van with the engine still running, and scarper off to a better world whilst shouting and giggling like a carefree anarchic teenager on a binge-drinking high! Then, when I was unable to hold in the cocktail of alcohol for a moment longer, revel in the glory of throwing up my innards all over the plastic 'Middle Class Wanker' who smugly resided in the bloody boring little cul-de-sac and, predictably, failed to tip me a dime! One thing to be said for the 'Working Classes', not the 'Chavy Underclasses', is that they, more often than not, shout you a drink… I suppose it is a kind of solidarity, as they know how knackering hard graft can be.

Needless to say, I survived being sandwiched in a *cul-de-sac* and continued with the ordeal. Trust the French to come up with the idea of a dead-end street with housing on every side! Anyway, I fulfilled my contractual agreement, with no break yet again! It always seems to work in favour of the supermarket giant at the expense of the humble worker. Was it not ever thus! Still, I do have one perk, a permanent stiff neck and shoulders from all the lifting, loading and delivering up and down copious flights of stairs to dodgy-looking flats.

Tonight was no exception. After more than my fair share of elevated dwellings my last customer's home was, you've got it, a flat… The block had no entry system so anyone could stroll into the communal areas, paint was peeling off the walls, the skirting boards had at least half an inch of fluff and grime encrusted on their narrow tips, the iron balustrade was rusted through, and the lighting dim and oppressive. As if that wasn't depressing enough, when the 'online customer' opened his door an unstoppable wave of bad odour quickly enveloped me. Seeing how I was out of breath from the mammoth ascent to his vile-smelling abode I had no choice but to inhale. Despite my brain telling the rest of my body that this was a bad call that was likely to leave me feeling nauseous, my lungs rapidly filled themselves with the foul acrid air. It was truly hideous, though I had to keep breathing to fulfil my contractual obligations, as well as staying alive! I hope my *Spineless Managers* have noted my dedication to duty!

Three more trips ensued, mainly laden with cheap cordial. On the last foray I had no choice but to fully open my eyes, whereupon I was greeted by a short, foreign-looking man with dark greasy hair, abundant facial stubble, and the thickest glasses imaginable... As he struggled to see to sign the paperwork I noticed a young girl half-hidden behind his right side. I couldn't see her face properly as she was very timidly gazing downwards, but judging by her height she couldn't have been a day over six. He appeared far too old to be her father, more like a grandfather I should say. For her sake I hoped he wasn't the father as it would be intolerable to live in that flat on a permanent basis; for, apart from the rancid stench, the general state of repair was even worse than the communal areas, and that takes some beating I can assure you... I could just see into the living room, where a huge wide-screen television took pride of place and was switched on with no sound. The sofa and carpet looked mutually filthy, the centre light was bare of a shade and the green synthetic curtains were held up, intermittently, with drawing pins. This was a modern-day *Dickensian* scene: squalid, depressing and seemingly without any hope of betterment... So, even after another shitty shift at *Supermarket Heaven* I was left knowing that I was still somewhat lucky, as, all things considered, there were people in far worse circumstances than mine.

However, having wound down with strong coffee and reflected on the whole business, save for feeling anxious for the little girl, I concluded that the guy was still able-bodied and quite fit enough to clean up his dirty flat...! Being poor, if indeed he is, as most of these people appear to have greater disposable income than I do, still no excuse for low personal hygiene and living in squalor whilst in charge of a minor.

After all is said and done, one less bottle of cordial would buy two of strong bleach!! The moral of the story being: 'Buying copious amounts of cordial belies the path to cleanliness'.

Wednesday 29ᵗʰ October

It's exactly a week since I discovered this little gem and I'm back on my bench at *Temple Place*… The sky is cumulus-free. The air, however, is cooler than last week, quite chilly in fact, which is only to be expected as we are fast approaching November. On the plus side my coffee was hot, and I didn't spill it! However, I shall have to venture indoors soon as even that has failed to warm me up.

I tuned into *Savile Row* again last night. My old friend *Sean* made another appearance, albeit a fleeting one: another walk-on role. On the other hand his father was ever-present, with copious lines. He was clearly relishing the limelight, the star of the show and all, so he is unlikely to be handing over the reins any time soon…That's the thing about a family business, you normally have to wait until the older generation die, become infirm or even insane! Only then do you inherit the mantle, become the absolute boss and thus wield power and control over the next in line of accession, invariably your eldest son or daughter… Fortunately, for my elder brother this has not turned out to be the case as he gained control of the 'Family Firm' in his mid-thirties. My father let the whole thing drift into his hands quite willingly as he couldn't be bothered with the responsibility any more, preferring instead to take a mediocre salary as the *quid pro quo*.

The traditional 'Family Firm' tends to be fraught with disagreement and is very often a curse. Unless you are the eldest sibling, that is! For, being first through the door, you can immediately start the process of getting the wheels rolling in your favour! My Elder Brother is a true testment to this theory!

The freehold premises of our particular family business is in the process of being sold to property developers, who aim to pull it down and construct flats to sell to an ever-burgeoning London population. They have already paid a large deposit, which my elder brother has taken the lion's share of, for expenses! My father insisted the rest had gone to pay off the debts of his feckless brother, which may well be the case as we all have at least one liability in our dysfunctional families..! My elder brother successfully smooth-talked my father into keeping the intended sale hush-hush... He's never really credited anyone else with any intelligence, therefore he's too blinded with conceit to realise that I have a mole right under his nose, sat in the adjacent office in fact, so I've known what he's been plotting for ages! Though it remains to be seen how purposeful this advanced information will be as my brother, possessing an amazingly firm iron-like grip on my father, has successfully brainwashed him into his camp, intent on keeping him onboard to supposedly share future spoils between them, throwing the rest of the family to the wolves! It's incredible what you can get away with, quite legally it would appear, if you are a Company Director with a minority shareholding and you have your father, The Chairman, tightly spun around your little finger! But greed has always been a powerful and delusional fuel for the failings of the human mind.

It's a mystery to me! We always used to get on so well! Weekends away with our respective partners, holidays at his house in France, time spent with me and my wife when we lived in the sticks. We never lived in each other's pockets, but we had lots of laughs, shared interests and a brother's bond! Consequently, in frustration, regrettably, during a fraught telephone conversation I recently told my elder brother:

'I've heard of *selling* your own grandmother… But your mother and brothers really is a dirty trick…!'

Still, it's all the rage today, look what the *bankers* in the *City* have got away with! If you see something you want and it doesn't belong to you, just take it! That's modern family values, I'm ashamed to say… Not that my romantic view of a more honourable past holds any credence. As I gain a little more wisdom with every passing line on my ageing face I realise that the vast majority of the human race is, and always has been, corruptible….

Enough of this subject, it's depressing the hell out of me. Besides, there's nothing I can do about it anyway… I'm off for a walk to warm my ageing bones, poor old soul that I am turning into… *Julie*, my female companion, is meeting me at lunchtime. I have managed to score us two tickets for the new musical *Piaf* at the bargain price of £10 each. Front row of the stalls as well; there must be a catch. Perhaps we won't be able to see anything!

Friday 31st October

Halloween, All Hallows Eve, the night before All Hallows Day, whatever your beliefs, if any, it has come round again... As a child the week between *Halloween* and *Bonfire Night* was a magical and memorable period. A time full of wacky, spooky parties that seemed to intensify in excitement the older I became, reaching their climax around my late teens. These were the 'hoorays' my mother used to put on in the woods by our house. My younger brother and I would collect firewood from fallen branches of oak, birch and pine, kindling from the wood's floor, and dried-up leaves for firelighters. I had the operation of bonfire-building down to a fine art and my younger brother was always ready and willing to assist; he was a great number two. My elder brother, by a mere two years, rarely helped us as he was busy building up the Family Empire! Even if he was home he tended to delegate, assuming his preferred managerial role or, more often than not, he simply made himself unavailable when the prospect of manual labour loomed.

I am a good few years senior to my younger brother but regardless of the gulf in age, me being in my late teens at the time and he just about to reach adolescence, we worked well together, always assembling a mammoth *Bonfire...* A hard-graft work ethic has stayed with me throughout my life, whereas my elder brother gives the appearance of working hard but still assumes the arrogant, smug role of an overly confident manager. Smugness naturally stemming from megalomania, an overt sense of satisfaction with your lot, regardless of how you obtained it! Still, this tactic has definitely worked for him... I think entering a family business, never having had to go for a job interview or take instruction from others is, quite possibly, the overwhelming factor in this embarrassingly greedy and selfish attitude in my elder sibling. Though he would probably maintain that he turned the business around and we are simply scavenging off his back! Undoubtedly, he has given years to the enterprise, with some success, but that doesn't entitle him to other people's shares! Regardless of right and wrong, I really do miss him. Such a waste of valuable time, feuding…!

'Sour Grapes…!' It's easy to presume this to be the case, the 'heir' sorted and the 'spare' left in limbo! Then to add insult to injury along comes a younger male, leaving *moi* with 'middle child syndrome', which only increases the paranoia inherent within *Highly Sensitive Persons*... I convinced myself that it was me being bitter and twisted because my life, like most people's, had not turned out how I had naïvely and arrogantly assumed it would. However, age brings some degree of reason, an increasingly philosophical outlook, a slightly pathetic resignation to uncontrollable, uncomfortable facts. After all, we are all frail beings with an intrinsic need to find something or somebody to blame or worship in this fast-paced modern world… We have become conned into thinking that assets and bank balances are the most important yardsticks for measuring happiness and, above all, success. Once you realise that this is bollocks your life path becomes less restricted, your mind freed from the conformist shackles of a duplicitous, consumerist society. It's akin to rebirth. I should know, granted I'm still a bit nuts, but when you try new things in life, venture out of the cosy little bubble we all tend to inhabit then, boy oh boy, suddenly anything seems possible! Naturally you'll be as poor as a church mouse, but even sanity is costed..!

Just a year ago, if someone suggested *meditation* to

me I would have considered them a 'frigging, lazy, whole-nut crunching, deluded, unwashed moron'. How wrong I was, suffocated by my own fears and entrenched paranoia! Meditation truly is remarkable, a discovery of regions of the body that you never knew existed! The depth and contrast of sound within the human voice is amazing, and once you know your *chakras* a complete revelation. If you want to quit smoking, or curtail a drug or alcohol addiction, I strongly recommend you give meditation a go. Oh, also, if you love sex but haven't been getting much lately it's ten times better, literally out of this world... I know it sounds totally crass. I'm the world's biggest cynic. But meditation triggers inexplicable sensations, enabling your soul to float away into a calmer parallel universe beautifully devoid of toxic 'white noise'. It's HSP heaven...

Returning to the subject of 'Bonfires', firstly we would celebrate *Halloween*, then five days later we would build another one for *Guy Fawkes Night*... Sadly, the 'P.C. Police', particularly in our multicultural cities, have successfully hijacked and obliterated the history and meaning of 'Bonfire or Guy Fawkes Night' altogether..!

Last year I went to an organised *'do'* with my brother, mother, and young nephew; the whole thing was such a total farce that we may as well have been celebrating the winner of *'Big Brother'* rather than a major historical event in *'our(!)'* nation's history. No *Guido Fawkes* burnt on the 'Bonfire', no bonfire even, no 'Remember, remember, the fifth of November', no history of the '1605 Catholic conspiracy to blow up Parliament', no 'costumed parade', not a single reference to *The Gunpowder Plot*, just a mediocre fireworks display to overtly loud music..! It was shit... The kids didn't know what the hell the whole thing was about.

The dull and uninterested-looking parents more than happy to stuff burgers and candyfloss into their children's anaemic –looking faces, rather than teaching them how *James 1* was saved from annihilation by a cocktail of high explosives. Still, at least the Frankenstein garbage shut the spoilt little '*Wannabes*' up for five minutes!

In stark contrast, I fondly remember the wonderful procession through my local village. The floats, the Puritan torch-bearers, the Conspirators and the King all parading, in character, towards the bonfire ground. Everywhere was pitch-black, electric street lamps turned off, the only light coming from hand-crafted lanterns and torches of real tar, cloth and sticks. Onlookers and marchers mysteriously silhouetted by the fanning flames, the stage was set and we were catapulted into a time when 'England belonged to the English' and patriotism was a badge of honour worth fighting for… If this were re-enacted today, *Health and Safety Zealots* would be standing by with high-powered water cannons at the ready, and the *Race Relations Runts* would have the unequivocal power to arrest anyone who wasn't a *Catholic, Muslim, Hindu, Buddhist* etc. etc. Basically, all the *White-Trash Protestants* and any other *Indigenous Non-Believers* would be rounded up, bludgeoned with truncheons, showered with plastic bullets and pepper sprayed into oblivion…'Diversity rocks man!'

There are still a dwindling few beacons where some sense of our history is upheld, the old county town of *Sussex, Lewes*, being one example. The town has five 'Bonfire Societies', and after a spectacular joint procession through its ancient streets they hold their own displays in various quarters of the town… The one I went to, several years back, had some guy dressed as 'The Pope'. Just prior to the 'Bonfire' being lit he stood up on a low plinth and, as is customary, the 'Royalists' threw firecrackers at his conspiratorial feet. In this ancient *Protestant stronghold* it was tradition to then shout *'Burn the Pope!'* Keen to enter into the spirit of our cultural heritage my younger brother and I loudly reiterated the phrase as the man dressed as the Pope passed us by. The ensuing silence was palpable; you could have heard a pin drop! We were somewhat taken aback. I really didn't understand why there was a deathly hush!

After all this was tradition, a celebration of the downfall of the murderous 'Catholic Plot' to blow up 'King and Parliament', and we were upholding it, for posterity!

The far reaching tentacles of the intolerant *P.C. Brigade* had obviously extended to one of the last bastions of free speech. They probably had informants planted in the crowd! With the luxury of hindsight, I suppose we were quite fortunate nobody reported us to the insipid, lily-livered *Hitleresque* zealots. So at least we were spared our fate and lived to tell the tale... Fear envelopes most people in this day and age but if you are of the *Protestant* persuasion, white, and English, then you have rational justification to be scared of free expression. Good job I'm a *Pagan...!* The youth of *London* stand more chance of learning about *Diwali* than the intricacies of 'The Gunpowder Plot'. 'The Festival of Lights' is being celebrated in *Trafalgar Square* at this very moment, whereas *Trafalgar Day*, save for an unpublicised word from *Boris*, wasn't even deemed important enough to be mentioned, let alone celebrated in *Nelson's* very own square! Not that the continual denial of our history and culture is much of a revelation nowadays... How does it go? 'A country that forgets its past has no future!'

My mother has always loved to dress up, throw a party and all. So *Halloween* was as good an excuse as any… She would spend all day cooking stew, carving out pumpkins, mixing lemonade with gory colours of food dye, and bake a Halloween cake which she'd ice in putrid green, a black spider's web and blood-red fangs dripping off one side… We were encouraged to dress up for the celebrations and despite our initial grumpy protestations it always turned out to be immense fun.

There's a lot to be said for tomato ketchup and bandages in the pursuit of horror..! The guest list included my friends, my brothers' friends and friends of my parents. My mother has friends in their twenties to the ninetieth year of life. Being a gregarious and fun-loving soul she is the perfect host and people-magnet, so there was always an eager queue hoping to be invited to her legendary parties.

As the night progressed, having consumed piles of tasty home cooking, apple-bobbed to *Brighton* and back and spooked the guests half to death, my mother would appear, as if by magic, from the surrounding woods to menacingly circle the flaming *Bonfire* on her broomstick… She was the ultimate witch. The crooked nose, black hair, green eyes, blacked-out teeth, blood-red lips and pallid complexion were a masterstroke. The costume was just as meticulously thought out, the witch's hat had just the right amount of crookedness, her huge black cape cleverly concealing her body, the only other visible parts being her leather boots and long, curly bright-red fingernails… After delighting, mesmerising and beguiling her dutifully assembled fan-base with terrible witches' tales she would go round the fire once more, cast a spell on one of her unassuming victims, and gradually stir it into her witch's cauldron whilst reciting the list of vile ingredients and prophesying a fateful curse…! How lucky was I! You would have to pay a fortune to see that today; trawl up to the 'West End', sit in a hot and uncomfortable theatre, and the performance wouldn't be a patch on my mother's enigmatic spectacle…Wednesday night's performance was, however, a complete exception, one of the most convincing I have seen for a very long time.

After I met *Julie* we walked through *Covent Garden* which was bustling with the usual mix of tourists, day trippers, and office workers watching varying skill levels of disparate Street Performers. Somewhere between *Covent Garden* and *Leicester Square* we stopped for a coffee in one of those chain-branded cafes. We queued for a short while, *Julie* ordered her drink and we agreed to share a caramel slice. I then asked for my usual double espresso with a little warm milk and froth on top…! Having worked in catering myself, including a coffee shop our family once owned, I'm used to customers' idiosyncrasies and would always try to oblige them; after all, it is supposed to be a 'Service Industry…!' But when the *Young Lanky Eastern European Gentleman* presented me with my beverage he gleefully informed me 'Now you have a macchiato!' This scenario has happened to me on numerous occasions, so I decided to say nothing to the 'Prepubescent Twat' and off we went to find a place to sit and enjoy the dull, corporately global, experience.

Upon the first sip of my now tepid coffee my taste buds began to notice that something was amiss. Of course, how predictable, I thought to myself, there was no warm milk, only froth; as per every time I have ever ordered this bloody drink in a branded central London coffee bar. So off I traipsed to confront the *Barista!* A rather stupid grandiose title, it probably explains their delusional self-importance.

'Macchiato is espresso with a little frothed milk... I asked for warm milk as well, so may I have some please..!' I explained to the uninterested, rotund girl, as at the time 'Mr Lanky' was busy correcting other customers. A debate ensued; finally, she delighted in gutturally telling me how great she and her colleague were and, moreover, up to now nobody had ever complained! In other words, you are the problem!

Choosing to ignore her childish insolence, I again asked for my coffee as I had originally ordered it. Begrudgingly, she started to remake my coffee but decided to serve me coffee in one paper cup, milk in the next, and froth in another... In no uncertain terms I told her she was petty, pushy, insulting, and deluded, and that her colleague was arrogant and totally bereft of customer service skills. Last, but by no means least, I told her to keep her coffee, drop her imported attitude problem, and give me my money back. Witnessing her jaw drop, like a stone, off her plain, pallid face, adulterated further by her oversized conk, was a sight to behold. For she was obviously used to dishing out orders in harsh clipped tones that would leave a camp commandant feeling cold. As for being challenged, well, this was obviously a completely unexpected and unwanted novelty in her domineering little world...! Needless to say, she and her 'Lanky Twat' colleague soon regained the use of their lungs and continued to huff and puff at us as we left their jolly establishment! Had we been in Poland we would have probably been lynched on the spot! Thank God they didn't call the 'P.C.Police..!'

I know 'Talk to the hand service' is prevalent in this country but as for *Eastern European* newcomers being harder workers than us *Brits*, what a heap of divisive bullshit... However, in my tortuous experience they are definitely less friendly, more strident, fearless, and ten times pushier than 'Lazy Brits', as our 'Tossing out of touch Overlords' like to blanket-label us.

The day did begin to improve, the *National Portrait Gallery* a perfect tonic to wilful obduracy. If you have a spare few hours after being patronised by a couple of 'bloodsucking migrants' in a central London coffee bar it truly is a wonderful place to lose yourself! After immersing ourselves in the art world we stopped off for some classically under-flavoured British comfort food at *The Stockpot* in *Panton Street*. But without doubt, the day's tantalisingly tasteful highlight was the performance of *Piaf* at the *Vaudeville Theatre* in *The Strand*. The £10 front-row seats were exceptional value: although you had to crook your neck slightly you could practically touch the actors' faces… The set was grey and austere, and the stage had a cobble-effect floor which successfully recaptured a bygone Parisian street scene. You felt as if you were there, reliving *Edith's* life with her. The cast were undeniably brilliant but *Eleanor Rogers*, who played the diminutive 'Piaf', stole the show. She was pure genius, an absolute pinnacle of unsurpassable perfection as she successfully imitated an inimitable icon….! *Julie* and *I* were mesmerised, enthralled, totally spellbound. We can't wait to book again, especially for £10! It beats two pints of lager and a packet of crisps. They should send some of our yobs to see it, if only to try and broaden their narrow little daytime-TV minds!

Monday 3rd November

My neck, shoulders and lower back feel like they have been stretched to twice their original size, and are struggling to return to their natural alignment. As anyone who suffers with back trouble will know, it's a recurring nightmare which usually occurs when life's problems ratchet up a gear or two, financial worries or family feuds being fine examples of the extra stresses required to bring on the aforementioned condition.

Anyway, here I am sitting on my burnt orange sofa, having spent *le weekend* delivering orange plastic carrier bags laden with groceries, and minutes after ending a phone call to the mobile phone company of the same colour! I could not understand a word the *Glaswegian Call Centre Lady* was saying, though she seemed to be having the same problem with me. And all over £2.80! But in this credit crunch £2.80 is two fillets of fish. All I need is the proverbial five loaves and I could feed the nation out of the crisis! Food prices would consequently fall through the floor and we might finally have some disposable income...! However, the government and big business are not that stupid! Without a doubt they'd find a way of regaining the upper hand by recouping any additional disposable income through taxes and trading cartels. A little extra Council Tax, a VAT hike, more tax on fuel, in order to save the planet of course! Their options are endless, until the revolution. Mind you, with the track record of the law abiding *British* that might be a few millennia away!

I did manage to have *ten pence* refunded for a data charge! Apparently, unbeknown to me, I used my mobile phone to access the World Wide Web! After much to-ing and fro-ing this charge was revoked as a gesture of *goodwill!* I suspect I unwittingly pocket-dialled the internet as I have no clue how to lock the keypad, and I'm too afraid to try in case I can't ever unlock it again! However, I certainly wasn't about to admit this to the *Glaswegian Lady!* The remaining £2.70 charge was apparently my own fault as free phone numbers and local call rate numbers are chargeable. I do vaguely remember an automated voice informing me 'Your network may charge you for dialling this number...', which is about as helpful as an atheist at a christening! 'May charge you' or, very unlikely, 'may not charge you' doesn't have, in my book, a definitive ring to it!

I tried to relay this point to the *Glaswegian Lady*, but I wasn't getting anywhere. We were communicating in a parallel universe. We could have gone on all day. I was starting to see the funny side of the situation. Though she clearly had a sense-of-humour failure as, after the fifth time of asking her what my basic bill amounted to, before the little extras they put on for the Executives' bonuses, I was unceremoniously cut off! This is the type of 'Customer Service' one has to endure today. I have had my call terminated on numerous occasions by condescending *'oiks'* from all four corners of the globe! I have circumnavigated aggressive, angry, wilful, uninterested, sad, pathetic, mentally unstable and even semi-sane behaviour. All to no avail!

Huge companies absolutely adore internet and telephone customer service. They have total control, keep you at arm's length so they can earn money as nefariously as they like, then if you become too demanding the connection mysteriously falters or they simply inform you: 'There's no need to be aggressive. I'm going to have to end this conversation now.' CLICK... Your blood pressure is now dangerously high but you have absolutely no redress… Even if you can release yourself from your contract and change provider you'll have to go through a long and arduous process only to be treated at best the same, but quite possibly even worse! The odds of the game are loaded against you, for you have signed their contract and the small print is doing its job. To add insult to injury you probably pay by their beloved 'direct debit'. You are their little *cash cow* whom they love to squeeze a little extra creamy milk out of on the first day of every month. All you get out of it is false promises, a 'Houdini Contract' and some useless 'Loyalty Card'; this, they call PROGRESS!!!

I did have some downtime over the weekend… Yesterday afternoon was very cathartic. After a long morning of *Supermarket Heaven* I set off for the Surrey/Sussex borders. Arriving at my parents' home I was met with the sound of lilting *Irish* folk songs, which were swiftly followed by fast and furious jigs. My nephew was wearing a skeleton cat suit and a mask in homage to the film *Scream*, my mother back in the Emerald Isle showing off her Irish dancing, which then drifted to tap, Cossack kicks, jazz, swing and finally a high-kicking cabaret routine. She can still kick her legs up to head height, which is quite impressive for a lady of retirement age. What with my back and all, I can only just about manage to reach my burgeoning waistline!

My brother and I joined the party, throwing ourselves into its madness. At one point we fitted the dogs with Halloween masks, transforming them into four-legged barking 'gremlins'. The atmosphere reached fever pitch as we upstaged one another with more and more ludicrously elaborate routines. It was akin to a voodoo frenzy in *Haiti*.

Eventually, we were all totally high on adrenaline, our choreography becoming increasingly avant-garde as we fought for mirror space to vainly marvel at our weird and wonderful performances. *Strictly Come Dancing* could have learnt a thing or two! We definitely scored 10 out of 10 for 'artistic impression!' Dancing around upstaging each other is a recurring part of our family life, as I'm sure it is in houses throughout the land. In our family this trait comes from my mother's father's side; they're the ones with the *Irish* roots.

A late *Sunday Lunch* was a welcome break from the frantic exertions… The roast beef, home-made Yorkshire pudding, roast potatoes, roast parsnips, courgettes, carrots and peas were absolutely delicious. As is always the case, my mother's 'Yorkshire' was at least six inches high. My grandmother, who is the grand old age of ninety-two, was suitably impressed. It is a bit of a standing joke, which my lovely grandmother always enters into in the spirit intended… 'Yorkshires' were never her forte, as they always forgot to rise! They harboured plenty of flavour but more resembled the Cambridgeshire Fens than *the rolling Yorkshire Dales of my Mother's puddings!*

Dessert was equally delectable, a huge high-rise *mille feuille* crammed with strawberries and clotted cream.

After lunch, my nephew, brother and I went for a short ramble over the misty autumn fields, returning through the dense woodland surrounding my parents' house. We then spent the evening seated in the living room, entranced by the roaring log fire, paying scant regard to the lame televisual offerings before us… The comforts and familiarity of your family home can be very settling, reassuring even, despite the fact that you and your father are barely on speaking terms any more…. I remember watching *Dallas* and *Dynasty* as a child and naïvely thinking it was glamorous entertainment! I never imagined that the double crossing antics of that family would, decades later, come home to roost in a leafy corner of Surrey! Needless to say we are no 'Oil Barons', but the consequences and repercussions are similar all the same. Power and greed is a universal curse that can implode to tear even the strongest of families apart… Fortunately, naturally talented people do not normally have to sink to the depths of duplicitous subterfuge…! I'd like to see my elder brother or father replicate my mother's superb lunch! To be fair my elder brother, whom I miss dreadfully, is quite capable in the kitchen and my father is more than proficient when he sets his mind to it. Sadly they are lost to me at present as they have both become enslaved by the 'God of Cash…'. Though I'm sure the mistrust won't last forever. I don't think their intentions were as sinister as, on the surface, they appear. I reckon they thought they could make some money out of the down-payment then divulge the whole deal at a later date. My shattered faith hopes so at least!

I have always been a bad judge of character, a total sucker for charm and manners as nowadays they are pretty well non-existent. I, therefore, felt a complete 'twat', yet again, on finding out that *Bhupinder* had been *sacked..!* Having idolised him, been inspired by his charitable work, good karma and philosophical attitude towards life, it transpired that he was dismissed for repeatedly phoning in sick during his probationary period! It just goes to show that it really is impossible to 'judge a book by its cover.' Was he genuinely sick, or just messing them around? The latter, I sadly suspect, is closer to the truth… With hindsight, I recall him telling me how the antisocial hours could become an invasion of one's social life, which never registered at the time as I thought he was simply philosophising, being objective! After all, he was from a wealthy background and had previously said that he didn't really need the money. Clearly, I was a gullible fool to elevate him to status of modern-day 'Saint!' But *John*, the online manager, who suffers with the worst back and neck I have ever seen, obviously saw right through his sickness charade and dumped him before he really screwed up the schedules.

Last week *John* was telling me and a fellow driver about his pending hospital appointment. He has suffered from psoriasis for some years now, and his specialist has recently diagnosed him with arthritis and some awful bone-crumbling disease. He is obviously in perpetual pain and was joking about going to Switzerland to be 'put down', so I asked him if he was flying 'Euthanasia Airways?' We all ended up pissing ourselves with laughter, and ratcheted up the silly self-deprecation even further. *John*, above all people, should be the one phoning in 'sick'. In his condition he shouldn't even be at work in the first place!

So *Bhupinder*, it would appear, was just a 'flash in the pan...' Stupidly, I was taken in by his charm. It's the same old story, the same mistake I always tend to make. I can be so gullible..! The *Johns* of this world are the real heroes, the links that hold the chain together, the cogs of the wheel and all. Now I shall just have to idolise my great *Supermarket Heaven Manager* instead. *John* holds the number one spot now, his lead one hundred per cent unassailable. At least until it becomes public knowledge that he beats his wife on a daily basis!

Wednesday 5th November (Guy Fawkes Night)

I nearly forgot, last Saturday afternoon I was in receipt of two tips for my capable product delivery and appealing doorstep manner. To my complete surprise, my hitherto prejudgement and generalisation of people's characters was confounded yet again! The two households in question were both in *Worcester Park*, one being a nineteen-thirties semi, the other a grander detached abode. To make matters even more equal, one was a man of similar age to me, the other a 'mumsy', bossy type of lady in her late forties. I was beginning to think that my theory on the profile of 'Online Grocery Tippers', which is borne out of my limited experience to date, had been shot to pieces! Maybe it was time for me to stop socially profiling people, to start liberating myself from my own preconceptions, for it would now appear that middle-class people can tip too!

Despite the above, last night's round reverted to type! Lots of smiles and middle-class 'thank yous', but not a dime in sight! That is until my last delivery, an end of terrace ex-council house. Bingo! I'd hit the jackpot! A whole gold sovereign kindly placed into the obliging palm of my grateful hand... Obviously it was not a real gold sovereign at all, but a piece of Her Majesty's coinage to the value of one pound sterling. The value was immaterial, the gesture very much appreciated and the fact that they live on my estate, a mere two streets away in fact, made me feel quite proud.

My theory on tipping had been reaffirmed. So, consequently, the bag of chips I indulged in at the end of my shift tasted particularly delicious... The fried potatoes were perfectly crisp and crunchy, with just the right covering of vinegar and salt. The flavour was divine, hedonistic perfection: the whole experience so pleasurable that it was as if *Sir Walter Raleigh* himself had sliced and fried the newly discovered tubers in front of me, and being *Queen Elizabeth's* personal taster I was the first person in the whole of Merry England to eat such exotic fare…

I have just come off the phone to *Julie*. Wednesday is one of her 'days off', so we usually tend to have a little chat before the highlight of our weekend outing! However, last week we also enjoyed each other's company during the week too, although it is still usually the weekend we meet… Invariably the fun takes place on a Sunday, but if we are feeling up to it we throw in Saturday night for good measure…! Anyhow, we were debating the American elections and the subsequent victory of *Barack Obama*. Sorry, we were discussing the most historic, amazing, life-changing, marvellous, apocalyptic event ever! Not that one could say that the whole process has been over-hyped by the deluded, self-ingratiating liberal media from the comfort of their urban bubbles! Apparently 97% of *Black* voters voted for *Mr Obama*, as did well over 40% of *Whites*, to give us the first 'Black President' of the good old US of A… There's no two ways about it, he's a great orator, a man of intellect who may help to improve America's standing in the world. However, it remains to be seen whether 'the economy stupid' will be quite such an easy nut to crack, seeing how most 'blue-collar jobs' have already been exported to China and the like!

'90% of voters say, 'Race is not an issue!' This was perpetually trailed across the news bar of the BBC's Election 2008 coverage. The good old 'Beeb', along with the usual rabble of presenters, kept on trying to re-electrify the story by feeding a new slant into the exhausted subtext with yet more fantastical metaphors, analogies and statistics… One statistic that is hardly ever mentioned is the compelling argument for his lack of total blackness. Am I a racist for noticing this fact? There must surely be other people walking this earth that have heard a rumour that he is half-white! I know in this equality-obsessed world we are all meant to be 'colour blind', but surely this is taking things just a little too far..! The media simply love to jump all over these stories, determined to outdo each other in the process: 'We love ethnic minorities more than peanut butter sandwiches.' 'Well, we love people of any colour and we love your minorities too.' 'Hang on a minute, we love people of any colour, ethnic minorities and peanut butter sandwiches, so stick that in your pipe and smoke it. We win, you lose. I'm the biggest Democrat and you stink like a Republican loo...'

At least we now know who's who in America; the 'Racial Election' having provided us with the proof in the 'butt-licking journalists', you guessed it, statistics…! Around 40% of *Whites* are liberally minded, forward-thinking and tolerant. Sadly, this quite obviously, in the *'Do-Gooders"* eyes, makes the remaining 60% intolerant, illiberal and inward-looking hillbilly-loving 'Red Necks'. Finally, there are the 97% of *Black Voters* who voted for *Barack Obama*. If we follow the same argument to its natural conclusion a large percentage could be racist, as they seem to have spurned *John McCain* because of his whiteness! No, wait a minute, the exit poll states that '90% of voters say race is not an issue'; which means only 10% of American voters, of any creed, are in fact racist. Then there are the 3% of *Black Voters* who did not vote for *Obama!* Did they vote for *McCain*, or are they the most racist of everyone, as they couldn't bring themselves to vote for *Obama* as he is half-white, or did they simply spoil their ballot papers in sympathy with other minorities without a representative?! Though, the biggest *racists* of all appear to have been the naïve liberal media; as, in their self-righteous quest to deny that any *Blacks* or *White Liberals* voted along racial lines they have completely neglected *Latinos, Orientals, Asians,* or, last but by no means least, *Native Americans…!* These groups were not included or categorised in any of their damn statistics! How racist is that!!

Remember, remember the fifth of November:
Gunpowder, treason and plot.
I see no reason, why gunpowder treason
Should ever be forgot.

Guy Fawkes, guy, t'was his intent
To blow up King and Parliament.
Three score barrels were laid below
To prove old England's overthrow.

By God's mercy he was catch'd
With a darkened lantern and burning match.
So, holler boys, holler boys, let the bells ring.
Holler boys, holler boys, God save the King.

And what shall we do with him?
Burn him.

Today is a day without 'Popery'. 'Tis an important day in the history of our once Great British Nation... Though this November fifth the 'Gunpowder Plot' will have to take second billing behind **'Obamamania...'.** Which is probably just as well, for legally it is now more than likely a racial crime to burn an effigy of the traitorous *Guy Fawkes*. I'm sure the *Do-Gooders* have already made sure of that..! If caught attempting such freedom of expression, firstly you would be pilloried, then stripped of your assets, naturally they would be handed over to superior *Eastern Europeans*, probably to the couple from the hellish coffee bar, after which you would be imprisoned for having the sheer audacity to re-enact part of your national heritage!! There would be a ubiquitous follow-on TV series where they would track down the long-lost descendents of naughty little *'Guido'*, the bemused distant relations presented with compensation cheques by some gushingly hormonal minor celebrity who has just won a contrived stage-managed talent show on Channel Nine Hundred and Ninety-Nine....! All achieved in order to maintain the well-oiled, biased and bigoted 'Monolithic P.C. Machine' that successfully rules every aspect of a British person's life...

My journey back from London tonight was absolutely horrendous: it took two hours! *The Northern Line* was so packed that I missed four trains before I eventually managed to squeeze myself on to a carriage. Packed in like sardines. The temperature rose quickly. It was stifling. An unpleasant smell of sweat was soon hanging in the air… To make matters even more uncomfortable, the train was travelling unusually slowly. I was beginning to think the driver had had a bad day and was now exacting his revenge on his poor unassuming passengers. Just happy to be moving, albeit at a snail's pace, I took a deep breath and thought of nothing… I'm sure everyone else was doing exactly the same thing, thankful to be on their way home, grateful that the nightmare was gradually fading into recent history… Alas, this was not to be the case! Unbeknown to us, our fun had only just begun! We proceeded to pass through *Kennington Interchange* without stopping; muttering, tuts and minor expletives abounded at our end of the 'cattle truck'. To make matters worse the driver then informed us that due to overcrowding on the platform he had been instructed to circle the loop once more. This he did, into the tunnel we went, around the loop and out again, passing the platform which was still bulging with trapped commuters going nowhere. Then, the driver's muffled 'cockney' voice re-appeared over the tannoy to inform us that we were now to be transported back to *Waterloo...!* Within minutes we were there, a stone's throw from *Embankment*, only one stop short of where I began my onslaught home! Albeit facing northwards instead of south. As the doors opened the human mass exited with some relief. The adjacent southbound platform quickly filling to dangerous levels, this was definitely the definition of *overcrowding!*

After what seemed like an unpleasant lifetime the 'Bravehearts' amongst us who had not scarpered for the exit were rewarded with a tube train that had just enough space for us to be catapulted into… Crushed once again, off we set, slowly ambling southwards along the *Northern Line*, hoping that we would, at last, reach our respective destinations. The *English* stronghold of *Clapham Common*, where the platform is dangerously sandwiched between the tracks, was also heaving with people, so the train passed straight through to *Clapham South*. Apparently, they were not waiting to climb aboard our airless smelly shuttle, but patiently queuing to leave the crowded station and head for the 'Fireworks on the Common!' Somewhat ironically, despite my earlier lamentable manifestations on the subject, it transpired that my journey home had been disrupted due to an overload of people intent on celebrating 'Guy Fawkes Night!'

Since arriving home, fireworks have been going off in all directions. The sky is a rainbow of colour, the smell of sulphur filling the night-time air. All in all, the homage to the failure of the 'Gunpowder Plot' has been quite a spectacle. Although I'm sure there are those among us who believe it a celebration of the victory of *Mr Obama!!!*

Thursday 6th November

Well, today is the first day of a better life for us all…! If you are one of our American cousins who bought into all the hype you will, presumably, be totally convinced of this fact! Although your reasons for voting in *Barack* may have been genuine and honourable, I can't imagine the plight of the hard-working poor will be any better by the end of his presidency. Cynical, granted. But I suspect that the rich will become richer and the vast majority will still be struggling. The only winners, if indeed there are any, are likely to be some of the people dependant on 'welfare'. Post *Barack*, 'hard-working mugs' in the developed world will still be trapped in the rusty cogs of an awful 'Globalised Corporate Society' with mortgages the size of a small African country's national debt.

'Change is coming' may be a great rallying cry to the faithful, who would, I should imagine, follow *Barack* over the precipice of *Niagara Falls* if they thought it would lead them to the *Promised Land!* But the truth of the matter is that *change* is not about to rear its hopeful head in Alabama, Kentucky, Illinois, Pennsylvania, or anywhere else you choose to think of. No new liberty is hovering on the horizon, just 'the freedom to wash dishes and shine shoes'. Granted, the inauguration in January will see a changing of the puppets, goodbye *Bush*, hello *Obama!* Same strings, new face, that's all…

So, please forgive me if I am not quite as excited by this supposedly systemic shift to a better, fairer world. The racial profile of the president has undoubtedly changed, but for the rest of us a lifetime of fear and exploitation at work, suburban drudgery, increasing taxes and death by exhaustion or binge-drinking is still the only show in town. Real *change*, releasing us from the shackles of this awful materialistic suppression, is certainly not on the cards. An obsession with *growth*, which inevitably requires more and more spending to keep the whole insane project on track, will still be propagated as the one-way road to enlightenment. The choice to opt out of bills, rent and mortgages and barter your way across the world on a just ideological breeze is, sadly, definitely not part of the mantra of 'The great winds of change'. Last, but by no means least, *change* will have only really occurred if people in Britain and America who do not subscribe to this nonsensical, wholly deceitful, supposedly left-leaning doctrine are allowed their unequivocal freedom of speech!

It has always been fashionable to mock any Republican, Conservative or Nationalist-leaning figure (save the Scottish Nationalists of course!), or anybody who dares to agree, in any part, with their opinions. Indeed, naïve Students, most of the Media Class, the majority of Hollywood Stars, countless British Celebrities, many 'Oh So Clever' Satirists, and the usual suspects on rather tragic and unfunny shows like *Mock The Week* all partake in a game of sneering superiority, playing to their adoring sheep-like gallery that wouldn't dare question the validity of their far higher intellect...! Besides, most of them can well afford to be as arrogant and self-congratulatory as they see fit! To these overpaid, under-talented, conflicted self-worshipers it is positively *de rigueur* to make fun of 'Poor White Trash', for they have now gravitated themselves away from their, quite often humble, origins... In modern Britain the aforementioned 'Poor White Trash', along with the 'Toffs', are the only groups who can be publicly mocked without recourse! For they, in the judgemental mind of the *'Liberal'*, are the untouchables, the *Racist Class!!*

In the main *Do-Gooders* are fantastically wealthy 'liberals' with free rein to say whatever they please. However, the apologetic self-loathing cause of these misguided morons has abruptly hit the buffers with the first *Black President* (remember, no white blood!) now in charge of their 'Free World'! The litmus test is upon us, affirmative action no longer required! So will the 'Non-Liberals' (anyone who doesn't match up to their stratospheric principals) finally be afforded equal rights and the freedom to openly criticise a Democratic President, especially a black one, without cries of *racism* ringing out all over Washington...?! Please God, now make these boring, repressed, dull, champagne-swilling, money-laden hypocrites shut the fuck up, for they have reached *their nirvana!* Also, instead of preaching to the struggling masses and encouraging redistribution of wealth from people on modest earnings and impoverished pensioners, why don't they lead by example and dish out some of their own millions and billions to the deserving poor...? Hallelujah, Lord. Should this happen, the Messiah will definitely be upon us. Don't hold your breath though!

Rock stars like *Bob Geldof* and *Bono* are another bunch of duplicitous bullies, forever jumping on the latest self-promoting, lecturing bandwagon. Sure, they offer their services for 'free' to whatever charitable cause is fashionable at the time. But in return they gain massive amounts of unpaid publicity, besides earning them the much craved, laughable status of 'Celebrity Saint...' Egged on, vociferously, by sycophants in all four vacuous corners of our foul-smelling media, they naturally become delusional. Believing their own hype, they're convinced they are blessed with supernatural powers, so increasingly they adopt the persona of an unelected dictator... 'Give us your bloody money', they demand...! Well, 'Bob & Co', why don't you relinquish some of yours? After all, you have plenty of it. You could even donate a few quid to the struggling *Ancient Britons..!* Although I suppose that would be a little too unfashionable. Besides, your *Do-Gooder* mates would definitely frown upon it, shutting off your visceral oxygen in disgust!

The whole 'sorry bunch' proclaim themselves to be on the side of the weak and downtrodden, whilst becoming nefariously wealthy with every passing minute, their dynasties further expanding as their naïvely cosseted, usually untalented, offspring fill our TV screens with yet more highly paid drivel. They think they are unique, a breath of fresh air, out there saving the planet on behalf of us mere mortals...! No, they are simply a gaggle of boring, cloned, greedy fashion victims with an insatiable appetite for jetting around the world in *Lear Jets* and stealing from the poor while they're at it. They claim to abhor class privilege, unfair advantage, nepotism, but use all these facets to their full advantage whilst continuing to smugly judge and mock their detractors..! Why don't they renounce their worldly goods and give all their wealth, or a very large portion of it, to the vast array of good causes they profess to hold so dear to their hearts, and insist on repeatedly ramming down our plebeian throats! Because they are egotistical, duplicitous, little, interfering control freaks, that's why...

Charity, I thought, began at home; caring for an elderly relative, doing your sick neighbour's shopping, maintaining your grandparents' garden, to name but a few examples of true altruism. Still, the manual side of life doesn't concern these deluded demigods, after all they have staff for menial and mindless tasks! Their concern isn't deep enough to actually dirty their hands or break into a sweat for the cause; they are far too important for that: they are intellectuals! If they are to engage in charitable acts they presume to enter at the top end of the food chain as overlords and ladies: they must have self-gratifying fun, a 'gala dinner' the very least they would expect… Lest we forget, it's all about them: massaging their egos, increasing their profits and expanding their profiles. *Vive les Bourgeois!!*

1 pm:

The train has just pulled out of *Morden* station and entered the darkness of the underground network. Yes, I'm off up to 'town' yet again, the modern-day equivalent of *Dick Whittington!* I used to reside in Gloucestershire so the story has some authenticity, the only real difference being our respective ages at the outset of our life-changing journeys! I'm not one to give up at the first hurdle so, like *Dick*, I soldier on believing the streets of London to be paved with gold! Although my ambitions differ slightly from *Dick's* as I certainly do not want to end up as *Lord Mayor of London*. No, I am set to become the most versatile *Singing Sensation* the world has ever known; which is why I have, for the last year, been regularly trudging up to London to attend voice-training classes.

The day America became a little bit cool again, reads the idiotic headline on one of the free papers… I suppose we are in for a fair few years of these crappy taglines, along with the accompanying meaningless editorials, like the 'Cool Britannia' bullshit some of the lemmings within the media class hyped-up when *Tony Blair* was elected 'Emperor'.

Though the propaganda machine soon ran out of steam, the hyped-up, unrealistic expectations were well and truly sunk when 'G.B.', the dour Scot, took over the mantle...! Enough of this political babble, I'm starting to give myself a migraine. In the end, when all good and bad is done in the name of 'Democracy' it will be the 'same old, same old'.

Más tarde:

My singing was a triumph! I was a veritable success... For all four minutes of my solo performance!

Wednesday 12th November

'Far from the madding crowd am I', for Central London at least! The air has turned chilly but the sky is bright. Big Ben, the tower of the House of Lords, and the Millennium Wheel are a dappled delight through the half-bare plane trees. A painter would be positively drooling, itching for a canvas, paints and easel; for the broken bubbly cloud behind the *Houses of Parliament* is being lit up by powerful streaming shards of sunlight, which, in turn, are reflecting these majestic buildings onto the mighty river below… Yes, I'm back at *Temple Place*, in my usual top right-hand corner… Seeing as I have now finished my lunch, the pigeons, two magpies and several seagulls have all but buggered off. The only other sign of life is the homeless man who is fast asleep on a bench in the opposing corner.

It is over a week already since *Barack Obama's* famous victory. The obsessively effusive and jovial euphoria is slowly subsiding… The *Irish* have claimed him as one of their own, *O'bama!!* Which is perfectly possible, as the man seems to have blood from all corners of the globe running through his saintly veins. Perhaps he represents the real modern America after all, the true global melting pot. After Britain, that is!

In hindsight, I suppose you can't blame *'black people'* for voting for him nigh on unanimously. If it was the other way around I'm sure the *'whites'* would have acted in the same compulsive manner. The slave trade was, as we all know, an indefensibly cruel betrayal of humanity; which, especially in America, is a wound that is deep-rooted, conflated by the apartheid that remained there until a few decades ago. The struggle of the African Americans has been long and arduous, so I hope the election result can advance us from this shameful period of America's recent history. Perhaps we can all now play on a level field, with far less wingeing and excuses from the lazy, work-shy elements of black and white people, or indeed people of any colour or ethnicity.

In this 'new age of enlightenment' let us have the courage to be totally free in speech, and completely honest with regards to the world's ills! Surely now we can challenge and tackle today's slavery and discrimination, which exists around the world in the supposedly civilised twenty-first century..! Countless African countries still have *Slave Markets*, Black Africans buying and selling other Black Africans. The caste system is rife in India, and in Malaysia the 'Bumiputeras' (Muslim sons of the soil) are given preference in education and government jobs, receive lower mortgage rates, benefit from discounted house prices and higher bank interest rates! When are we going to close the 'Black Police Officers Federation, the Lesbian Mothers Interracial Adoption Forum (I made that one up, although it is bound to exist somewhere.)', etc. These are flagrantly racist and discriminatory institutions, accepting or refusing people solely on the basis of colour, gender, sexuality or lifestyle choice. Irony, oh irony! Nowadays, even the Gentlemen's Clubs of St James allow women members for fear of contravening race and equality legislation. However, one has to remember, *'The Magna Charter of Do-Gooders'* allows for 'Affirmative Action' to prevent the curse of unintended meritocracy... Lastly, but by no means least, if the 'Indigenous Population of Britain' is inherently *racist*, why did so many people follow us back from their colonised countries as soon as independence was granted? Why are the number of new arrivals, especially from *Eastern Europe*, ever rising!? Because they know, as do we, this is the most tolerant and liberal country on earth, where 'minorities' are protected to the hilt. 'The proof of the pudding is in the eating' and boy oh boy do we have some tasty desserts…! As far as I am concerned every new arrival, illegal or otherwise, we mustn't 'discriminate' after all, should be given a free 'Sticky Toffee Pudding and Custard' along with the keys to their new home in our (sorry, their) 'Green and Pleasant Land'.

On that muscle-tensing note I'm away to the last bastion of Englishness, *el pub..!* Anyhow, it's getting cold. Daylight is fast fading, the dial of 'Big Ben' has just been illuminated, and twilight is darkening the Thames.

Later:

The church of *St Anselm and St Cecilia* was a welcome interlude from the hustle and bustle of the pavements of *Kingsway*. It turned out to be a Catholic church. Not that this is a problem, particularly for a *Pagan Ancient Briton*. Catholic, Protestant, Methodist, Presbyterian, it makes no odds to me. However, it turned out to be a very peaceful and enticing place to rest awhile.

The exterior of the church is very unassuming. Tightly sandwiched between late Victorian office buildings, it hardly bears any resemblance to a conventional church at all. Blink and you would be bound to miss it. The doors have that fifties plate-glass appearance, so the idea that you are entering a place of worship doesn't cross your mind in the slightest. What caught my eye, and so revealed this little gem, was the display of 'Charity Christmas Cards' in the small foyer... After praying for divine intervention in my quest for 'Superstar Singer Status', relaxing in the church for a while, and purchasing a rather overpriced pack of cards, I now find myself a few doors along in *J.D. Wetherspoon's* public house. I know it must seem rather hypocritical for a *Pagan* to be purchasing *Christmas Cards!* However, as far as I am aware, it was the Romans who cleverly and deliberately introduced Christmas around the same time as the pagan festival of the 'Winter Solstice'. Anyway, it's fun to send cards, an easy way of keeping in touch with old friends… If Jesus Christ did exist and lead his short life on earth, as is written, I have no problem celebrating the birth of such a humble humanitarian.

Some of those *Irish* genes must be catching up with me again! First the church, then the pub, all I need is a betting shop next door and I'll be back in a small village in *County Mayo!* Although, 'to be sure', I'm really not a drinker in the classical sense, but the occasional 'dark rum and Coke' on a chilly November's eve certainly helps to warm the cockles of your heart whilst you people-watch and think of very little.

Returning to the subject of church, apparently November is the 'Month of the Holy Souls'; derived from *Samhain*, the name of the pagan festival marking the end of the harvest season and the festival of the dead, now known as Halloween or All Hallows Day, and so on. Another Christian adoption into their ecclesiastical calendar, along with the use of holly and ivy at Christmas, and so many other pagan rituals… I suppose it is a very clever way of enticing people into a monotheistic religion, after all worshipping a single creationist god saves time and energy dancing around stone circles and the like!

Pagan or Christian, or whatever you fancy, fate does play funny tricks! Earlier, as I was leaving my bench at *Temple*

Place, a young *Black Man* approached me and informed me that I had some white stuff on the side of my cheek! I wasn't sure if he was winding me up or not. He seemed quite genuine in his concern. So I did that thing we all tend to do when we receive this type of information, I duly licked my index finger and began to brush it across my cheek. Alas, no white residue found its way onto my finger. So I tried again, the *Black Man* still standing in front of me, vacantly watching as I now proceeded to wipe two fingers around my cheeks. All the time thinking to myself, 'Was it pigeon poo? Surely I would have felt that landing on my face! I would have definitely smelt it, wouldn't I? Was it toothpaste from this morning's brushing? It certainly wasn't semen! Ah, perhaps it was some residue of the paper tissue that I wiped my mouth with after scoffing two "pigs in blankets" for my luncheon…!' After what seemed like an eternity of licking my fingers and rubbing my cheeks, without questioning as to why I was repeatedly doing this with absolutely no success, I eventually came to my senses and stopped. For a brief moment he gazed deeply into my soul. I must have looked completely puzzled, startled even! He did not flinch, his demeanour calm and still. Then, after some motionless time, he spoke:

'Are you homeless too?'

For some reason, maybe it was a subliminal reaction, empathy I suppose, I replied:

'No, but I used to be.'

He then asked me if I could spare some cash for a place in a hostel. Knowing that he more than likely wouldn't be spending it on a hostel, as they are usually free for the homeless, I gave him a pound and went on my merry way.

It must have been the mackintosh and the two

rucksacks that I was carrying which made him think I too was homeless. I did look a little laden and the mackintosh, although not cheap, a 'Burberry' no less, has seen better days; in fact it is somewhat short in the arms and is now more dirty beige than cream, partly due to the substantial residue of newspaper print! I am also feeling rather tired after *Supermarket Heaven* and I didn't bother to shave today so I probably do look dishevelled, which for an HSP over forty could easily lead people to believe you are homeless. Not that there is any shame in being homeless, for we are all but a few misfortunes away from a crisis in our lives… These are the very cases the state should be spending taxpayers' money on, not feckless yobs and the like!!

We never really know people, any of us… Paths come and go. They cross, meander, sometimes they meet, only to part again at some point in the future, near or far. Maybe the homeless guy wasn't homeless at all, but simply a fellow thespian going about his research! In class we've been experimenting with the *Stanislavski* technique of method acting. He was probably just living a day as a homeless person and is about to transfer his purism onto the 'Silver Screen', Hollywood and beyond..! I've just noticed, the *Christmas Cards* I bought claim to be supporting *Homeless Charities*. So it is a 'win-win' situation. I have either starred in some completely cutting-edge method acting rehearsal with a future *Sidney Poitier*, or I have twice helped the homeless in one afternoon!

Speaking of which, I had best get myself off to the college of mega-stardom. Although I already hate the fucking place! It has the usual ratio of ten administrators per tutor, their sole purpose dishing out copious amounts of 'P.C. Diktats' and generally creating an atmosphere of uninspiring fear and intimidation… I think I'm just too free-spirited to become shackled to the world of the superficial *'Luvvie Darling'*. Not that I'm getting ahead of myself!!

Thursday 13th November

Someone has just sneezed over my head! Despite them sporting a well-cut grey flannel suit, they didn't even bother to put their hand to their mouth! I'm on the tube early today, 9 a.m., consequently it's rather crowded and other people's germs are far too close for comfort… My default reaction when someone coughs or sneezes in my personal space is to curve my body inwards on itself into the protective foetal position, then hold my breath whilst averting my gaze downwards and praying I don't catch some virulent strain of influenza. I just can't stand being ill, not that anybody could possibly like it! It's such a waste of time and energy, notwithstanding the damage it could do to the vocal folds of a *Professional Singer* in the making, with a sub-skill in *Method Acting!*

----- *Stockwell* -----

I had to change here as, today, I have my second ever private singing lesson, at the extortionate rate of £60 per hour! I have to travel all the way to *Acton Town* in the deepest depths of west London. That's two whole shifts of *Supermarket Heaven* for an hour of vocal coaching, which, let's face it, is a bit of an expensive gamble for someone over forty! After the first lesson, when I was obliged to part with the monumental fee, I was full of self-doubt, but, if you don't have faith in yourself, blind or otherwise, who the hell else is going to?! It's a bit like those school reports most of us, save the all-round geniuses, have in a dusty cupboard somewhere, 'Could do better, has potential, has not reached his full potential,' etc, etc. So, if £60 per hour and a shitty driving job is what it takes then I have no choice but to suffer for my cause. Besides, at my age it is now or never!

----- *Victoria* -----

Everything is running like clockwork today, off one train and straight onto another... I am now on the *District Line*. We've just pulled out of *Sloane Square* (I remember hanging around here with friends in the 80s. Imitating *'Yuppies'*, collars up, sweaters loosely draped over impressionable shoulders... Maybe I was one for a while. After all I was from a semi-wealthy family. How life changes!). The long amble to *Acton Town* and superstardom is underway. It is bloody slow compared to the 'bullet train' speed of the southern stretch of the Northern Line. Of course, I haven't a clue whether this is necessarily true or not, but it does feel as if we are being dragged along by an overly tired mule on a double dose of morphine.

I had an 'Actors Voice Class' last night. The course began at the end of September, so I have been going for several weeks now. I'm not sure what I'm getting out of it! But we are an eclectic group and the teacher is clearly nuts, so it's entertaining to say the least... We are far too many people in a small classroom on the top floor of the plush new premises of the 'P.C. Further Education College'. The class starts at 6 p.m., but seeing how our drama-based lesson has been scheduled into an academic classroom prior to this we are expected to clear away copious amounts of cumbersome fold-up tables! Cutbacks no doubt..! There are over twenty of us in the class and on arrival the usual suspects, myself included, set about the chore. The noise is horrendous. Added to which, for every two successful folds one table is broken! The aluminium clips are no way strong enough to hold up the tubular metal legs. Invariably they bend, snap, or if you lean too hard on the wooden table tops as you try to fold them, they simply collapse.

----- *Acton Town* -----

Here I go, step by step to the maestro's door and a brighter golden future...

Wow! That was great! My Singing Teacher lives in one of those lovely late-Victorian Terraced Town Houses with big bay windows, proper wooden sash ones of course. Inside, the ceilings are high, the floors real old wood, oak I think, fancy architraves abound, and everything is in keeping with the period and in good taste, one thing the 'English Upper Middle Class' have in abundance. They have a perfect grasp of simple understated elegance which lends itself very well to renovating period houses and gardens... The usual large ground-floor extension had been added to increase the size of the minimalist eat-in kitchen. It was equipped with all the latest brushed-steel appliances, marble tops, the ubiquitous double 'Belfast sink', the must-have antique pine table with matching period chairs, a painted wicker sofa with twin armchairs, muted soft furnishings, walls painted in pastel green and off-whites, ample wooden-framed skylights, wall-to-wall 'French doors' which lead into the perfectly designed garden complete with a 'Cotswold stone' terrace surrounded by box, standard photinias, lace-capped hydrangeas in dried autumnal bloom and two olives in huge terracotta pots, all making for a perfect *al fresco* dining oasis, weather-permitting of course...

Naturally, the attic space has been fully utilised too! One of the rather spoilt children has it as a separate living area/bedroom and it is, more than likely, equipped with an en-suite 'wet room', complete with personal loo, huge designer basin and the latest, largest water-wasting shower head available on the interior design market! Wet room envy a must..! There are streets full of such properties all over the more 'well heeled' parts of London, and dotted around 'up and coming' suburbs such as *Acton Town..!* Sometimes people of taste are obliged to live in these more challenging locations, what with the bloody oligarchs and the like pushing up prices all over the place. They're a hopeful 'island of style' in a sea of 'Ikea'! Although I hope *Acton Town* isn't too 'up and coming', otherwise singing lesson fees will be on the rise and I'm not sure I could hack that.

Owners of such properties who haven't yet upgraded the *attic* probably have the *'Au Pair'* billeted up there, normally on around fifty pounds a week, so then the state of repair is pretty inconsequential. After all, she is barely ever there! Invariably spending the majority of her time running errands while simultaneously playing the role of 'Nanny', 'Cook', and 'Housekeeper'. Still, food (probably leftovers), board and lodging is included; which would cost her a small fortune in some of the areas where their naïvety is willingly exploited by their duplicitous saccharine hosts! Added to which, she has her weekly 'afternoon off!' Her chance to attend some dingy language school, where they will willingly relieve her of her hard earned fifty quid. After all, she did come to learn English so she shouldn't really complain, despite being sold a pup! Anyhow, her *Liberal-Minded Captors* are simply too busy racing between dinner parties, attending gallery openings and fundraisers for some poor *African Village* to worry about the welfare of the sleep-deprived prisoner in their own lavish home!

'Cynical, envious, bitter…!' I hear your cries. Surely, in this day and age, people would not be treated so! Wrong, I tell you, believe you me this type of feather-cushioned exploitation, abuse even, goes on all the time… I once had a very attractive German girlfriend, along with several other 'friends!' who reside in the same area of south London, who were consistently treating *'Au Pairs'* as if they had four sets of hands, a degree in social work and a drawer full of professional childcare qualifications. Then when something went wrong, often through exhaustion or resentment or both, guess who bagged the blame…!? I'm not saying that all *'Au Pairs'* are perfect: I'm sure some are complete nightmares. However, many Middle Class Parents lure them over under false pretences… It will be *'fun!'* They want to leave Prague, Rome, Lisbon, a myriad of European cities, for the bright lights of London, have an adventure and learn *English!* All they have to do is help a little in return for their keep, babysit once a week, do the occasional school run, and even receive a little pocket money for their trouble. It all sounds a perfect trade-off. Which, I suppose, it can sometimes turn out to be. Not that I have witnessed such an outcome, only a very pissed-off French girl who spat venom under her breath in a *patois* I could barely understand, even though I once worked in the Cognac region of south-west France. Nevertheless, *Heidi* was oblivious to her disgruntled demeanour! So one day, after a stiff drink, I plucked up the courage to confront her on the subject. Her response was typically dismissive. Her Germanic lilt became uncontrollably guttural, making her sound even more uncaring than she intimated. If that's possible!

'It is zee free market… If she doesn't like zeee work she can give her notice… Only vun month required!' she spat at me.

Needles to say, after that the relationship soon petered out!

Returning to *singing*… Due to the weird and wonderful anatomical routines I have been subjected to over the past year at 'The P.C. College' I thought I had all but mastered the technique of *breath control!* However, after two lessons with *Miriam* I now know to the contrary and have some idea what the bloody hell *breath control* is all about. *Control* being the key word that has so far eluded me..! It transpired that my usual habit of gulping huge amounts of air, thus expanding my diaphragm to the size of a beach ball, is not actually an effective way of supplying invisible life-giving gases to my lungs. At least, for the purpose of singing! Nor is singing through to the point that your breath dies in mid-phrase, causing your diaphragm to suddenly collapse, thus requiring you to inhale yet another gargantuan quantity of oxygen to sustain the next line of lyrics; by which time the piano accompaniment is two beats in front of you, or the pianist has simply had to, embarrassingly for you, pause on a single recurring note until you catch up again! All in all this has the effect of producing a performance littered with troughs and peaks. Sometimes you are brilliant, other times when the air abruptly cuts away your face turns a worrying shade of blue, your diaphragm collapsing as your voice, once more, grinds to an embarrassing halt... Subconsciously, you know you should have stopped singing before the air supply ran out in order to refill your lungs in good time for the upcoming phrase. However, for some bizarre reason, nerves I suspect, you are too scared to stop and your body keeps on exhaling lyrics which, as you squeeze out the last few parcels of air, become painfully high-pitched as your throat muscles naturally tighten before the inevitable abrupt ending in the middle of a now unintelligible phrase. Your body then does all the things you were taught not to allow it to. You become more and more tense and sweaty. The cycle is repeated throughout your performance as you nervously race yourself to the finish line, finally shouting out that last note with gusto, naïvely thinking you are a modern-day *Louis Armstrong* or *Matt Munro*. The reality being that you have just made a complete *twat* of yourself in front of your peers. The only consolation is that one of them has to perform next. You just hope it is not the one with the note-perfect voice! No, you want the 'class joker' to be called up, for he will humiliate himself to a far greater degree as he is even more contrived than you are! Anything that detracts from your *Karaoke*-style 'Knees up Mother Brown' charade would be a welcome diversion... Thank God I found my own guru in *Miriam*. 'The P.C. College' better watch out! Come next week's class I shall 'knock 'em dead' with my newfound confidence and professional technique...!

A *Piccadilly Line* train to *Cockfosters* arrived at the eastbound platform first so I decided to ditch the *District Line*, give it a shot and change at *Green Park* for my *Victoria Line* connection back south... So far so good: within the blink of an eye I'm at *Hyde Park Corner*. It remains to be seen how long the 'route march' will be at *Green Park!* If I remember rightly it is one of those interchange stations with a never-ending labyrinth of underground walkways.

----- *Green Park* -----

As I thought, it turned out to be a good brisk walk. However, it wasn't without its advantages. It certainly helped my delicious lunch push its way a little further down my stomach to the direction of my bowels... Following my singing triumph I indulged in a '£5.95 Eat as Much as you Like Oriental Buffet'. They can be a little hit and miss, but this one was delicious. Added to which the restaurant was as clean as a whistle, especially the toilets, which was a welcome surprise. There are definitely some benefits to the 'Credit Crunch'.

I only have one more stop until *Stockwell,* so I'll soon be back in the familiar safety of my beloved *Northern Line…* In the meantime I can sing 'Summertime' to my throngs of adoring fans! Well, seven actually, that's the grand sum of fellow travellers in this particular carriage. If they had *déjà vu* they would be aware of the magnitude of being seated in the same carriage as *moi…* Should they be daring enough to try and subtly touch me, a few specks of my unadulterated 'stardust' might inadvertently sprinkle over their downtrodden souls. Alas, they are none the wiser about their missed opportunity!

'HONEY, I'M HOME…!' … Silence…! Well, what did I expect? After all, I do live alone! Yes, I'm back in my tiny little flat, which, as usual, is totally devoid of activity, unless that pedigree *pussy* is prowling around my beautifully landscaped garden again. Even the cat is 'off' with me of late..! *Julie* has also fallen into this evasive, cool and rather displeased category! I suppose I am somewhat to blame as recently I have become so wrapped up in singing, the remainder of my spare time being taken up with the vileness that is *Supermarket Heaven.*

It seems whenever I am working *Julie* is free and vice versa, Sunday being the only day we are off together. By which time we are both knackered, irritable and, consequently, quite argumentative with one another… Last Sunday we went up to town for the 'Remembrance Service' in Whitehall. The whole occasion was naturally very moving. Seeing those brave men and women, many very old and frail now, march past the *Cenotaph* to honour their fallen comrades, was a humbling experience to say the least... We had both wanted to go, to pay tribute and thank them for their sacrifice in keeping the world, but especially our country, free from *Nazi* tyranny. Even so, we still succeeded in rubbing each other up the wrong way! On the way home we managed to have an argument about 'Yorkshire puddings' of all things!

Friday 14th November

Shit! It's ten past one! I'm off for a swim! I'm feeling rather lethargic today. Maybe the sight of *The Grey Ladies* will get me going...?!

Back again...! I cycled, frantically, to the public pool near *Mitcham Cricket Green* only to be greeted by herds of screaming kids and not a single *Grey Lady* in sight! Naturally, I left immediately. Cycling just as frantically I returned through picturesque *Morden Hall Park*, the 'National Trust' jewel in the tired rusty crown that is modern-day *Morden*. After which I stopped off at *el banco espagnol*, waited for the usual infuriating length of time to deposit some cash into my increasingly negative bank account, and I am now sat back at home downing hot tea, before racing off to that fucking supermarket again!

Wednesday 19th November

I feel like I have been used as a 'punch bag' for the last week or so…! The 'rum and Coke' is certainly helping me to relax. I'm back in *J.D. Wetherspoons* at the *Holborn* end of *Kingsway*, chilling out prior to my 'Actor's Voice Class' at the increasingly unbearable 'P.C. College'. My entire body is so exhausted that my muscles are hardly able to function! I am a walking, well, sitting at present, 'blob', liable to collapse at any moment!

Thank you *Daniel and Isa*, short for *Isabella*, you have turned me into a sleep deprived madman..! Yes, my latest tenants keep the most antisocial hours. *Isa*, in particular, should move to the Middle East for the summer and spend winters in the dry heat of the Australian desert, as she has an insatiable appetite for 'central heating'. I have been remiss to not mention that to support my *'mid-life crisis superstardom cause'* I have chopped my little red-brick, ex-local-authority, end-of-terrace house horizontally in two. They are up, I am down!

Both flats have a kitchen/diner, theirs being somewhat larger in size than mine, a newly fitted bathroom and a double bedroom… Their double bedroom adheres to the description of a double room in every facet; mine, on the other hand, houses my five-foot-wide double bed, a huge sliding beech-effect wardrobe, a chest of drawers in the same style, my grandfather's old mahogany bureau and several crater-sized clear storage boxes that are unable to fit under my bed because of all the other clobber that resides there. The top of the wardrobe is also piled high to the ceiling and the bed must be entered from the south-west corner, as it is all but enveloped by the sliding wardrobe and the partition wall that I myself constructed. Basically, the lounge of this small dwelling house is now my flat. Consequently, the bathroom is squeezed under the staircase and the galley kitchen leads onto my beautiful, in comparison to the flat, large garden. My bedroom and the door into my *bijou sector* are at the front of the property, right next to the shared main entrance; which means that when in bed I can hear, loudly and clearly, the handle of the nowadays obligatory plastic front door being violently thrust up and down as these 'arseholes' come and go.

The tenants prior to the toxic combination of *Daniel and Isa* always left early for work, so I was regularly woken at seven in the morning. However, after six months, I became used to the gruesome procedure, accustomed to the pattern, accepting of the pounding feet on the floor above, seeing as the upstairs flat's kitchen/living area is partially above the minute area known as my bedroom... Despite our close proximity, wooden joists and a few floorboards apart, the arrangement worked well enough as I and the previous 'Twenty-Somethings' frequently retired for the night at a similar hour. My living room being situated beneath their bedroom, more often than not we would be at opposite ends of the 'Manor' so, save for the odd loud copulative indulgence, I could hardly hear them, or them me. Mutual harmony prevailed. Well, as much as is humanly possible, when through the recklessness of an 'open-door immigration policy' courtesy of *Messrs Blair and Brown* we are forced to live in ever-decreasing circles. Space, due to the relentless pressure on houses and the stratospheric cost of purchasing one, is more valuable than gold.

Voices are not a pressing problem, as unless raised substantially they do not seem to travel between the flats.

Faint banging of a headboard is not a problem either, in fact it can be quite funny, titillating even, just knowing what they are up to a mere few feet from your head as you are sat staring less than half-heartedly at 'Newsnight'. You feel like 'egging them on', having a peek even, as all that bumping, grinding, headboard-banging, screeching, moaning and groaning suddenly climaxes with a caveman-like war cry and a reciprocal high-pitched shriek….. It's the 'fucking floorboards', that's what drives you insane! The constant little creak here and there, then there is the one that squeaks like a rusty coffin that has been opened after lying dormant for a thousand years, immediately sending your body into contorted convulsions of pernicious, frenzied fear!

Irritating at times, but the small *South African Guy* and his *English Girlfriend* were definitely not an ongoing problem... These two *Poles*, on the other hand, have so far managed to keep me awake every night since they moved in! Tonight is the ninth night in a row, so I am literally dreading my head touching pillow for fear of the nightmare that will inevitably follow. All this from someone who can quite easily slumber through a minor earthquake and who, under normal circumstances, has a propensity to fall asleep within seconds… Bastards…

One-thirty, one o'clock, two o'clock. Friday was a new record, 3.20 a.m.! He *(Arsehole 1)* is a 'chef' and she *(Arsehole 2)* 'a plate-dumping waitress' in one of those crappy 'Gourmet Burger Chains'. Having worked in catering myself, *à la carte* service no less, I would like to think that I would be a little more considerate towards the *Landlord* residing below, rather than intently 'fucking him off' on a nightly basis...! I know I would have been! Even now I creep around, worrying about making excessive noise late at night.

Whenever I play music I keep it low, shut the windows, etc… Alas, *consideration* seems to be an etiquette which is firmly consigned to the recent past. These *'Arseholes'* are a prime example: they couldn't give a fiddler's hoot, a flying shit! They're as brash as you like. Not a care or thought for the poor *Middle-Aged British Pagan* who has housed them to a high standard, and at very reasonable rates to boot! *'Crash, bang, wallop… half a sixpence!'* Slightly higher rent than that, I know. Maybe I can sing that tune at the 'P.C. College' next week! But seriously, thrashing around, putting up flat-pack furniture from Sweden and walking a half marathon at three in the morning just about takes the biscuit! They are the ultimate 'neighbours from the nemesis of hell'.

Come Monday night, having endured them for a whole week, I somewhat foolishly assumed I was in for a breather as they both had the day off..! 12.50 a.m.: Thump, thump, bang, smash, crash, stamp… 1.20 a.m.: Having continually tried to relax my quivering self, calm down generally, ponder gentle breezes lapping warm Mediterranean shores, then, when all else had failed, to ignore it and pretend I wasn't two seconds away from murdering the little *wankers* with a blunt kitchen utensil (after all I do have a spare key to their sector!), I finally flipped:

'Fucking shut up, fucking shut up, fucking shut up!' I yelled at the top of my voice... I then managed to calm myself down, very slightly, well at least enough to stop my hands shaking with rage so that I could send *'Arsehole 1'* a curt text message. A while afterwards noise pollution ended and I eventually managed to get some sleep.

The previous day I arranged ten minutes with the *uber gruesome duo* to talk about the heating as I had barely seen them, but of course heard them, since they moved in at 11.20 p.m. last Tuesday…! She is blonde, of average looks and has a rather dour, uninterested demeanour. He seems a little more with-it, but when you talk to him you get the impression he isn't really listening at all. He's polite enough, fixing his gaze upon yours as you speak; however, when his eyes rapidly start to glaze over you know he is only playing with you, humouring you even. Having gone through the boiler instructions and set the timer to their requirements, I then played my trump card!

The heating bills are shared, the boiler being located in the neutral *green zone* in the cupboard in the communal entrance lobby. Up to now this has not caused a problem as the previous couple enjoyed roughly the same ambient temperature as me. *'Arsehole 2'*, *Isabella* or *Isa* (I thought that was a tax-free savings account, not a stupid abbreviation for the name of a dull little girl!), only knows the Polish translation for the word 'ON' and is obviously accustomed to hermetically sealed sauna living! Clearly, she never intends to open a window in case the chill of 'FRESH AIR' should engulf their sector! I'm sure soon enough unpleasant smells will start to permeate their way down the stairs, under their sector door, through the *green zone* and into my quarters; not discounting the layers of mould that will inevitably proliferate in their bathroom! 'Selfish property-wrecking Bitch...'

I'm digressing… My 'trump card' was to inform them that I hate *central heating* and rarely have it on, an hour a day at the most during a cold snatch! Not that *Isa* is ever likely to suffer from a 'cold snatch', unless they are inclined to use ice cubes during sex!! Anyway, the ball was well and truly smashed into their court as everything was set to their preference… I pointed out that they were more than welcome to have the *central heating* on twenty-four hours a day if they so wished, but they would need to pay most of the shared bill. I also took it upon myself to inform the rather surprised-looking duo that one of my radiators was turned off permanently and the others were on a low setting. I also threw in a cheap line about nocturnal living habits, and explained that during winter historically the bill is usually £35 a month at the very most, that therefore this is what I should be paying half of, and that they could pay the other half, plus the inevitably huge surplus due to *Isa's* sterling efforts at single-handedly accelerating global warming...! Or words to that effect...

I don't think the sauna situation will change. They obviously love to live in one, so heating bills are set to soar... Standing in silence, at best paying lip service, will not alter that fact! Although, as I told them, whether they like it or not they will definitely be paying for their unmistakable thirst for heat, not me... They certainly do not want to mess with *moi*. They've already fucked me off enough, and they haven't seen the half of it yet! A pissed-off *Highly Sensitive Ancient Briton* in his own backyard cannot be held responsible for his actions. I am sleep-deprived to the max, so watch this space: one more mental push and I may just SNAP!!

Bloodbath in Morden – Polish Chef and Waitress Couple slain by Landlord in rented flat! I suppose that is one way of having your name all over the front page of the local 'rag'.

Shit! I've missed the start of my 'Actor's Voice Class'. Bollocks... Seven o'clock already, too late to join it now. I think I'll head home and belt out 'Summertime' a few times: I need to practise for class tomorrow. Although I'm sure it's in the wrong key for me! What the hell, 'Summertime' can wait a little while longer, I need another 'dark rum and Coke' before I head back to vampire land! I'm not pressed for time, no orange plastic bag torture tonight... Singing rehearsals can kick off at 3.20 a.m. sharp! Then *Daniel, Isa* and *I* will all be on the same body clock. Maybe I could join them upstairs for a 'Singalong!' Introduce them to my *repertoire*, or they might want to include me in one of their *ritualistic nocturnal bloodsucking sex games!* It doesn't really matter, as long as we are done, dusted and back in our pits by daybreak...!

Thursday 20th November

11.30 a.m. Noise from above not too bad last night. *'Arsehole 1 and 2'* are still alive, so far as I know!

I am sat on my sofa, drinking strong coffee, staring down the garden watching squirrels ease peanuts out of the 'squirrel-proof nut feeder!' that is hanging from a branch on my little greengage tree. My mum, grandmother, brother, not my older sibling because of the family feud, and I have freezers bursting with this year's fruit. Copious amounts of home-made jams, chutneys, pies and crumbles have been lovingly produced in our respective kitchens. There must have been nigh on 200lbs of greengages, which, if you were able to find them, would have cost you a small fortune in any of today's clinical supermarkets. A clever little – well, rather humungous, to be precise – squirrel is now performing a precarious balancing act on the slightest of branches, successfully extracting its bounty from the even sturdier contraption that is 'the squirrel-proof seed feeder…!' Clearly, neither 'seed feeder' nor 'nut feeder' do 'what they say on the tin!'

Up to now I have only seen the occasional blue tit, great tit or oversized pigeon attempt to use the feeders, usually with the naughty *Grey Pedigree* or another estate cat looking on from the roof of my shed. If not the shed, then they tend to hang off the nearby fence or stalk them from the base of the tree itself. After all, this is a potential gourmet snack, a tasty appetiser prior to another bowl of man-made cat food.

Squirrels are by far the most daring of suburban wildlife, just ahead of the poor and cruelly maligned opportunistic *fox…* The *Felines* haven't a hope in hell of bagging a squirrel for supper. They could watch them all day without success, the feeders dangling tantalizingly close yet always a few insurmountable inches from their reach. The little grey rodents are well aware of this fact, revelling in the cat's torment as they scurry and prance about in a gleefully aggravating way… The more nervy and cautious *birds* have failed to realise the cat's limitations and are reluctant to put the *squirrel's* superior knowledge to the test, preferring to feed early in the morning when they hope the nocturnally active *cats* will be too tired to pursue them… *Pigeons* are the one exception with regard to avian caution! Being rather greedy in nature, somewhat slow, lazy and cumbersome, and of lesser IQ they are quite prepared to take their chances where food is concerned! I have a hanging basket full of red geraniums which is positioned near the peanut feeder, and in complete defiance of recent frosts still in full bloom. This creates a perfect suspended feeding platform. Just the right height for them to perch and safely peck away to their heart's content; which they are quite happy to do at any given hour, cleverly overcoming the tiny mesh holes designed for birds with far smaller beaks.

My resident *Grey Pedigree* becomes quite exasperated by the site of the out-of-reach meal some five feet from terra firma. He, or she, starts out by jumping onto 'the hot shed roof' from where he soon leaps on to the narrow edges of the close-board fence, which is nearer to his bounty but eventually overwhelmingly precarious so moments later he inevitably ends up full circle back on terra firma. This cycle is repeated until he becomes altogether too weary. So, still salivating at the prospect of the fat, juicy meal a stone's throw from his head, he takes a breather. Finally, he decides to give it one last-ditch attempt, without warning launching himself from the shed roof towards the narrow leaning trunk of my greengage tree. A few humiliating seconds later he comes tumbling straight back down with a bump. Yes, yet again he's back on terra firma, succumbing to defeat, for the time being at least... The delighted *pigeons* carry on regardless, smugly chomping away as he departs with his tail rammed firmly between his tired little legs. Though, renowned for its tenacity, the furry feline is probably mumbling: 'I'll be back.'

Pigeons are comparable to a jumbo jet, requiring plenty of space, and therefore time, to launch themselves skywards. Alas, for them, take-off space is limited in my enclosed suburban garden. This is not at all an issue for the smaller, lighter birds, who can quickly flutter away at a moment's notice... *Pigeons* are rather like *Labrador* dogs; they never know when to stop eating. If you put bread out they'll carry on until every last crumb has disappeared. So come take-off they are invariably laden with extra weight, making them less agile than ever. This, therefore, is the brief moment when the stalking *feline* must go in for the kill...! According to the evidence scattered over my lawn this morning, my theory holds water. The tenacity of the *Grey Pedigree* obviously prevailed, for you could hardly see the grass for pigeon plumes. I think I may need to purchase a bird table for their breadcrumbs, or else leave them to struggle at extracting peanuts. Scattering crumbs on my lawn will clearly not do, unless I want to eradicate the local *pigeon* population entirely! Which the arseholes among us would love, as, along with *urban foxes* and anything else that is not human, they consider them troublesome vermin! Some may say it's 'nature's way', as nature surely can be cruel. However, I'd rather be a 'Carnivorous Hypocrite', purchase a six-foot-tall bird table and customise it with a suitably long landing and take-off strip! Genius! Sir Alan would love that (now

Lord Sugar, I believe)!

Julie and I are on somewhat better terms! We've been a tad grown up, decided to 'bury the hatchet', 'rewind the clock', and meet up on neutral ground. Maybe we'll get along better that way…! She has been living with her mother for nearly a year now and is trying to extricate herself from her former life with her *Partner* of twenty-three years, with whom she says she has already wasted far too long! By all accounts he only eats salad, peas, chips, cheese and bread! He is a tennis coach, and as far as I have been made aware there begin and end his interests! He refuses to fly and will only travel on a short break within England! Apparently, so *Julie* tells me, he has no desire to socialise with anybody outside work, so when they were together she would invariably end up going out in a *threesome*. Which, I have often thought to myself, is not altogether such a bad thing!

On one occasion, when they did go on a night out with another couple, they ended up in a bistro in *Esher*... *Julie's Partner* (they never married) immediately made some excuse to leave the restaurant for a while, only to purchase some crisps and a fizzy drink! Two hours later he returned, sat back down and carried on as if nothing had happened! When I asked *Julie* what the other bloke and his wife said about his random behaviour, 'Nothing' was her reply! Apparently they had known the couple for years, consequently they knew all about *Julie's Partner's* dietary peculiarities and total lack of elementary social skills. By all accounts they felt rather sorry for him, and simply carried on regardless, expecting him to disappear again without a moment's notice. I suppose their disregard towards his behaviour was what made him feel comfortable enough to go in the first place! Although, nine times out of ten, *Julie* would still have to go on her own, which I'm sure would piss off even the most accommodating person in the end! Personally, I don't think I could stand living with a 'Lettuce-Eating Introvert', not without killing them one day…

According to *Julie*, his mother, who is in her late seventies, still brings him a bag full of his favourite salad and snack items on a weekly basis! This, understandably, really pisses her off… By all accounts his mother can't stand *Julie*, so I'm sure she revels in still mothering her over-aged son right under her nose! I must say, I'm not normally one to judge, live and let live and all, but it is a little freaky, a man in his mid-forties who has been in a relationship for twenty-three years taking in weekly food parcels from his mother! *Julie* is currently on a mission to rescue her son from the same ill fate as his 'Food Phobic Father', recently managing to make him eat roast potatoes! The other day saw an even greater turning point: he now likes carrots!

Julie's mother's flat is a mere ten minutes' walk from her former suburban semi, where her 'Partner of Disorders' and son still reside. She is, therefore, in and out all the time, ferrying her son to and from school, preparing his obscure meals and dishing out cash as and when required. Her son is fifteen years old now and quite independent, albeit not financially. He is currently in stroppy teenage mode, parents wanted one minute, a hated pain up the arse the next. So *Julie* is grappling with a sack full of crap at the moment, whilst simultaneously trying to carve out a new life for herself. Her baggage along with my own hang-ups making a perpetual itchy relationship… Timing being everything… I think we both know, really, if we are honest, that we are on a hiding to nothing…

It is now a whole year since we first met one another, at a Saturday morning 'Italian Class' in the lovely suburban town of *Sutton!* I was there to prepare myself for a new life in southern Italy, having sold my house at great profit, or so I thought! Of course my type of luck prevailed and it fell through, right at the peak of the market! Lots of 'blood, sweat and tears' with scant reward, 'so near yet so far', the metaphors are endless. Not that I can ever decipher one! Mild dyslexia is a pain up the arse. Oh well:

Life goes on
Love runs free
I'm a menopausal man
That's why Julie and I can never be.

One more line and I've created my first limerick! Maybe I should give up on my thirst for 'song and dance' and turn to poetry instead!

We never had sex while she was still with *Paul*, although she maintained that the physical side of their relationship had been dead for some time. Our first full-on encounter was back in June, over six months since we sort of started dating. Besides, once over forty the weight of accrued psychological baggage makes getting your kit off in front of another human being an activity best avoided for as long as is biologically possible! Anyway, after last Saturday night's meal at *La Dolce Vita* in *Wimbledon* high street, followed by plenty of middle-aged gyrating to 70s and 80s classics on the postage-stamp dance floor, we agreed to slow things down a little. We all detest our lives to some degree but, eventually, you have to come to terms with the parts you are not entirely happy with, or are simply beyond your control. Can I come to terms with being forty-one and still childless? Seeing how she is six and a half years older than me, if we remain together this is highly likely to continue to be the case, which all makes for an explosive cocktail! A permanent sticking plaster on an open wound, unless we have the good fortune to conquer this biological hurdle…! Apparently, according to a friend of mine, 'Resignation can help you move on with your life in a controlled and measured way!' The person in question has a naturally pompous air about him and duly turned out to be a duplicitous 'Back-Stabbing Tosser'. Naturally, he is now consigned to *'trash'*, firmly deleted from my 'Christmas Card List'. However, in some ways, I dearly hope he's right! Because this need to reproduce is doing my head in. I feel like a constant simmering volcano moments away from a catastrophic eruption.

Supermarket Heaven tonight... I am seriously starting to hate that fucking job too! Tuesday was absolutely dreadful, far too many deliveries in a short space of time. Added to which the 'Fat Cow' from the Human Resources office really pissed me off! I went to see her with regard to my 'Contract of Employment', which I'm still awaiting! She brushed it to one side and started going on about my holiday for the Christmas period! In very unpleasant terms she said I would lose my entitlement if I didn't book it soon; naturally it was the first I'd heard of it, and besides she was just deflecting her inefficiencies by spouting off a load of illegal power-crazed claptrap…! Added to which I still haven't got any safety boots, and only one of their hot and itchy polyester polo shirts to parade myself around in! Not that the 'Sulky Cow' gave a damn; on the contrary, in fact, she seemed to revel in being as unhelpful as is humanly possible. She obviously gets some kind of sick pleasure from being deliberately obtuse and antagonistic. She's about as useless as a 'willy' at a lesbian orgy! *Bitter Old Heifer!*

Consequently, by the time I had loaded my van with enough food and general crap to keep a 'Rebel African Army' in operation for an entire month I too was ready to go on an indiscriminate killing spree… I can see how easy it must be to totally lose it, suddenly slip into *road rage* and all. Fortunately, I managed to avoid this manifestation. Although, secretly, if I could have got away with it, I would have revelled in the prospect of deliberately crashing my van, along with my 'Capitalist Masters' Goods', into the central reservation of the busy A3…

1.30 p.m. already…! I suppose I should get dressed, eat a couple of those out-of-date sausages I cooked this morning. Having voluntarily elected to bunk off this afternoon's Singing Class I had intended to go for a swim today. I haven't been since Monday so I thought I should make an effort to do something enjoyable before tonight's inevitable hell ride. Oh well, it's getting a bit late now, the *Grey Ladies* will just have to cope without the stimulation of my muscle-clad body for another day. I think I'll take a trip to the garden centre instead. Maybe buy some 'spring bulbs'. Anything to take my mind off the hideousness that awaits…

Saturday 22nd November

'Well, what the fuck are you goin' to get 'im then…?' On leaving *'el'* money-sucking superstore *'esta noche'* this ephemeral line was catapulted into the ether from the vulgar mouth of a 'Thirty-Something' suburban mum, with badly coiffed spiky brown hair and tacky gold ear studs. The fact that her two young children were standing right next to her as she loudly expressed herself with inane expletives obviously did not concern her in the slightest! To his credit the poor husband, or more than likely nowadays 'Partner', steered away from profanities and somehow managed to constrain his reply to mild pre-watershed *English*. Besides, I suspect he's used to it! He probably rues the day he ever set eyes on the foul-mouthed *'Washer Woman…!'* Not that this was a particularly shocking one-off encounter. Swearing in public is a commonplace modern-day phenomenon. Especially, it would seem, among younger women. Even the best of us are guilty of swearing from time to time. I certainly am. But in a public place, and in front of your kids! Surely this is taking 'Yob Culture' that little bit too far?

Well, I suppose it is only to be expected! As an alpha female she will, quite possibly, insist on her browbeaten 'Partner' babysitting the kids tonight while she gallivants around town. She still feels she has youth on her side, although because of her drink problem the years are not being particularly kind. Blinded and undeterred, she's intent on behaving like a perpetual teenager. After all, it's Saturday night, her 'Chavy Mates' await her presence in the 'Cattle Market' of some swanky pseudo 'New York-Style Club Bar'. When she rolls in, literally, with half her midriff and nearly all her meaty thunderous thighs on show, her mates will be well on the road to inebriation, having already drunk their way through the 'Happy Hour' menu! Not one to be outdone, she'll go straight onto 'spirits' then cheap 'Champagne', followed by an orgy of high-proof 'chasers'. This mindless pattern continuing throughout the evening, then, as they become increasingly intoxicated the relatively few inhibitions they posses will rapidly subside. By now they have 'No Fear', the 'Cougars' heading for a state of euphoria! Obliging lingering men and boys are chatted up, groped, flashed at, sexually taunted and generally used as fodder to fulfil the group's sexual fantasies as a frenzied drunken climax is duly reached…! Before stumbling home in their overly high heels they will indulge in one of those hideous doner kebabs that are filled with all the gunge imaginable and taste like *Basics* dog food! Not that I have ever eaten dog food: I could be doing it a disservice! For all I know 'dog food' could be far tastier, definitely more nutritionally beneficial one would imagine…

Anyway, the 'Kebab' is quite likely to be consumed in the high street, as the shop is normally far too small and overcrowded with other drunken revellers to eat in. Most of the contents, as anyone who dares to venture out in their local town centre on a Saturday night will know, end up squashed into the chewing-gum-strewn pavement, and the environmentally unfriendly packaging simply dropped willy-nilly! If, by some small miracle, they have any change left over, instead of stumbling home they will opt to share a minicab or two. Thus providing a warm and relatively comfortable environment for the most-pissed *Ladette* to 'throw up' in…! If they haven't enough money for a minicab, can't be arsed to wait for one, or are just too damn drunk to stumble home, they can always phone up one of their longsuffering Partners/Husbands to come and collect them. So what if the kids are left 'home alone' for half an hour or so! If the other halves are stupid enough not to play ball and they still can't be arsed to waddle home on foot, as a last resort they may start a group brawl, smash a shop window, or flash their 'private parts' at all and sundry. Then, if they strike it lucky, they can all be driven home in a warm 'Pig Van' instead...! However, I could be wrong. It is feasible that the 'Poor Cow' is a very good mother! Perhaps she has had a bad day with the kids, or her husband has just lost his job due to the looming recession and this has, quite understandably, triggered another bout of her rather crude form of 'Tourettes'!

Well, that's enough judging for one day *Saint Ian*... No outing with *Julie* tonight and the remainder of my family are all busy, so a 'night in' is on the cards. The *Poles* won't be back from work until much later, so it's still relatively peaceful. Fuck it! Sweaty bollocks! Steaming beef curtains! If you can't beat the *Swearing Yobs,* join them! I'm heading for a stiff 'Gin and Tonic!' I've even submitted myself to tonight's *X Factor* debacle, so I reckon I'll need more than one... Besides, I'll have to be pissed if I'm to be kept up all night by the *Vampish Poles*...

Maybe I could round my cultural evening off with a 'Kebab' or two, then invite the partying *Lithuanians* over to meet the invidiously defiant *Poles*, smash the joint up and instigate a pan-European drunken projectile-vomiting competition...! Reality TV has a lot to answer for!!

Sunday 23rd November

A dusting of snow has greeted me this morning… *Equatorial Isa* will be absolutely delighted as, today, even I need the heating on full blast.

The *Lithuanians* were partying, as per usual for a Saturday night. I do enjoy their folk music, for a few hours at least…! As the evening progressed, the vodka-fuelled shouts of *dobra, way hay, kurwa, woop ya*, increased with equal measures of volume and intensity. The music then ratcheted up a further notch, then another, and another, until the bearable folk music was finally replaced by some awful 'euro rave shit' in combination with a stampede of anarchic drunken dancing…

By one in the morning, when the 'thriller' I was trying to watch had finished, I turned off the television and began, in a worryingly insane way, to indiscriminately pound the wall with the handle of my soft broom whilst shouting 'Go back to Lithuania, you fucking miserable cunts…!' Naturally, they couldn't hear a frigging thing for they were totally high, oblivious, intoxicated, flailing in a trance-like frenzy, or simply aggravating me on purpose, revelling in the fact that they were pissing me off to the max. Far more likely the case! Although I really shouldn't flatter myself by thinking that they would give me the slightest thought, not even a negative one! Quite clearly their track record speaks for itself… After all they are still relatively young, although one of them looks well into his thirties, so all they want to do is follow the herd, get pissed and party all night. They have no time for middle-aged neighbourly considerations. English Yobs, Lithuanian Yobs, they're all the same in the end! WANKERS… Although English Yobs have some concept of basic etiquette, 'please, thank you' etc. And at least you can understand them. And it is their country, supposedly!

I really couldn't be arsed to march round next door in the freezing cold in order to smash their front door down. Besides, I would have only been told to 'Piss off, you mother fucker!' So I tried to adopt the role of a mature adult! I endeavoured to calm myself down using the 'breath control' technique I learnt in singing class, then nervously ventured to the bedroom for an attempt at self-hypnotised sleep… As my 'fucked up' head hit the pillow *Daniel and Equatorial Isa* returned home from the posh burger joint. Great, now they're going to start their long, noisy, post-work wind-down, I morosely concluded, despite trying to pretend I was hearing soft rolling waves gently breaking on a deserted tropical beach! And all because of *Tony Blair and Co's Open-Door Immigration Policy* forcing us to live in ever smaller portions of our unaffordable overpriced houses!

Sleep deprivation, it appears, can eventually work in your favour! As one becomes so tired that the reasons for not being able to sleep cannot, in the end, conquer the body's desire to close down for the night. Consequently, I slept like a log and almost feel normal this morning. Whatever normal is!

Following a long soothing soak in my 'under stairs bath' I have just dried myself, and put on my horizontally striped blue and white boxer shorts and ten-year-old T-shirt from Langkawi Island, Malaysia… I've spent the day tidying up the garden and planting spring bulbs, consequently I have removed a ton of dirt from the under reaches of my rather long finger nails. I now feel as 'fresh as a daisy', sublimely clean. The old adage rings true, cleanliness is definitely next to godliness… Whether you adhere to a monotheistic religion or a nature-based belief system, it makes no difference, the pure and serene feeling of freshly scrubbed skin is the closest and most relaxed the body comes to a state of *nirvana*. Not that I have a clue what *nirvana* actually feels like! But I can only imagine it to be so, for at this very moment in time I feel so completely relaxed that I could willingly give up my self-imposed control in order to break free into a non-materialistic world of kind and fruitful subjugation. Dream on, dude!

Julie called this morning... We had a very entertaining conversation, so I think we are kind of back on some sort of level footing... We still have little niggles that need ironing out so we agreed on a 'rain check' for tonight's trip to the 'flicks'. Anyway, the 'silver screen' is full of crap at the moment...'Time' is the proverbial healer, although with us two it remains to be seen. I suspect things will take their natural course and we shall plod on as a seemingly odd couple: whether that is purely as friends or part-time lovers, only time will tell. We certainly shall not be settling down to start a family any time soon. However much that would please me it ain't likely to happen, considering her age and all. It's just a sad unfortunate fact of life, timing! Needless to say, the fault could lie entirely at my door! For all I know, I could be firing blanks...

Anyhow, I'm off to pour myself a 'Gin and Tonic'. Two nights in a row! If I'm not careful I'm in danger of turning into an alcoholic. I'll need a stiff one to see me through the tension of the 'Strictly Come Dancing Results Show!' That's as exciting as my Sunday evening is likely to get, unless the odious *'Arseholes'* upstairs have a game of psychologically sleep-deprived torture in store for me!

Monday 24th November

'Hello, is Mrs Davison there please?'

'No, I think you have the wrong number!' I replied.

'No, me don't have de wrong number, me have de right number, alright...' The lady's lovely rich West Indian accent gradually faded away before the receiver was loudly replaced.

You could tell she was probably one of those wonderfully buxom, perfectly presented, hat-wearing, old-school ladies who originally came over with the *Windrush* generation in the 1950s. The fact that her phone still makes an old-fashioned clicking noise as the receiver re-engages with the dial-around base is the trigger that throws your mind back to a more orderly, respectable age... I love fantasising about the 'good old days', when communities were far safer, more inclusive, more caring, and the young didn't just pay 'lip service' to their elders but had a healthy fear of them, and any form of authority for that matter. Of course there were the ubiquitous cheeky little blighters who pushed their parents to the margins of tolerance, but when they duly crossed that line parental discipline won the day. Should it be deemed necessary, it was commonplace for the back of an adult hand to leave a sore reminder for *Poor Little Johnny* to mull over for future reference... As I speak I can hear the cries of outrage from the lunatic fringe of the *P.C. Mob* ringing in my ear... Well, sod them, because, generally, it worked. There was far more respect, parents were in charge of their children, unlike today's *'Pol Pot'* generation egged on by the 'Human Rights Fanatics' and people who insist on only ever wearing black clothes and small retro glasses! These boring misguided *clones* believe their own ridiculous propaganda, genuinely thinking they are enriching the pattern of everyday life! The opposite, as the 'even-minded majority' well know, being true. The overbearing zealots deliberately stifle debate in the name of 'discrimination' and successfully crush anyone's individual point of view because they are causing 'offence'! They, along with the *Obstreperous Selfish Lefties* at the BBC and the predominantly *Barmy Judiciary*, will use any part of their 'Legal P.C. Armoury' to quell the rational voice of the common man. Unless it concurs with their mad minded-mantra, whereupon the airwaves will part like 'Moses and the Red Sea' to allow the newly enlightened *puppets* to evangelise the rest of the *Great Unwashed* from their carefully scripted scroll of 'Politically Correct Commandments'.

Well, the telephone call did force me to rise from my 'pit' at least. The time being well past ten-thirty! Yes, I have been a 'dirty lazy lie-in' this morning. If only the reasons were as genuine as the mad sexual dream that passed through my subconscious in the wee small hours! Some 'Metro-Sexual' creature was busy combing what is left of my thinning hair! While it was gently preening me it began to whisper in my ear:

'You are the most beautiful man in the whole universe and I shall attend to your every mortal need, earthly desire and extra-terrestrial fantasy! You need not tell me when I should begin to indulge you, or how, for I already know what satisfies you, as well as the time that you require such feeble human relief!'

I momentarily looked down under my duvet! A raging *hard-on*, mine I believe, was standing proud, totally rigid with a *'one eye'* staring wantonly back at me. A thin green hand grasped my *shaft!* It felt rather chilly, but very smooth. Soon it began to rub me up and down. As it gained momentum the hand changed colour and my penis grew larger and larger with every stroke of my manhood. My legs were quivering with pleasure. My toes started to tingle. My whole body was ready to explode. Then moist translucent lips encompassed my throbbing head. I was lost in a wet, warm tunnel...! Stamp, stamp, stamp, thump, squeak, stamp! 2.30 a.m. End of dream...

The *Vampish Pole* was up and about. I'm sure it was him, as she seems too sluggish to even bother to stay up so late... They returned home around nine last night, so God only knows why he wanted to partake in 'squad-bashing' at such an unearthly hour...! He left at eight-thirty this morning, so he obviously requires nil hours of 'shut eye'. Maybe he is the 'Metro-Sexual' creature entering my psyche! His blond 'stooge' would be preferable, but if it is he who metamorphosed into an obliging *Alien* then who am I to complain! If I had to choose I'd rather he was servicing my nether regions than driving me mad with his nocturnal shenanigans...

Upon last night's second *Polish* awakening I leapt up from under my far-too-hot duvet, screeched a mental diatribe, and flung my fucking clock across the room. Even the old-fashioned-sounding 'tick-tock' of my Chinese retro Victorian carriage clock is starting to annoy me now! I genuinely think I'm going mad. Well, let's just say madder! Without consent I am living their lifestyle. They are gradually taking over my soul. Soon they shall possess me completely! I have never been particularly early to bed, usually around twelve to twelve-thirty, but this insane time-keeping is testing me to the outer limits of reasonable tolerance. I feel an air of inevitability, fate one could say, theirs and mine inextricably linked. The conflation accelerating a reaction, a time in the near future where, to regain my sanity, I'm obliged to slaughter the pair of them. That is if I can, by some small miracle, catch them asleep at the same time!

After the snow, sleet and icy rain of yesterday the sun has decided to grace us with its chilly rays. So before I commit murder I think I shall take the opportunity to plant the rest of my spring bulbs. I'm too late for a swim now, which is rather a shame as the pool is normally deserted on Mondays; not a *Grey Lady* in sight! However, I still need to get off the premises for a while to sort my sleep-deprived head out. So after I've planted my bulbs a spontaneous bike ride might be a good idea! There's nothing like brisk exercise to get the mind racing. Besides, I might just come up with the perfect unsolvable murder!

Wednesday 26th November

Only a calendar month now until we shall all be completely bloated, rolling around like 'Teletubbies', having spent the previous day gorging ourselves silly on rich festive foods, lovingly digested with a cacophony of high-strength alcohol. Once again, come Boxing Day, the nation's lavatories will be in constant use. A strong scent of overindulgence fighting its way out of every nook and cranny of the vast majority of 'lavs' in this green and pleasant land… Unusually, for me, the thought of Christmas hasn't even entered my consciousness! By now I am normally quite advanced with purchasing presents and all the other timely trimmings. However, this year things are different: my one and only obsession right now is the removal of the *Poles* from upstairs. One way or another they will have to be *vaulted…!* My neck, back and shoulders have done what they always do when I am overloaded with stress: constricted into an increasingly tighter ball of wrought iron, making me stoop so low that I look like the *Hunchback of Notre Dame*... Well, enough is enough. The pain is excruciating. I can't take any more. So I have had to be proactive. I have asked *Daniel and Isa* to look for new lodgings.

Monday night followed the interrupted pattern of Sunday. Bang on 2.30 a.m. I was woken up. Expletives once again followed… I could feel that I was just about to lose it, big-time! Although I calmed down just enough to stop myself from unlocking their door and running up the stairs, with all the consequences that would inevitably follow, the law being on their side of course! Anyway, I managed to halt my primeval urge to slaughter *Daniel* and texted him his notice instead. A surprisingly grown up-message, considering the circumstances...

Yesterday morning as he attempted to sneak out unnoticed I caught him in the *green zone*. I asked him if he had received my 'text..!' 'Yes,' he declared... A polite conversation ensued. He just stood there looking blank, uninterested, exuding arrogance. However, he did not deny that he is late to bed, noisy, selfish, and totally inconsiderate! It must be drugs, or drugs and alcohol judging by the amount of empty bottles in the recycling. For a man in his thirties, he is behaving like a spoilt teenager! Anyway, the 'royal we' agreed that he would look for a new dwelling house to accommodate their annoying nocturnal habits. The sooner the better... Two weeks, that's all they've been here. Though it feels like a lifetime, a miserable one at that... They have also managed to break the glass door of the fan oven, so I dread to think what kind of state the rest of the place is in!

I have decided to apply for planning permission to sell off upstairs and extend downstairs to create another bedroom and more living space. Hopefully gaining some peace and quiet! At least I shall then have an area without human activity just a few feet away from my fragile head. I'll have to make sure that the rafters are stuffed with sound insulation and the creaking floorboards screwed down tightly, for if I do rid myself of ownership of upstairs I shall have foregone the power of eviction. Then murder will definitely be the only option available, which is worrying as I know I am quite capable... The loss of rent during the conversion will be a struggle, as will the building and planning costs. Thank God for the *credit card cheques* I have just received from one of those government-owned banks. Does this mean I now have to vote *Labour*, on top of all this bloody stress and misery?! Well, torture techniques are designed to gradually wear you down. Maybe the *Poles* are undercover *Labour Party Operatives!* Not that they have destroyed me yet. When all is said and done, I am *British!* 'I shall fight them on the beaches', even if they were supposed to be our allies! Something they have clearly forgotten...! Mind you, come to think of it, when they first moved in, all that time ago, *Daniel* did mention that he came from a town only a few kilometres from the German border! Maybe he is a *double-crossing German* masquerading as a dour *Pole!!*

Later:

'Yes, I would love to get to some mountains this winter. Do you ski?

'Yes, I have been once.'

'Oh well, you know what fun it is then. Last year was amazing, so much powder. We went to my friend's chalet in Courchevel... Amazing place and the chalet was amazing too.'

The twenty-something Tall Blonde Girl with tied-back hair, small silver earrings, posh squeaky voice and a well-cut black business suit was positively delighted, quite determined to loudly impart this *amazing* information about her and the circles she mixes in. Leaving her dull, uninterested-looking Middle-Aged Male corporate guest no choice but to listen intently, nod at the correct moment and say 'Yes' as and when required. *'Amazing'* what you hear as you wander up *Victoria Street...!* They carried on up towards the Westminster end and I peeled off through *Strutton Ground*, purchased five pairs of socks for £4.50 from an old 'Cockney Market Trader', and I am now sat at cafe XLNT!

'Get off me then... Fuck off... Fuck off you English

CUNT..!' A short, crude diatribe delivered by the *Irish Bag Lady* who is now limping past me and still muttering her displeasure... She's around fifty years old, not your stereotypical rough sleeper, neither dirty nor particularly unkempt but just a little mentally rocky... I feel for the harmless suited *English Cunt* whom she was berating, he looks totally embarrassed, quite shaken actually, poor unassuming soul. He's only a young guy, around thirty-odd, plain-looking but with the most amazing straw-coloured hair. After all, he was merely going about his business, paying his taxes, popping out for lunch to escape the humdrum of some nondescript office. His only crime that he happened to be positioned on the wrong bit of the pavement at an inconvenient moment, in her eyes anyhow. Consequently, I am currently feeling rather ashamed of my smidgen of *Irish* heritage; who said 'The Troubles' were over! Scratch the surface and old wounds reopen. The *English* being, unfortunately if you are *English*, an easy target, favoured scapegoat for the world's ills, both past and present.

'Excuse me *Bruv*... do you 'ave a spare fag mate?'

'I don't smoke. No...' the Middle Class Businessman replied.

The White Cockney Guy, probably in his sixties, then moved on and repeated his request to the next unassuming passer-by... Why do so many white people feel the need to substitute their natural voice with some sort of *Gangster Rap?* And at his age too! He must be rather confused, starting off with the black urban phrase *'Bruv'*, presumably intended as an endearing ice-breaker short for 'brother' or 'blood' or 'homey' and the like, only to finish his sentence with the white-working class classic: MATE... I suppose it all comes down to the muddled 'mockney' identities of the global village! Although, personally, I have not succumbed! I am so firmly rooted in my *Ancient British*, *Pagan*, slightly *Irish*, hopefully *non-Germanic*, *'Englishness'* that I do not deem it necessary to acquire a modern 'Politically Correct Non-Idiomatic Identity...'

Anyway, that's enough on the downside of multiculturalism... I have always been a sucker for nostalgia. The past has a comforting allure, giving one a sense of passage, a belonging. Maybe that is how I, quite unintentionally, ended up at this café in *Greycoat Place*, opposite the *Greencoat Boy* public house and in view of the lovely Georgian building that is *Greycoat Hospital*, which I believe is now a school... Being back in this little patch makes me feel somewhat youthful! I fondly remember the raucous lunch-breaks spent in the *Greencoat Boy* or the little 'Greasy Spoon' that lay a few doors down from the pub, the trips to *Strutton Ground Market*, and the passing through on our way to the green spaces of *St James's Park*... Now it seems like a lifetime ago, but from the tender age of seventeen to twenty-one this was my backyard, the rat run to and from college... My buddy *Caroline* is now living in Melbourne, Australia. *Ali* in Surrey with a husband and two kids, *Martin* in urban Kent, and *me*, well that's a long story. But twenty years soon passes you by...'Innit Bruv!'

Tea time:

Actually, a little after tea time, in the traditional English sense. It is more like 'High Tea', eight minutes past six to be precise. I am on the *King's Road*, sat in one of those newfangled 'French Refectory, Bakery, Light Lunch, Dinner, Breakfast 'fuck up' places'. There is probably one near you!

They seem to be popping up everywhere, something about *Pain* and *Quotient*, that's part of the title! The interior is very pleasant, lots of antique pine tables and chairs, wide wooden floorboards, chalkboard menus and, to my surprise, very pleasant staff. They haven't gone for the now commonplace Eastern Europeans, but opted to stay much closer to home; French, a stunning Italian girl and boy, even an English waitress has passed my table! All with beaming smiles and only too eager to help!

A *Czech* friend of mine told me that in 'Communist Eastern Europe' it was considered rude, bad manners, to serve someone, as people were meant to be on an equal footing! So etiquette at the dining table was for everyone to serve themselves. However, as is always the case, I'm sure 'some people are more equal than others'! Anyway, maybe that explains why, when I went to the Italian restaurant with *Julie*, the sour-faced *Polish Girl* just dumped our bottle of wine on the table, without a 'by-your-leave'. On the other hand, she firmly informed us that she didn't receive any share of the 'house service charge' and that we were free to leave her a little extra, should we so desire! We politely declined and both agreed on the reason why she probably didn't receive a portion of the 'house service charge!' There wasn't a modicum of warmth in her entire body; she certainly had no personal touch, just a characterless cold demeanour and the ability to process people efficiently, like 'lambs to the slaughter'... The only 'personal service' she unwittingly delivered was when she leaned over to place my *pollo con funghi di bosco* in front of me! Her mammoth breasts obligingly brushing my shoulder blade, then my right-hand cheek, as they followed the trajectory of my less than gastronomic pile of cream-laden food. Having released control of the very hot plate, her smelly service cloth met with the corner of my mouth and, once more, her huge nipple brushed my cheek as she retracted herself upright to fetch our *pommes sautés*… If I was daring enough, during that moment I could have 'rogered' her over the table: her face resting on my creamy chicken dinner, *Julie* looking on aghast as I pumped her until she became so wildly wet that she ate up my meal like a primeval cave woman desperate to be seeded by an alpha male's sperm so she could dominate the oestrogen-fuelled competition, becoming *Queen Bee* in an instant, with all the juxtaposed privileges of a restaurant manager controlling her flock!! Though still not worthy of extra tips…! I have digressed again, but the rarity of good service is a joy to savour and highlights the cultural differences between *East* and *West* in the *'New Europe'*.

For the second time this week I have just watched a film in the lovely retro cinema on the *Fulham Road*; *Changeling* this afternoon, *Easy Virtue* last Monday night. They are both set in the 'Roaring Twenties', one in America, the other in the Home Counties of England, and I can't recommend them highly enough… *Changeling* is completely harrowing, with a fantastic performance by *Angelina Jolie*. *Easy Virtue* is brought to life by the consummate professional that is *Kristin Scott Thomas*, who, along with *Colin Firth* among others, is just brilliant in this light-hearted, hilarious insight into the complex relationships of a struggling aristocratic family between the two world wars… On route to the film I also managed to purchase two 'Christmas Presents', beautifully gift wrapped 'Smellies' for Mum and Dad. You know, those expensive liquid soaps Upper-Middle-Class People always have in their downstairs loos. Not that my parents are particularly Upper Middle Class. Granted, we all have

Public School overtones, but we 'aint posh, or particularly rich either, certainly not with all the squandering that's going on in the family firm right now anyhow. However, family politics aside, I think we are posh enough to have a superior-quality air freshener in the family loo! So, in an act of altruism, before leaving the upmarket perfumery I frivolously splashed out an extra £14 on an incredibly small, but immensely stylish, bottle of 'Room Spray' to mask those invariably smelly *Christmas Poos…!*

I have missed 'The Actor's Voice Class' again! I'll have to practise the technique of assuming a trance-like state tomorrow morning, while I warm up for my 'Singing Class'. I'm not copping out of that, I'm definitely going, sleep deprivation or not! Which reminds me, I need to photocopy 'Summertime'. Please God, let it be in the right key. I'm in no mood for another public humiliation!

That is the wrong attitude, *Ian!* You will be a triumph, after all success was built in 'cans', not 'cants'. So sock it to them, especially the *Craggy Auburn-Haired Cow* in the front row, if she's there! Mind you, she, along with the *bitch* of a teacher, is bound to be there! They're unlikely to pass up the chance to sneer and superiorly mock all around them… Besides, where else would she be? It's not as if she has a real stage to sing on!

I've just realised its *Le Pain Quotidien…* Daily bread…! Quite clever of *dem Frenchies!*

Friday 28th November

£1... Predictably, this was handed to me, once again, by an old-school *Working-Class Gentleman*. He wasn't hiding his real personality, frailties, delusions, being plastic or superficial. He was a straightforward, decent 'salt of the earth' type of guy! Mind you, for all I know, as he closed his front door and I made my way back to my three-and-a-half-tonne delivery vehicle, equipped with 'on-board chiller', he could have quite possibly landed a 'backhander' on his longsuffering wife's face, or vice versa...!

We all tend to assume so much from first impressions, duly conforming to old-fashioned stereotypes. However open-minded and non-judgemental we may try to be our subconscious invariably leads us to the same predetermined conclusion in the end. Hence we are quite often wrong in our analysis of human character in relation to upbringing... I had never set eyes on this gentleman in my life. But when I registered him as a proper aspirational *cockney*, and he then tipped me for my impeccable service, I instantly warmed to him like 'stewed eels' to 'pie and mash'. Revealing my own psychological flaws I was 'judging a book by its cover!' I could have been right, the man may have been as warm in character as his demeanour pervaded, or extraordinarily cruel to his kith and kin, as those who are kind to strangers can sometimes be. Either way, it shall remain a mystery, unless I recognise his face on this evening's local news bulletin: *Cockney on-line shopper suffocates longsuffering wife with orange plastic bag!*

The home should be a sanctuary, a place where you and those around you can freely express themselves within the protection of your particular group. Sadly, usually unbeknown to friends or extended relatives, it can often be a place of fear, subjugation, repression, and in the worst case, violence… I wonder if there is any correlation between social class and violence!? Rather a taboo subject in this P.C.-mad world and probably not one worth looking into, as I'm sure just as many pompous solicitors beat their partners, as wives beat their drunken tradesmen husbands.

However, when it comes to *tipping* there is not so much a divide, more like a chasm the size of the Grand Canyon, the 'Middle Classes' as tight as arses in comparison to those further down the social scale. Money doesn't come into the equation either, as a 'Working-Class Lad' 'done-good' is still far more likely to tip than a 'Middle-Class Bore' of equal wealth... That's one thing this God-awful job has taught me... Although, on the whole, our 'Middle-Class Clients' are very polite. Lots of fake smiles, wishy-washy 'hellooos', but my absolute favourite has to be the overly breathy and insincere-sounding 'Thank you so much…!' To them this is quite enough in the way of praise! After all they have paid for your service, or purposely ordered over £100 worth of the bulkiest, heaviest items possible in order to qualify for *free delivery*... After you have repeatedly traipsed backwards and forwards to their suburban home, re-stiffened your neck and shoulders, been ordered to bring it through to the kitchen while a capable middle-aged husband looks on, the final insult is about to be delivered! An obligatory insincere *smile* now stretching to near bursting point, like the 'Joker' from a 'Batman' movie, the punchline quickly follows! By now they are almost hyperventilating with excitement, absolutely delighted, practically climaxing before you as they place a huge bundle of 'orange plastic bags' into your hand! 'You do recycle bags, don't you? We try to do our bit..!' She, or he, for they are more often than not a dull fading carbon copy of one another, clearly expecting you to be overwhelmed with admiration by their environmental credentials! Ready to *climax* with them, flow down a sea of organic, sustainable discharge on route to a green nirvana where BMW ESTATES run on chicken poo!! The fact that I have just carried crate upon crate of plastic wrapped water to their door, which has been removed from its natural environment only to be transported hundreds of miles to a supermarket, doesn't seem to have registered. Somehow they are too stupid to appreciate the irony of their situation! Besides, they haven't time to drink dreaded tap water as they are far too committed to saving the planet by returning their *orange plastic bags!* Unfortunately, these rather naïve environmentally aware consumers are quite unaware that their beloved bags, that have barely been used, are heading to some obscure, dangerously polluted town in a far-flung corner of China, literally, *'on a slow boat!'*

On returning to the store last night I managed to drop a skyscraper-high stack of blue crates on my unprotected foot. The pain was excruciating. Lovely *Ellen*, our warm and cuddly 'Night Time Supervisor', came to the rescue, marching me straight up to the 'H.R. Office' to demand that I have my safety shoes there and then. Unsurprisingly, there wasn't a 'sole' (!) about at that time of night. The fat cow who runs 'H.R.' was long gone and her persecuted army of 'pen-pushers' were also off barracks. That totals nine weeks now without 'steel-capped safety shoes', only one pair of trousers and a single company polo shirt! Still, unbeknown to the bullying *Fat Cow*, I am now in possession of a 'baseball cap'! One of the other drivers somehow managing to smuggle one out of the stockroom for me... I can't wait until the misery-spreading, overweight *'Old Suburban Heifer'* sees me fashioning it around the canteen! If she tries to confiscate it, as she said she would, she will only succeed in starting a riot amongst the drivers... Should it all kick off we already have a battle plan! We intend to abduct her as she leaves the store one evening, cram her into a shopping trolley and push the heavy, wide and unstable load down a decline on the A24!

Prior to *Supermarket Heaven* I attended my singing class at the P.C. College... As I entered the 'Politically Correct Cauldron of Mediocrity' I felt confident, pumped-up, in conquering mood, good to go, for I had spent ages warming up my voice at home.

'Summertime' was an unmitigated disaster! My singing was in tune, but hearing the piano accompaniment for the first time completely threw me. Consequently my timing was 'off' and the whole performance descended into chaos, an embarrassing farce... The delectable, overdressed *Lynn* was unable to conceal her unadulterated delight in my precarious predicament: her face illuminated by a broad smug smile, so insanely intense that it managed to produce hairline cracks on the thick layer of *war paint* generously plastered over her drooping facial skin. No time to ponder, her fashionable boots clonking loudly on the wooden floor, she paced across the room, stopping within an inch of my aura. Without further ado the overly glamorous bitchy *'Drag Queen'* began in earnest:

'A rather strange choice of song...! This class is not a place for you to practise. You need to come here having worked and prepared the piece... The class is supposed to be more advanced than this! You missed cues...! Are you counting in the notes? Are you even aware of the piano? Or just hoping it falls into place?'

Following yet another public humiliation courtesy of this sadistic lady, she allowed me to sing on in small phrases, which she then interrupted every few seconds in order to dish out more advice/criticism! Fortunately, the whole debacle soon came to a crashing halt. As intended, she had subverted my confidence, so I was more than happy to return to my seat and make way for her next timeless victim. However, her assassination of my character had only just begun! I had to be taught a lesson, once and for all, my face was to be well and truly dismembered, consigned to trash with a *stiletto-style purge*... So, in an act of sadistic absolutism she called up one of her *sycophantic groupies*. Naturally, instead of further public humiliation mutual adoration ensued. The bipartisan pianist was in on the subterfuge, suddenly far more tolerant of the slightest vocal malapropism, the huge woman in question effortlessly sailing through *Lynn's* dumbed-down assault course, licking as much *'arse'* as she could possibly bear along the way! The whole thing stank! It was a set-up, to make my hatchet job look even worse... The Fat Blonde Woman, who on the surface seems all right, although devoid of personality, has only ever sung one song: 'Oh What a Beautiful Morning' from *Oklahoma*, which she is still singing from the score! Basically, as long as you are prepared to kowtow to *Lynn* and her ridiculous ego you can be as repetitive, unprepared, and boring as you like... Not that I could ever lower myself to the status of *'Twinkle Toes'*! Anyway, what's the point? Call me old-fashioned, but surely the whole reason for being there is to improve, progress! Though she is running a *Stalinist* project, so I shouldn't be so unreasonable, deluded...!

Later on I sang the 'Sondheim' number which she

makes us all sing on a weekly basis. This performance was quite successful, at least in comparison to my earlier car crash. I was even applauded, although, unsurprisingly, not by the 'Craggy Old Witch' who always sits in the front row. The sad 'Old Sow' gets off on messing with your head, deliberately staring at you in a very disapproving way as you try your utmost to ignore the 'Bitter Old Trout' and carry on regardless… Being a gentleman I have not, until now, lowered myself to her level of pettiness! But, when the 'Auburn-Haired Craggy Cow', who is without fail smothered in red and gold from the top of her 'turkey neck' right down to her 'plates of meat', rose up to take centre stage and show us how uninspiring, consistently dull and note-perfect she is, was the moment I decided to take my 'gloves off'. The time had come! My tolerance was all spent. Unbeknown to her she was about to taste a little of her own bitter medicine, served icily cold of course!

When the delusional bitch began her measured performance my pharmacy opened for business…. I stared at her, intently… As her 'floor show' continued my stare transformed into a glare…. At first it was blank and disinterested. I was looking straight through her. Though my nonchalance soon turned more sinister! My jaw pushed forward, my face tightened, my eyes met her gaze, my brow rose and I looked right into her callous soul. Cruel thoughts racing around my mind as I surrounded her vision with a look of despicable hate… *'Cunt'!* That's all I was thinking….. Although the *'Old Sow'* could not hear my inner thoughts, my outer demeanour unnerved her considerably! She looked surprised, uneasy, her boringly tuneful voice frequently wobbling… It's true, *revenge*, as I discovered, is definitely *'a dish best served cold'*.

I can't say I am particularly proud of mimicking her unpleasantness. But *bullies* have to be challenged! I learnt that at school. Once you stand up to them they, usually, sit straight back down. Sometimes, the only way they will take any notice and understand that you are not prepared to be a 'whipping boy' for their psychological insecurities any more is to engage them with their own antics... In the end they nearly always respond to their own mindless behaviour. Though I still haven't cracked the pitiful obdurate that is *Lynn*.

Lynn has already banned me from singing 'Old Man River'! When I sang it a few weeks ago she was positively squirming in her 'upmarket lingerie'. When the opportunity arose she stopped me in what she thought was a masterstroke of subtle 'politically correct' intervention:

'You're far too young to sing this song, Ian...'

'Why?' I replied in a teasingly theatrical tone, knowing full well what her real reasons were.

On she went, predictably:

'It is okay for a Black Man to sing it. But if you want to, you must sing it in plain English. No "de's"or "dat's".'

'But that changes the whole piece, the essence of the song…!' I quite frostily stated, shaking my head slowly and deliberately for all the class to see.

Nevertheless, I continued singing as to her dictum while she tried to provoke and unnerve me by standing very close. One of her favourite wind-ups...! When she decided it was time to interrupt me yet again my defiant streak was having none of it! I ignored her, deliberately. Simply carrying on regardless with bucketloads of gusto, plunging myself into the psyche of a downtrodden *slave* in the deep south of *pre-Lincoln America*, the Englishness of my accent reverting back in sympathy, my intonation lovingly embellishing the idiomatic patois of the period... Naturally, since that day my card has been indelibly marked by the bullying well-dressed sadist that is *Lynn*... I can't get my head around all that P.C. crap, not being allowed to play an historical black or mixed-race character if you are white, when the other way round it is, rather puzzlingly, quite acceptable, positively encouraged by the *'P.C. Fuckers'*! They are the true bigots! They just create trouble, where it doesn't, on the whole, exist, through their misguided moralising and sneering 'holier than thou' attitude towards us plebeians.

There are two Black Ladies at work, a Black Guy and quite a few Indians. None of them have issues with me or vice versa. In fact, the Black Lady of West Indian Ancestry and I have a great rapport. However, ironically, the other Black Lady, of African origin, and *Leona* cannot stand one another. There is also a Mixed-Race Driver who is somewhat scary and unpredictable who also hates *Leona*, referring to her as the *'Nigger!'* Apparently he hates her with a passion, addressing her by the 'N' word as a matter of course... He mentored me on my first day of driving. When we returned to the yard *Leona* was loading her van. As we parked up he turned to me and vehemently declared ***'There she is! The NIGGER'***... Obviously, I was extremely shocked. But he, perhaps because he has 'Black' blood himself, talks about her in this vein with total ease, much to the mutual embarrassment of all the other drivers. So, all the underlying prejudices at *Supermarket Heaven* are clearly, contrary to the *Do-Gooders* dogmatic assertions, coming from within the ethnic community of online shopping, with absolutely no compliance from the unfairly maligned indigenous *white* population!!

I was once married to a woman with *brown* skin, millions of Afro-Americans are 'Mixed-Race', and for all I know I may have some 'Black' ancestry myself! Maybe that's the reason I am so drawn to 'Spirituals' and old 'Soul Music..!' *Lynn* really should be more careful before she enforces the 'Stalinist Doctrine' of the 'Lunatic Oligarchs' at that insanely mad 'PC College'! How can she profess to really know people's ethnic make-up and their entitlement to sing songs that originate from the 'deep south' of former 'Slave-Ridden America?' Added to which she has proved herself somewhat inconsistent as she allowed my 'Chinese Friend', who is well into his eighties, to sing 'Old Man River' without question!? Even she couldn't work out how to enforce that one...! After all she had told me that only a 'Black Man' could sing it in its original form! However, my *Chinese Friend* was clearly intoning in a deep southern accent pertaining to the period, his rendition littered with 'de's' and 'dat's'! I could kick myself now for failing to mention this fact when she ticked me off the other week... I should have also asked her if under unforgiving house rules a 'Black Man' should be allowed to sing 'Summertime'?! For the original is sung by a woman! That's where the peddlers of *Political Correctness* fall foul of the very liberties they claim to promote! They consciously set themselves up as 'judge and jury', selecting people on the basis of colour, gender, or the latest in vogue mantra, then deny anyone else freedom of expression according to social history! How liberating and forward-thinking is that! If I pass a DNA test which discovers a modicum of a 'Black' gene, will I then be entitled to sing 'Old Man River'?! Or, at the very least, the relevant percentage of the song!

There was, in the not too distant past, an *Austrian chap* who used *race* as a yardstick to decide who was more eligible to be part of his warped sense of perfect society, and look where that got us. And from a man with Jewish blood too...! I'm not suggesting *Lynn* is on a par with *Hitler*, but by wielding their disproportionate power to curtail our age-old freedom of speech and self-expression these *Do-Gooders* have managed to create a sea swell of public animosity towards any form of authority. When the *revolution* comes, the likes of *Lynn* and her band of naïve idealists will be the first for the guillotine! Ironically, although they are too stupid to see it, they have turned themselves into the modern-day, power-crazed, out-of-touch *Elitist Bourgeoisie* that they purport to detest, and we now want to rid ourselves of with a French-style chop.

I'm sure the *Queen of England* wouldn't object to me singing 'Old Man River'! So there may be something to be said for '*The divine right of kings*' after all...

Sunday 30th November

7.58 am:

Insomnia has well and truly taken a stranglehold now... *Julie* is still asleep. She came over around nine last night.

It was a long, hard grind at work yesterday. Two large *Gin and Tonics* certainly lightened my spirits, pardon the pun; helping immeasurably with the post-servitude winding-down process. It has been nearly two weeks since our last meeting, we were chatting so incessantly, that the time whizzed by; consequently we never made it to the 'Chinese Buffet' at the Karaoke Restaurant, or the 'Shindig' afterwards at the Irish Pub in Morden High Street. So, I quickly made us some *Cheese and Finest Sausage Pasta* instead, which admittedly sounds like a rather peculiar combination, but believe it or not is extremely tasty.

Julie has the appetite of a mouse and only managed to polish off her usual starter-sized portion, leaving me to gorge on the rest, which I demolished without hesitation. Consequently, I feel totally bloated, full to bursting point with fat, protein and carbohydrates. My stomach has expanded to the size of an overindulged Pot-Belly Pig's, my *six-pack* sunk without a trace!

Julie's son is becoming more and more adventurous with regard to his eating habits: not only is he into carrots and roast potatoes, he will now eat chicken and sausages! Only organic ones though, which is to be commended... Despite the cripplingly high cost of non-Frankenstein food to us lowly-paid mortals, she's delighted, triumphant even, that her son is finally deviating from the path of his father's 'food phobias' towards the realms of healthy normality with regards to day-to-day sustenance. Although she's hoping he doesn't gain a taste for organic seafood and caviar just yet!

After she had finished recounting her current trials and tribulations, I naturally shared mine, colourfully filling her in on the ongoing saga of *Daniel and Isa...* The front door opened at 1a.m., shortly after which we turned in for the night. I lay there waiting for it to kick off, with *Daniel and Isa* I mean! There was an initial disturbance from above, which thankfully soon petered out. Maybe they were too pissed and needed sleep, I thought, and nervously hoped to myself: even *Vampires* need an occasional night off! Then at around 2.30 a.m. my hopes were confounded when we were awoken by a heavy artillery attack of antisocial noise which lasted for some ten to fifteen minutes. *Julie* calmed me down like some oversensitive child, gently stroking my shoulder and middle back. As 'sod's law' decrees the rest of the night passed without a murmur. The *Lithuanians* were not partying this weekend either! Not that I am complaining, but it does lull you into a rather false sense of security and make you appear to be an oversensitive, paranoid 'Scrooge' with nothing better to worry about in life! Or maybe I'm right: *Julie* could be in cahoots with them all!! After all, she is still narked, ever so slightly seething with me under her disguised outer shell of pleasantness. Maybe it's pay-back time! *Julie* a double-crossing mole in a 'Cold War'-style plot to avenge all our previous arguments!?

The 'Sleeper Cell' might be waking up soon so I had best act normal, not at all suspicious, nervous or paranoid... I'm looking forward to today. We're off to town to have a wander down the *King's Road*, and take in the *Saatchi Gallery*. It's great to have a cultural partner to venture out with. As for the more romantic side of our peculiar coupling, I couldn't possibly say where that's heading as I haven't a clue, and I don't honestly think *Julie* does either.

I've just heard her turn over again. She's becoming restless. I'll make some coffee to pacify her with when she gets up... Sharing a house with strangers can really fuck your head up, roll on *Daniel and Isa's* leaving date...

Wednesday 3rd December

A *Walking Zombie*, well a *Sitting Zombie* in fact! On the underground, heading for my 'Voice Class'.

The wonders of the 'E.C.' that is purportedly so beneficial to the 'working poor' of this once great nation has just passed by in the form of a perfectly tidy and extremely well-dressed *Romanian Gypsy!* Her baby covered from top to toe in brand new designer clothes. Nevertheless, she still deemed it necessary to commence her farcical, duplicitous begging ritual! The young *Englishman* sitting next to me gallantly, but naïvely, jumped up like *Zebedee* from *The Magic Roundabout* to offer up his seat to this supposedly child-laden figure! She also had one in the oven, although it looked more like a strapped-on cushion! Unsure and somewhat bemused by this 'old-school' gesture she raised her capped right hand to within a whisker of his nose and began to sorrowfully shake the few coins therein at him. The poor chap was extremely uncomfortable. She had invaded his personal space and looked as if she was about to embark on some sort of desperate wailing ritual. At this moment I just couldn't help myself and off went my 'Un-P.C. Mouth':

'She doesn't want your seat... She wants your money.'

The fresh-faced young lad smiled wryly, then rapidly sat back down. No one else uttered a word. They simply bowed their heads, too scared to agree or disagree, in the P.C.-ravished madness that is twenty-first-century Britain. Thankfully, her shameful charade did not work! Not in this carriage at least. We silently closed ranks! Nobody was sucked in by her pathetic excuse for a con trick... After all, along with her suffering child, she was far more expensively dressed than most of us tired and downtrodden workers put together.

Maybe she'll fare better in the next carriage?! Or, if her transparent subterfuge keeps faltering, which is highly likely as there aren't enough unsuspecting tourists at this time of the year to fill her deceitful coffers, she'll have to bugger off home! By 'HOME' I mean the house that our 'Barmy Government', I would wager money on that being fact, have freely provided for her and her contented tribe. All at the expense of the *Great British Taxpayer*: you, me, and all the other law-abiding mugs...

She probably claimed asylum due to the 'persecution' of the 'Roma' in her homeland; despite Romania having been admitted, by the hypocritical 'Bourgeois of Brussels', to the 'altar of sovereign sacrifice and fanatical human rights' that is the 'E.C.'. Logic would suggest that she couldn't be eligible for asylum, for she comes from a country that had to pass 'human rights' tests before being allowed into the ultimate 'Bullies Club'! Still, we are undeniably the most stupid, compliant country in this rancid gabble of nonsense. We know exactly what type of reception she would have received from our 'French or German Allies', and so does she! Or anyone else for that matter:

'*Nil Point...*'

Temple Place:

I have a friend... A *pigeon* is perched on one end, and I on the other, of my favourite iron-framed, wooden-slatted park bench. Curiosity has got the better of him and he is now moving tentatively closer. Realising the cupboard is bare he's thought better of it and hopped off onto the floor to join the rest of the gang who are frantically pecking away at the last few visible crumbs… I can't stop thinking about the cheek of the well-heeled woman on the tube… Now they've all fluttered away, seeing that there is nothing left. Between them they have managed to reduce my sandwich to half a round.

We *Ancient Britons* are just too damn soft and kind-hearted for our own good! We protest about the state of our borderless nation, but as we are neither cold nor ruthless we begrudgingly accept the rapid change going on all around us, even though we never voted for it! Then, when we are served by a pleasant-mannered African Woman, as I was when purchasing my snack lunch, we are instantly thrown into turmoil, consumed with uncontrollable guilt for wanting our 'Spineless Government' to curtail their endless 'open-door immigration policy' in the first place… At the end of the day, as we all know, it's simply a question of numbers on our already overcrowded island. That's what terrifies the average man in the street. Some diversity is to be celebrated, enriching our lives, but we strongly need a sense of proportionality within this madness…

Our tolerance will surely be our ultimate downfall! Most indigenous people I speak to, at least in *London*, just want to emigrate. They have had their fill of 'Political Correctness' and are sick to the back teeth of being continually ignored by successive ARSEHOLE GOVERNMENTS. If we dare to, quite logically, suggest that in order to have good 'race relations' the *indigenous peoples* must remain in the majority and the thousands of years of our social, religious and tribal history have to be protected as it has been fought for with the blood of our brave forebears, we are derided as, you guessed it, RACISTS!

Many people from ethnic minority backgrounds,

especially the 'Queen's Subjects' from former British Colonies whose ancestors have also fought and died for this country, often concur and espouse a similar point of view. Feeling just as *British* as the *Indigenous Tribes*, they too want to protect our uniquely civilised way of life. So when will these idiots understand that by nature we are not *European*. The land bridge across the *North Sea* disappeared at the end of the last 'Ice Age', and we have developed our own unique culture and wit that is far more akin to our Commonwealth Friends' than the dull, dour, humourless hordes on the European Mainland. Save for some life-loving *Italians*, and fellow island dwellers, like the *Greeks* and the charmers of the *Emerald Isle...* 'To be sure!'

I am, self-evidently, a bear with a very sore head..! I was right not to celebrate the brief interlude in the nocturnal shenanigans of the 'Polish Double Act!' Around 4 a.m., after texting *Daniel*, telling him to 'shut the fuck up', the marathon being paced out in the kitchen above finally ceased, and with it the unbearable sound of creaking floorboards thankfully dissolved altogether.

It has been nine days since I politely asked them to find new accommodation. *Daniel* said he would get back to me the next day. In fact it took him a further week! Then, as is the modern cowardly way, he merely texted me, asking if they could stay put as the creaking floorboards were not their fault and they were endeavouring to be quieter. He hoped that I had noticed this fact and even offered to have a thick carpet fitted to help reduce the noise. Seeing how their combined salary is well over 40k this would be a drop in the ocean to them, rather dispelling the widely peddled myth that 'Immigrants' from Eastern Europe are filling unattractive low-paid jobs! There certainly isn't a queue of them seeking a job like mine. Mind you, who can blame them; a near-death experience for £7.29 an hour is hardly an attractive proposition... Consequently, ever since his text I have been grappling with my conscience. As a fair-minded *Ancient Briton*, an HSP, and a person susceptible to bouts of paranoia, I was thrown into mind-numbing analytical guilt:

'Am I a complete Ogre? A Dickensian landlord throwing his tenants out onto the street to be picked over by charlatans, hunted down by a pack of hungry urban foxes?'

My sympathy swung towards anger and resentment, then back again to an over-emotional sympathetic guilt. For the last week my head has been like a rumbling volcano, modulating the scales between two psychological extremes, bubbling with uncertainty, full of deep analysis and an uneasy justification of the situation. Oh to have a thick, uncaring skin..! *Daniel* obviously has one! Two, three, four, five in the morning, it's immaterial. If he wants to be up and about, he will. Thicker carpet or not, he still won't go to bed at a reasonable hour. I could cope up to one or even two in the morning, but this is quite clearly never going to be late enough for an insatiably hungry bloodsucker like him! So before going out today I left them a carefully coded note using all the sarcastic *double entendres* I could muster from within the confines of my slightly dyslexic mind. To them it would have come across as plain in-your-face English, something they seem to be familiar with; however, to fellow deep-thinking *Ancient Britons* the nuanced, layered convolutions would be easily deciphered, instantaneously understood. In essence, it was a final, politely 'British', request for them to 'fuck off' out of my house once and for all... Maybe the penny will finally drop and I can have one full night's sleep before Christmas! It's up to them now! My only other recourse, as I have previously hinted, being extreme violence. A rather unpleasant and bloody last resort...

It's so cold now that my *bollocks* are starting to freeze onto my inner thigh, so I'm going to vacate my favoured seat for warmer climes. But not before I snap a picture on my mobile phone! As I speak the sky above the *Houses of Parliament* is slowly transforming into the most stunning shade of honey yellow, akin to the mellowest stone of the prettiest cottage in a sleepy Cotswold Village... Right, I've taken the photo. A good one to hang on the wall in my Southern Italian Villa! I can gaze at it every time I become homesick, and feel the need to reminisce about old *Blighty*. How often that will be remains to be seen!

There are only three of us left here now, all 'White Males'. I think one of the others might be a 'Homeless Man'. He is unkempt, wrapped in a huge beige raincoat, head covered in newspaper, lying flat out on one of the other park benches. They may well think I am, myself, a 'wanderer', for this was the spot where that 'Black Guy' asked me if I was a 'Tramp'. Although I am far less dishevelled today, wearing my faithful old camel coat rather than my grimy mackintosh. So maybe I shall be overlooked as a 'Vagrant' on this occasion!

I hope the 'Guy' on the bench isn't spending the night out here. He'll freeze to bloody death. Why can't we help these people properly? I thought 'charity' was supposed to begin 'at home'! Unfortunately, that is something that has long been forgotten by successive generations of our treacherous foreigner-obsessed rulers! WANKERS... *Blair...* *Brown...* They should all be tried for treason, crimes against *Ancient Britons*, etc...

J.D.Wetherspoons:

As I passed the *London School of Economics* my auditory senses were treated to the colourful Italian tones of two young lads in their twenties. Immediately after which a football team of Oriental smiles shone out of the 'Sushi Bar' nearby. Now back in the 'Holborn branch of J.D.'s' I am sat on a comfortable high-chair, resting my cold, sleep-deprived body, slouching over the Victorian-style talltable, sipping my welcoming 'rum and Coke' whilst listening to the garrulous hum all about me.

There are quite a few tables of Japanese students who seem to be quietly enjoying themselves, visibly relishing the freedom of being unchaperoned in the far-flung city of London. They appear a little tipsy, as they are giggling in that rather shy and understated Asian way! The girls shrouding their mouths with the palm of their hand every time the atmosphere turns a little raucous, whereupon they giggle more quickly, their bodies then start to shake ever so slightly as they unsuccessfully try to stave off any feeling of embarrassment... Even if they do become totally intoxicated, I'd wager money that they don't end up in an unsightly state of *Northern European public vulgarity...*

Studying their social interaction has made me reflect on my past, yet again! It's high time I left the dark and depressing continent of Europe for the allure of the Orient. It is over seven years now since I was there. Then I was still married, visiting my 'in-laws' in Malaysia... I do feel a trip coming on! It must be a sign from above! I think the 'seven-year itch' is starting to manifest itself in my irritability of late. So maybe it's not all *Daniel and Isa's* fault after all, nor my increasingly boring and uncommunicative relationship with *Julie*.

I need a break, with sleep! The Philippines has always interested me and come hell or high water I've set my mind on it... I'm going... I think about it every day, the famed Chocolate Hills, rice terraces, white sandy beaches. Yes, please... However, I shall certainly not be eating any *canines..!* I mentioned it to *Julie* the other day. But every time we have tried to organise a holiday a spanner has always been thrown in the works! Back in the summer we thought we would be spontaneous, romantic even, so we tried to head off for a week's adventure in Italy. We had it all planned: fine wines accompanied by classical food, eaten *al fresco* on a warm Mediterranean evening in some medieval 'piazza' overlooking two-thousand-year-old ruins. Dreamy perfection! When we checked flight availability we realised it was going to cost a small fortune at that time of year. Added to which the only times that were left fell slap bang in the middle of her son's birthday. So that put paid to that. Other people's kids can be a right pain up the arse...

Sunday was a prime example of our luck lately! The day was freezing: grey, cold and drizzly. The *Saatchi Gallery* full of crap. The only inspiring artwork the beautiful period building, the minimalist whitewashed walls, the 'piece de resistance' being the polished hardwood flooring.

Julie's son was ill in bed... Poor chap, he's only fifteen... His *Food-Phobic Father* preoccupied at work. Consequently, *Julie* was feeling guilty for leaving him on his own, so her mother had agreed to pop in and see how he was doing. I think her son likes to lay it on thick, playing one off against the other: *Mother, Food-Phobic Father* and *Grandmother*. Despite having a 'Private Nurse' in the guise of his *Grandmother*, for what later transpired to be a bit of a cough, the phone calls were endless! *Julie* to *Son*, *Mother/Grandmother* to *Julie*, *Julie* to *Mother/Grandmother*, *Son* to *Julie*, *Julie* to *Food-Phobic Father*, *Julie* to *Mother/Grandmother* at 'death bed' of *Son*, *Food-Phobic Father* to *Julie*... You get my drift! The whole awful day revolved around her bloody son. Anyone would have thought he was dying of CONSUMPTION...

I like *Julie* and I think she is quite fond of me too! Dating women with children seems to be a serial pattern in my life! It never works. You are always in a precarious position. You have no 'chips' to play with, no bargaining power at all. It's just you, childless, without dependents... Therefore, you are the one who ends up bending in favour of the other. Invariably fitting in with their life, playing second fiddle, whether you like it or not. And I have come to the conclusion that I DO NOT...

Why the 'fuck' did I end up with this desperate, pre-menopausal, childless life? The majority of my contemporaries have been blessed with at least one child. I have been, I believe, far more giving and conscientious than the whole damn lot of them combined. And this is how I am rewarded!! None of them, so far as I know, are *Pagan*, they don't necessarily believe in *God* either. They haven't been *sanctified* for endless good deeds to fellow humanity, nor given up their homes to needy 'Immigrants'! They don't cycle everywhere, they are not vegetarian, teetotal, self-sufficient, psychic healers, nor, by any stretch of the imagination, are they modern-day 'paragons of virtue'. I'm no more fallible or mortally flawed than the next person, although at the best of times, I do feel somewhat Extraterrestrial..! It's quite true, 'good guys never come first', 'always come last', 'second', however goes the back-handed complement..! I'm sick of metaphors that seek to soften the blow of unfairness... I know someone halfway around the world is starving or dying of thirst as I speak. We are bloody lucky in the great scheme of things. But why do those that suffer continue to suffer more while some overweight arsehole of a 'Merchant Banker' or 'Benefit Scrounger' is blessed with babies galore???

I'm in dire need of some *Divine Intervention*. Come on *God*, show yourself. Everyone seems to be converting to *Islam*, so you had better hurry up before your flock dissipates entirely! I need reasons, definitive answers, justifications, before I quite possibly go completely barnstorming mad... While I wait, very impatiently, I shall try and keep myself calm by dreaming of what may happen on my holiday in The Philippines. Perhaps it will be the making of me?! God may be testing my patience?! Maybe my destiny is to meet the love of my life there, convert to *Catholicism*, settle down near Manila and produce endless children! Not that they need any more 'little ones' on that overcrowded Archipelago... On that upbeat note I must dash, my 'Voice Class' awaits. Besides, I need a few hours of fun before the inevitable late-night debacle kicks off like clockwork... *Daniel* must be watching 'porn' on the internet! Why else would he stay up half the night! He probably waits for *Isa* to go to bed and then gets down to it. Maybe she doesn't like too much sex precisely because he is an uncontrollable *porn addict..!?* Rather than getting all uptight about never being able to sleep during the hours of darkness, maybe I should just go and join him. Besides, *Julie* and *I* are not up to much in the bedroom department at the moment. *Daniel* and *I* could become a couple of mutual late-night WANKERS...!

Thursday 4ᵗʰ December

I have just been ejected from the telephone by some 'spotty-nosed intern' from one of those 'banks' that we all now own! I find it incredible how busy all these people seem to be! Their only mission is to get rid of you, and as soon as possible. All I wanted to do was check my balance. Alas for them, mere mortal customers seem to be an inconvenient intrusion, to be avoided at all costs. 'Customer Service' must be their nemesis... Still, apart from the unhelpful little *'tosser'* from the very dreary bank, all is quiet at the moment; the *Vampires* having left together, at ten-thirty. Hooray...

Last night, after my 'Voice Class', I caught up with *Mike*. Neither of us are confirmed drinkers; nevertheless, we downed far too much alcohol, chatted like perverted overgrown school kids and tried, but failed, to eat our pre-packed Sushi out of sight of the wandering eyes of the bar staff... On leaving the pub, both rather worse for wear, *Mike* accidentally stumbled, falling directly into the cleavage of a pretty 'buxom brunette'. She didn't appear to mind in the slightest, simply giggling, uncontrollably, as *Mike* slowly raised his drink-laden head from the midst of her sizeable pert breasts. As their eyes met she giggled again, licked her lips in an extremely sexually provocative manner, and suggestively pushed her tongue out of her mischievous alcohol-soaked mouth, whereupon *Mike's* head duly fell back into her mammoth frontage. There it rested for several seconds. She giggled again, then began to run her fingers through his wayward hair. It was at this point that I stepped in to protect *Mike's* honour! Jovially declaring his marital status, I quickly escorted him to the tube at *Charing Cross*. I'm not sure whether he'll thank me for that or not when he's sobered up! Assuming he actually remembers anything about his accidental foray into the assets of the obliging young lady..! Why wasn't she saddling up to me? I'm better looking, and divorced..! Anyway, I succeeded in manhandling him to the tube, whereupon he needed the loo, yet again! After visiting the urinals, fortunately he stuck to urination, and not vomiting, we headed off in our usual opposing directions of the *Northern Line*.

Mike and I first became acquainted with one another whilst on a 'Drama Course'; which, with hindsight, was a comically juxtaposed ironic interlude into a life that has, to this very day, definitely not been lacking any sort of dramatic effect… It was an overpriced 'Summer School' at one of the many secondary 'London Dramatic Art Colleges'. Packed with all types of deluded people, ranging in age from twenty to sixty… For me it was a manifestation of the early stages of my *mid-life crisis*, which, thankfully, I think I am starting to come out of now; acceptance of middle age gradually creeping up on me. I hope it is graceful acknowledgement and not sluggish resignation! Anyway, to begin with I never took much notice of *Mike*, or anyone else for that matter, as at the time I was far too introspective. Besides, he was in a different group from me so our paths rarely crossed… He made a beeline for me at the pub one evening, after class. Apparently, it later transpired that he had recognised someone with gravitas! And thought we would make a good *Comedy Partnership..!*

As we got to know one another I warmed to him, but had never even considered that I would find someone to collaborate with on an artistic level. Thanks to a persistent mother he had done some child acting, and was therefore more advanced in his quest for artistic rebirth. I just wanted to be a star of stage and screen and assumed that after the three-week course I would be halfway there! Rather romantic and somewhat naïve to say the least, but I am, generally, 'a glass-half-full' kind of guy. At least when I am not feeling like a suppressed *Highly Sensitive Ancient Briton..!* Anyway, on reflection we decided that the live performance thing probably wouldn't work as we were both a little over the hill, and we really didn't want to sign up for all that public humiliation. So we are now formulating an idea for a 'screenplay' instead! You never know, we might be the next big thing, or just a couple more delusional 'wannabes!' Time will tell…

As I was tanked up on 'Double Gin and Tonics', my obsessive paranoia about *Daniel's* nightmarish activities was set at a very low level last night. Hence, I managed to sleep through the intermittent nocturnal shuffling and totally forgot about going up there to join him for a *'double wank'*. Predictably, I still haven't had a response to my 'official letter' asking them to leave. Sure, they are probably pissed off, but I really couldn't care less now. He clearly has a rhino's skin, couldn't give a 'shite'. They always say you need to watch the quiet ones; 'still waters' and all. So 'fuck 'em' both. They're just a couple of closed-lip wilful arseholes, Polish hicks, recalcitrant bastards.

I know full well why they are resisting eviction! After all, the flat is brand new, very reasonably priced, and they are unlikely to find as good a deal anywhere else in the area; which they should have considered before they became 'Sleep Deprivation Terrorists!' Well, that's their look-out failure... They have obviously never stumbled across the word 'consideration' in the Polish/English Dictionary! Maybe it doesn't exist in Polish? Anyhow, I'm counting down the days now... I still have some spring bulbs left to plant, so I'll have to calm myself down with a bit of light gardening.

After last week's ongoing 'dressing down' I have decided not to venture up to town for the *singing slaughter* at the P.C. College... I hope I'm not turning into a coward! I'm not normally one to run away and hide from problems, but I just can't face it this week. Added to which, my newly appointed and very expensive 'Singing Coach' rang me this morning! I had forgotten to turn up! I thought it was next week! I had visions of her asking me to send her the £60 through the post for wasting her valuable time, as she is supposed to be at the top of her game! Hence the £60 per hour... Fortunately this was not the case, and we rescheduled. I've only been a few times, and once a month at that. The meagre wages of an *Online Delivery Driver* could hardly afford much more, unless they were *whoring* on the side. Now there's a thought!

The recent greyness has finally been replaced with a sky as vivid blue as a sunny Caribbean island's... Seeing how I've chickened out of singing, maybe I'll take a trip to the swimming baths. It's been ages, and my 'six-pack' needs redefining before the Christmas onslaught...

Much later:

Daniel and Isa are at it! Their headboard banging away like billio, the joints of their conformist europhile *Ikea* bed squeaking exponentially... SILENCE... I think it's all over!? Far be it from me to complain about the sudden exhausted peace, it's a welcome interlude of late. Although listening to people having sex is certainly less annoying than general racket. At least you know what they're up to. It gives you something to focus on. There's logic to the vibrations, bumps, chorus of groans and grunts. It's actually quite enjoyable, in small doses, mechanical human sound without sight or smell. Far easier to handle than thoughtless random noise, it is both purposeful and mildly titillating… Hang on! The cogs have started to turn again. He was probably taking a breather, conserving energy for an explosive finish… Of course, if he didn't insist on staying up half the night he might have had the energy to finish the job properly in the first place! It's a tip he might well want to take with him upon departure! Needless to say, when the time comes I doubt we shall be sharing convivial wisdom. It's bound to be somewhat awkward, possibly fraught, but hopefully not dangerous!

This evening's grocery round was not too stressful. No tips, little traffic, a pleasant enough experience. That is until a group of '*White Trash Hoodies*' tried to jump into the back of my van and help themselves to my mobile bounty. Fortunately, for me not them, I spotted them in the nick of time and they dispersed, save for a tall lanky guy and a stocky shorter kid. They both looked around fifteen years of age; the shorter kid was quite clearly the ring leader, the taller one appeared to be less aggressive but obviously impressionable and certainly under the '*runt's*' influence. The tall kid didn't have the guts to speak, he was definitely being led, probably just wanting to belong, seeking acceptance while he tried to navigate his way through those hormonally challenging years of adolescence. Anyway, the '*runt's*' mouth was more than big enough for the two of them! As I was soon to find out, he was the official spokesperson for the whole ramshackle 'gang'.

'Can I help you?' I asked, in a deliberately posh voice, as I returned to the back of my open van. At first he appeared a little flummoxed, unsure. But as the self-appointed leader he couldn't lose face so went on anyway:

'What! I'm just standing here, *Bruv*. You gotta problem with that *Bruv*?' Replied the ugly, short-arsed little '*hoody*'; hands in pocket, slouched over, slowly and deliberately swaying his head and torso in that nonchalant arrogant manner they love to adopt. Silly boy..! The cocky idiot was a stereotypical little '*Slutton Yob*'; '*Slutton*' being the derogatory vernacular for the town of Sutton... Visit its faceless 'downtown' on a Friday or Saturday night and you will see why... Although to be fair the majority of Britain's town centres suffer from much the same sort of degeneration. However, '*Slutton's*' '*Drunken Yobs*' and scantily clad '*Ladettes*' fighting, groping and willy-nilly vomiting must come close to the top of the leader board in the competition to find the most 'common public vileness' in this 'Disunited Kingdom!'

I felt like hitting the 'little shite', though thought better of it in case the sorrowfully pathetic attempt at a 'Jamaican Yardie' was tooled-up! So I said nothing. I closed the back door, slowly made my way to the cab in an exaggeratedly confident manner that mimicked the '*runt's*' idiocy, then climbed aboard and prepared to drive off. As I checked my mirrors, there they were staring straight back at me. The 'tall lanky one' was just standing there, looking gormless, without purpose, a mere spectator. The 'short-arsed runt' was, predictably, much closer, a few feet away from my wing mirror, trying, but failing massively, to look like a hard-nosed menacing 'gangster'. If only he could have seen his infantile reflection. He looked like a silly baby-faced twat, an utter buffoon. I wanted to laugh but thought better of it. After all I was supposedly the grown-up, a professional driver representing my fabulous community-minded capitalist supermarket..! Despite my quite legitimate concerns for my personal safety I still wasn't about to let this 'little shit' think he was intimidating me. So, following a full assessment of the road, I started the engine, checked my mirrors, indicated to pull out, then lowered my electric widow to half-mast. As I drove away I began, in the plummiest voice I could muster, to impart my words with gusto:

'Why don't you go and find yourself some brain cells, you silly, pitiful little boy?'

Flabbergasted, he was unable to stop his jaw dropping onto the pavement... As he brought it back up to its natural alignment with the rest of the unpleasantness that constituted his face, he proceeded to spit and curse. Alas, before he could think of a clever little 'street' retort, no doubt full of threats and expletives, I was off to my next drop. To piss him off even further I gave him a little wave, like the Queen's... His pasty white face reddened with rage, he angrily shouted *'Bruv'* along with a tirade of inane swear words, in more ridiculous *Mockney Jamaican Drool..!* On reflection, I suppose it was cowardly of me, only confronting him when I was secure in the cab with the engine revved ready for a quick getaway! Oh well, I didn't fancy being stabbed or kicked to death by a mob of spotty children. Which has happened to several middle-aged white males in this thug-ridden country. His face was an absolute picture, though. It was a complete pleasure to put one over the little *'runt'*. Let's only hope they're not hanging around there the next time I'm obliged to deliver...

It's fast approaching 2 a.m. so I think I'll head for my pit and get some shut-eye. That is if the *'Vamps'* allow it..! Oh, I nearly forgot, I made it to the swimming pool today. I swam like an Olympian, showing off my washboard stomach as I sped up and down. No *Grey Ladies* though! They seem to have vanished without a trace!

Tuesday 9th December

Julie came over last night… 'Gin and Tonics' in hand, we 'vegged out' in front of *University Challenge*; feebly answering the occasional question but spending most of our time being silly, outdoing each other at mocking and mimicking the contestants' youthful puppy-like eagerness and general naïvety… Little do they know, but by the time these *'Guardian-Reading Do-Gooders'* reach forty the exuberance of youth will have undoubtedly flown their nests of blinded optimism. The unkempt mad scientist hair turned grey and straggly, their liberal ideals tested to the point where they all vote 'Tory' and are obliged to hire gun-laden 'Security Guards' in order to protect their 'Capitalist Assets'. To cap it all, their new mother tongue will most probably be 'Polish', with 'Extreme Islam' the 'State Enforced Religion'.

Sunday was just as barmy! After we had finished hysterically prophesying our beloved *Blighty's* 'Doomsday' scenario, the demise of our ancient 'British History', the final assault and conquest of our unique identity, sense of humour, and once tolerant 'Green and Pleasant Land', we had to get out of the house in order to bring ourselves back from the precipice of mass *Indigenous Suicide*... Something the 'British-Hating Fanatics' would surely welcome..! So off we drove to 'Wimbledon Village', true patriots in *Julie's* little white *'Rover'* (The sad demise of 'Rover Cars' dismissed as inconsequential by our own supposedly Socialist Government!), to find some hearty 'English Pub Food' and stroll the 'Common' with fellow *Britons*, ancient or otherwise. 'The Grapes', 'The Crooked Billet', 'The Hand in Hand', all these old 'Ale Houses' were bursting at the seams with fellow escapees from the 'Urban Jungle'. Seeing as we were far too ravenous for a long wait we hopped back into *Julie's 'Rover'* and sped around south-west London in search of an alternative 'Roast Dinner', an hour and a half of patriotic hunting later ending up back in *Multicultural Morden* chomping on 'Chicken Madras' instead!

Lately, I have been feeling even more fragile, nearing the edge of sanity, than is usually the case in my oversensitive, slightly paranoid, fantastical, occasionally delusional mind... My descent of the proverbial 'slippery slope' began in earnest on Saturday afternoon. Having just pulled up outside a hideous block of concrete flats, close to the A3 in New Malden, my mobile phone, which contrary to company rules was nestled in my trouser pocket, rang out its usual heartstopping tune! I hate the bloody things. I always expect the worst. I don't know why I get so anxious! I suppose, subconsciously, I'm thinking that if someone needs to call me on it while I'm working they are either about to give me some horrific family news, announce the death of a long-lost friend, or they are an overeager debt collector from one of the numerous credit card companies I am beholden to, or, failing all the above, some arsehole from my bank intent on calling in my personal loan etc.

Anyway, thank God I was out on my round and not back at HQ! *John*, my manager, wouldn't have given a shit, but the maniac who oversees the whole shebang would have been apoplectic if he heard a personal mobile go off at work. Apparently, he has already been involved in an 'in-store brawl', and not with a member of staff either, but a customer! So the gossip goes, The Store Manager rugby-tackled the guy to the ground and they both ended up in a Sumo-style contest, rolling around, wrestling one another between the fresh meat and fish counters... The Store Manager was suspended for several months, on full pay of course, while the incident was investigated. After what amounted to a highly paid sabbatical the 'powers that be' deemed it appropriate to reinstate the psychotic megalomaniac! One has to admire his tenacity. He must have Rhinoceros skin! Apparently, the customer was notorious for being irritating, generally difficult and curt to staff. So, in hindsight, he should be commended for sticking up for his longsuffering workers, albeit a little too violently...

A principled man is hard to find, a dying breed in these visceral modern times. Nevertheless, in this 'P.C. World' it is quite remarkable how The Store Manager held onto his job! He must have had some good 'dirt' to sling at 'Head Office', for I doubt I would receive the same treatment if I were to assault one of my demanding 'on-line customers...' Although I can think of several that I'd like to sock it to...

Well, back to the call... As it was dark, and therefore nobody could see me to report my misdemeanour to the 'nutter' of a Store Manager, I answered the unrecognisable number; which soon transpired to be a big mistake, my sense of victimisation and descent into general despair quickly gathering pace! It was the BITCH, *Lynn* from the P.C. College!! She had seen her opportunity and not being one to miss a trick had seized the moment with both hands:

'Hello Ian, this is *Lynn*... (pause) from the Musical Theatre Class... Are you able to talk? Do you have a few minutes?'

I must confess she took me totally by surprise. I certainly hadn't bargained for a call from *'Mrs Glamour Puss'* whilst dishing out groceries around the dullness of suburbia.

'Well, I am at work... But I can spare five minutes,' I replied.

She went on, 'It's okay, don't worry... when is more convenient to call?'

Ever an obsequious fool, 'No, no,' I insisted, 'I can speak now. I'm not busy at the moment.'

So off she went on her, clearly, pre-planned ramble... It transpired that she was of the opinion that I had not fulfilled her class remit of singing that bloody song 'He/She Is No Good' followed by a verbal link to my own chosen score! As she condescendingly went on to explain:

'The whole idea was to give a complete performance and tell a story at the same time... This is an advanced class, and you have to do most of the work away from college... I don't feel you have done this during the term, and seeing as I have given you many opportunities to do so I feel you would be better off in the other class.'

'In other words, the one I was in last year!' I thought to myself, steam bellowing out of my ears... She had quality ammunition to fire at me, as, unable to face another ritualistic public humiliation, I had failed to turn up to last week's excuse for a class where I was supposed to perform my 'two-song play'. As for giving me opportunities! Delusional would be an understatement. But, to her mind her intimidation had worked.

I was toast. She'd run me out of town! Or, so she thinks! By demoting me now she's assuming I won't turn up to the last lesson of term, but leave quietly with my tail rammed firmly between my legs... Will I? I would like to think not, but I probably shan't go as I cannot stand the sight of her. However, if I could be arsed it would be fun to turn the tables on her, humiliate the past-her-sell-by-date *'Glamour Puss'* in front of her sycophantic *lieblings*... While I had the chance not to mince my words I could also tell the *'Craggy*

Auburn-Haired Wizened Eye-Balling Old Witch' what I really thought of her, as well as the second most invidious pupil, the 'Condescending Slap Head' that is the *'Safa Queen!'* The effeminate 'South African Bitch' with a nose as long as Pinocchio's, that he loves to look down in a superior, disapproving manner, would also feel the wrath of my lucid tongue. He has one of those faces that needs punching, pompous little twat, sat there like 'Queen Bee' with a Middle Eastern Headdress wrapped around his weedy neck, the tassels cascading down his chest like some dinner shirt from the 1970s. He looks like a camp Yasser Arafat. Sure he has a perfect 'Musical Theatre Voice', but, along with eighty per cent of the rest of the group, about as much charisma as 'Osama Bin Laden's Social Secretary'. No wonder I feel incongruous…

As I tried to keep my mind focused on the conversation, not the aforementioned thoughts of revenge, our five-minute chat turned into a twenty-five-minute marathon… When she had finished laying her cards on the table I furnished her 'Middle-Class Mind' with my own opinions. She was somewhat aghast, horrified even, as I declared that on several occasions I felt humiliated by her severely 'dressing me down' in front of the 'boring compliant mass'… Naturally, I didn't use the term 'boring'… She asked me to give her an example, which I duly did… I then informed her of the negative behaviour of the aforementioned classmates and asked her why she never checked them. I also questioned her as to why the atmosphere was so tense and why the pianist was deliberately so unhelpful. I wanted to know what the purpose of the class was, what her input was supposed to be?! I told her, firmly:

'I am sorry to have to say it but it seems to me that you

are simply there to criticise, me in particular!'

Before she could draw breath, I went on:

'It's all very well to say that we have to prepare everything away from class. But, if we are to be that perfectly polished before we perform, how do we progress and challenge ourselves? Yes, there are some people in the class with very pleasant, listenable voices; but they are belting out the same tunes every week. It seems like they are stuck in a safety net of repetition..! I know I have a lot to learn, but I am not afraid to make mistakes in order to move forward... It seems to me that you want a class full of repetitive sycophants?!'

Finally, I informed her that I have only been singing for just over a year and that last year I managed to memorise and perform numerous numbers to a much higher standard. In no uncertain terms I told her that she had sapped my confidence, bullied me, and put me off to the point where I had begun to dislike singing and become incapable of holding even the most basic tune... Obviously, this was not music to her ears. However, surprisingly, she did actually apologise! She said I should have spoken to her earlier, which was an easy cop-out... Way back in October I had approached her, said I wanted to speak to her. However, I never followed it up straight away as I didn't want to appear oversensitive and get into some kind of negative situation with the *'Glamour Puss'*. Besides, I already had the measure of her! There was no way she would take any criticism or dissent, especially from a new whippersnapper like me... A couple of weeks ago, when I did pluck up the courage to speak to her, was the fateful day she humiliated me in front of the class for daring to sing *Summertime*.

'A very odd choice of song..! You should be more advanced by now. Be prepared!' she loudly declared while deliberately stooping over me, conquering my male odour with her upmarket pheromones. Hence my reason for avoiding her savage bloodbath last week... In the semi-simmering exchange on my mobile I forgot to mention this most recent cruelness. Not that it really mattered, as she couldn't fail to be in sync with my disapproving, unflattering thoughts on the whole debacle she dresses up as *Further Education!!!*

I had definitely overshot the mark now. My outspokenness having really got to her, the tone and pitch of her voice was starting to wobble. At least I had had a small victory by succeeding in cracking the outer shell of her dictatorial armour. Much to her surprise, I think... The well of defence and discontent had now run dry, there was nothing left to say, the twenty-five minutes of grating discourse came to its fruitless, for me at least, climax, as she delighted in reiterating her entrenched point of view on the future course of my singing endeavours at the 'P.C. College'.

'I shall transfer you to Musical Theatre 1, and I hope you are able to rearrange your work commitments so you can attend!'

So, despite telling her that I wasn't available on Mondays, that was the grand sum of it. She didn't want me in her class any more. I didn't want to be in it either, but I wasn't going to let her get rid of me that easily... I could attend the less advanced class on Mondays, but being stubborn, obstinate, unyielding, intransigent, intractable, a little pig-headed and totally non-compliant, I wasn't about to move smoothly aside... I doubt I shall bother to go and cause havoc at the last class of term this Thursday, but, as far as I am concerned, it is still unfinished business. I shall be writing a letter of complaint about her and sending it right to the top. I also want my fees refunded as compensation. In hindsight, I think I'm better off with one-to-one tuition. Mixing with *'arse lickers'* has never been my bag...

'You do have a presence and talent, and should keep at it,' were her patronising, saccharin-soaked, parting words... Was she being sincere?! Or just having a laugh! I couldn't tell, for her momentary wobble had passed and her voice was back on auto-pilot. Perhaps her intention was to placate me by planting a seed of airy-fairy pleasantness in my overactive mind, in the self-preserving hope that I wouldn't remember her vileness and therefore not bother to make an official complaint..! Either way, I had that message to cling onto as I ascended the never-ending flights of stairs, weighed down by copious amounts of heavy festive consumables for my depressed-looking customer in his unappealing high-rise flat.

By contrast, Saturday evening proved to be quite entertaining! I joined *Julie* and two other couples at a Chinese Restaurant in North Cheam. Having rushed home to exchange my orange and blue uniform for smart/casual attire, more befitting a youthful-looking forty-one-year-old, I arrived around 9 p.m.

They had just finished their starters but had kindly saved me some mini spring rolls, prawn toast, chicken satay, and some fried cabbage that Chinese restaurants always refer to as seaweed. *Julie* and the other two women had dressed up, mainly in black, but with vibrant flashes (of colour!). *Julie's* nails looked splendid, painted in a very lustrous, exotic aubergine. They had all made a concerted effort, as women universally do. The same cannot be said for the husband of *Julie's* workmate! He was wearing some nondescript trousers, and a 'dickhead' black and sand striped shirt which was aimlessly hanging over his trousers in that common 'lager lout' fashion... However, his mate, who *Julie* had never met before, could certainly not be accused of submitting to mediocrity in the wardrobe department. His pillar-box-red cashmere cardigan was startling. It drew your gaze straight towards his well-defined upper torso, then up to his cheeky twinkle-eyed face... *Dean* and his smooth-skinned wife *Bianca* were true *'Eastenders!'* At least according to *Julie's* workmate!

Alas, as the evening progressed, our expectations were slowly and painfully quashed! There wasn't a 'cockney knees-up between' them. The two couples were the best of friends and, apart from the occasional aside from *Julie's* workmate, hardly bothered to engage us all night. We soon became completely fed up with their rudeness. So after the main course we let them be, deciding to dance to the dubious-sounding band instead. Despite the absence of a 'Chinese Elvis' it proved to be the best part of the evening by far. We did ask one of the waitresses where 'Elvis' had got to, on 'Elvis Night?!' She just smiled and asked us if we wanted another bottle of wine! Unsurprisingly, we declined the offer of spending another £20 on average wine to go with the overpriced and undersized set buffet...! I think she thought it was a given. An English Couple on a night out with a bit of music thrown in, they're going to drink a minimum of a bottle each, along with a few beers and several chasers to round the night off. She looked a little miffed, pissed even. So to really get her back up we asked for two pints of tap water, with ice of course... The moral of the story being, *'Don't lure people into your restaurant under false pretences and then expect them to buy up your wine cellar'.* It's probably an old Chinese proverb! Either way, we did have fun flamboyantly gyrating to the *X Factor* equivalent of *Oasis!*

Needless to say, the other two couples, who were both in denial of their 'Working Class' roots, failed to join in. It was all a bit ironic! I was probably the most *'posh'* person there, with my *'Public School'* education and leafy rural upbringing; but I, as ever, was in for a penny, in for a pound. I could have spun around that small patch of decidedly dirty carpet all night long... *Julie* has absolutely no qualms about where her roots lie. She is proud of them, and quite rightly so. Even mine are only one generation removed from 'Working Class', which is probably why I feel so comfortable with a good old-fashioned 'Knees up Mother Brown'. Thank God I am heading down the opposite way of the dual carriageway of social mobility to *Dean, Bianca,* and the other *Pseudo-Middle-Class Couple,* back in the trajectory of the honest, aspirational *'Working Class Roots'* of my *'Grandparents'*.

Julie and I parted in good spirits, hot and sweaty from dancing and laughing at the ridiculousness of her impressionable friend, her friend's pompous husband and her friend's friends' *'Mockney Middle Class Identities'*... All was well, or so I thought! The 'slippery slope' had other ideas! As I was about to find out, the level plateau of the valley floor was still some way off!

3.30 am:

'Shut the fucking hell up, you absolute bastards!' I screeched at the top of my voice whilst simultaneously leaping from my restless slumber to pound the ceiling over my once comfortable, alluring bed.

The ever-creaking floorboards combined with the stifling heat, the uncomfortable consequence of *Isa's* refusal to ever turn the central heating off, had finally made me spontaneously and uncontrollably combust like a caged mad dog out in the midday sun… Following my assault on the ceiling I grabbed my bathrobe, flung it around my naked body, and began thumping the door of my flat. Moments later, still as crazed as a cornered bull, I broke free from my quarters, entered our communal hallway, and repeated the process on their door whilst madly screaming:

'Daniel… You are the most selfish person I have ever met. Do you ever go to bed?'

After what seemed like an eternity he replied in his soft, monotone, deliberately provocative, metronomic, highly accented English:

'We come in 11 o'clock… We watch TV… We don't want go to bed.'

I responded, quickly, 'I come back from work later than you, quite often in fact. But I am not noisily walking around my flat until nearly daybreak! You just couldn't care less…Why don't you look up the word "neighbourly"? And "selfish" while you are at it?! …Selfish, that's what you are…' A brief calm overcame me. But my blood soon began to re-boil and I yelled, psychotically, 'SELFISH. YOU ARE SO FUCKING SELFISH…'

Everything went silent. All I could hear was my racing heartbeat. A couple of seconds passed… I went on, modulating between speaking ever so quietly and uncontrollable ranting. My voice trembling as I tried to contain my anger:

'Are you there..? Why don't you come down here, instead of hiding up there like a coward?'

Silence…

'Daniel..! Selfish, selfish, selfish arsehole… Daniel!' My

voice was now clear, clipped in tone, almost Germanic!

After more deliberate silence, *Daniel* responded in his usual irritatingly downbeat, deep Eastern European accent:

'Yes... Why you keep repeatin' yourself? Selfish, you keep say selfish!'

His monotone dismissive drool was doing exactly what it said on the tin. Winding me up, yet again! Not that I had in any way started the process of winding down... I responded:

'You are so bloody arrogant!' Then, becoming angrier and angrier, I began repeating my, what in the cold light of day would seem insane, demands:

'Why don't you come down here instead of hiding up there like a coward? One, or even two in the morning, I could cope with that once or twice a week. But no, every bloody night! Three o'clock. Four o'clock. Even five-thirty the other night! You just don't give a shit... But why should you! After you've stayed up all night you can lie in until eleven... Maybe I should start playing loud music and stomp about all morning!? See how you like it! Let's see if you are so matter-of-fact then, eh..! Daniel..?'

Having clearly understood my entire rant, the *'tosser'* replied in a deliberately antagonising lyrical legato, 'Weee seeee..!'

'Yes, we'll see alright... Actually, let's see right now..! I want you out tomorrow morning. You can both leave...' I rather manically declared. Then, as I began to shake with pure unadulterated rage, teetering on hatred, the famed 'courage' of a 'British Bulldog' began to roar... He had finally burnt his last bridge. My natural 'British stoicism' had been tested to the limit! My voice went deep and I spoke with authoritative determination:

'I'm going to get the spare key and I'm coming up there

right now… I've had my fill of you people… How would you like it if one million Brits turned up in Poland with your arrogant attitude?'

'We see!' Same standard response, although spoken quite quickly for once. The habitual dull, monotone inflection was ever-present but for the first time his voice was somewhat shaky.

'I'll tell you now! You wouldn't like it, not in the slightest… We certainly wouldn't be welcomed, as you are here… Selfish arseholes… Out… I want you out.'

Having momentarily decided that accessing their quarters would be a rather dangerous step too far, my subconscious kicked in to calm me down. Though within moments I imparted a final barrage towards the *'Introspective Recalcitrant Wanker'*:

'I don't know why you are so cocky and think you are so bloody clever! You people have been ruled and conquered for generations. It was better under communism. Bring back the Iron Curtain, I say… You are so thick-skinned. Do you realise most British people can't stand you? Of course you do, but you don't give a shit! You look down your noses at us. God only knows why! What have you contributed to the world? You're only here for the money… So, FUCK OFF, RHINO-SKIN. This is my house and I want you out… Come back when you have learnt some manners, and etiquette. A thousand years will do.'

Needless to say, that was the straw that broke the camel's back. The *'Polish Vampires'* are finally packing up, they're leaving tomorrow. Thank God… If only they were civilised! If they had even the smallest amount of consideration this would not have been necessary… As a member of the overly *'Fair-Play British Race'* I have given them chance after chance after chance to show even a modicum of manners. But, there we have it! After far too much leniency, useless 'Chamberlain'-style diplomacy, the only option was a 'Churchillian' last stand.

The Do-Gooders' ridiculous softly, softly approach always comes back to haunt us in the end... However, I think *Daniel* and *Isa* are now well aware that regular *Ancient Britons* do not adhere to the *Do-Gooders'* insane policy of lying down and being walked all over in your own backyard! Although we will probably need 'Divine Intervention' before our cowardly self-serving politicians implement our wishes and start putting their own people first!

I think that is why *Do-Gooders*, along with most of the 'European Bourgeois', so clearly resent this once great nation. As much as they try to piss us off, mock our values, condemn, and generally undermine, they can never crush our resolve. Resilience, ingenuity, stoicism, and above all irony, wit and humour are priceless 'British Characteristics' that, with the exception of our Irish cousins, are seldom found far away from our blessed shores. ONE NIL TO BLIGHTY...

Thursday 11ᵗʰ December

I am sitting, peacefully, in a restaurant called *'So Asia'* in the multicultural melting pot that is *Acton Town*. The food is, as on my previous visit, freshly cooked, extremely yummy, and good value for money, and the South East Asian Staff very welcoming. Above all, the toilets are spotless!

My mood is more positive than it has been for the last turbulent month. I am feeling remarkably upbeat, despite the fact that I have just handed over £60 of hard-earned cash to my private singing coach..! No dreaded *Lynn* today! I am not attending her last 'farce of term'; which, subconsciously, I knew would be the case. I need to steer clear of overly critical Energy Vampires..! My one-to-one lesson with *Miriam* was poles apart from the *'Glamour Puss's'* soul-destroying debacle. Critiquing, yes; but in a mature, positive way. It was totally uplifting, an encouraging confidence-booster to be taught by a teacher with unpoisoned blood running through her veins.

This is my third lesson with *Miriam*... She was very welcoming, regardless of me totally forgetting about last week's appointment. As if that wasn't bad enough, I reconfirmed my poor time-keeping by rocking up fifteen minutes late, due to faulty signals on the approach to Acton Town Station… Seeing how my bed is so comfortable I rarely allow for unforeseen delays. I love my sleep. Nevertheless, my good upbringing shone through, as I had already called ahead to inform her of the situation. Maybe that's why she wasn't vexed with me, or perhaps she can see a star in the making!

She certainly managed to get the best out of me. I feel so relaxed, on cloud nine and a half, totally elated... Today

I sang *The Lady Is a Tramp* in a way that 'Old Blue Eyes' would have been proud of… All is well in my world. I'm so chilled-out that my mind is wandering all over the place! The faint oriental background music has a subtle festive beat which is transporting me back to my 'backpacking youth', to a shopping mall in Thailand or Malaysia, where, like other religious festivals, 'Christmas' is celebrated with gusto… However, the real reason for my calm state of mind is that I have just had my first continuous night's sleep for over a month. Yes, it has actually happened! *'The Vampires'* have finally fled their cave… Hallelujah…

Yesterday, I deliberately came home late to avoid bumping into the unwillingly departing 'bloodsuckers'. This morning I located the spare key and rushed up the stairs like an excited small child to see what state they had left the place in! True to my suspicions it wasn't a welcoming sight… In only one month they had managed to ruin the shower door, the once sparkling glass panel being now covered in dirty limescale. There was dried excrement all around the toilet bowl, an abundance of human hair and fluff, bags of rubbish were piled up in the bedroom, grime had taken control of the shiny new kitchen I had personally fitted, and the air was heavy with a strong-smelling body odour… God only knows what else I shall find when I return this afternoon?!

Following tonight's shift at the 'Retail Hellhole' *Daniel* is coming over for the 'Key and Deposit Returning Ceremony'. Which I'm sure will prove to be an interesting experience..! Despite the looming unpleasantness I'm determined to enjoy my main course courtesy of the tasty 'Oriental Buffet'. After which I shall amble home, savouring my singing successes as I go… I shall cross *Daniel's* stubborn bridge as it arrives. Then, please God, the recent 'slippery slope' will have well and truly hit the buffers, allowing me to pick up the pieces and continue with a less hysterical life!

Wednesday 17ᵗʰ December

A beautiful sunny day... I'm slowly entering into the *'Christmas Spirit'*. My shopping is nearly complete and today is the day I've decided to put up my festive decorations. Since the *'Vamps'* have gone the 'Season of Goodwill' has well and truly crossed my radar. I even bought a *Big Issue* the other day, although after giving the guy a couple of quid I left the magazine with him as they rarely contain anything worth reading.

I've just flicked the telly on to be greeted by an advertisement on behalf of *The Salvation Army*. Homeless people shivering under blankets and cardboard, trying to sleep on the pavements on a cold winter's day; all the more poignant seeing as it is bloody freezing out there. The 'P.R.' and 'Marketing' is sublime, and the voice-over artist has a wonderful melancholic tone that pulls on your heartstrings. His pitch is delivered sincerely and meaningfully, in perfect time with the sorrowful visuals:

'Cold homeless people can have some warm clothes, a hot meal and even a smile on their face as they are presented with a seasonal gift.'

All this can be achieved in a flash, as long as you part with the £19 *The Salvation Army* has calculated it will cost... But hang on a minute, I've already done my 'Good Deed' for the week. And I am a regular supporter of 'Animal Charities' too... But now the powers-that-be want even more! And they actually have the cheek to quote the price of your SALVATION! I know I said I was entering into the spirit of it all, but after the stressful debacle of *Lynn* and the *'Vamps'* I'm in sore need of a bit of guilt-free self-indulgence.

Self-Indulgence, that's the real underlying theme of

a modern *Christmas!* Let's face it, apart from a few saints among us, we completely overindulge, it's all about rich food and expensive presents. The narrative of the birth of *Jesus* and his subsequent dying on the cross for the greater good of humanity is completely sidelined by insatiable consumerism and the insane need for retailers to increase their year-on-year sales. It's all about growth, GDP, not falling into recession, bulging credit cards, getting pissed, groping your boss at the office party, seeing detested relatives, falling out with them, bitching about your in-laws, fighting with your husband or wife or partner, resenting your neighbours, fighting over turkeys at the last minute, bursting out of your new cords after Christmas dinner, eating pound upon pound of extremely rich chocolates, drinking weird festive cocktails until you vomit, then farting your way through to the New Year whilst eating the leftover turkey in sandwiches, fricasses, stews and soups… By *New Year's Eve* you must host or be invited to a party, otherwise you will be labelled a loser, slightly backward, a trifle odd, mentally ill, smelly, Johnny-No mates, a paedophile, or an in-the-closet poofter... Come January everyone gives up something for at least a week. We all feel euphoric for a while, *'It's going to be a life-changing year'* we naïvely mutter to ourselves as we prepare our mind for the new life we intend to lead. Then, by February 1st we are just as fat as we were at Christmas, depression is lingering on the horizon and we are back to square one. Until next year, anyhow!

Despite the modern-day hedonism of Christmas, most of us are still ruled by our subconscious! Guilt, melancholy, despair, anger, resentment, manic highs of near-hysterical laughter and suicidal lows are all part of the fragile pre-Christmas condition. And judging by the recent behaviour of *Julie* and *Mike* my theory has some weight to it…

The advert has really played with my head. 'I am a good person, aren't I?' That's what we all say when our sensibilities have been tested. We want to be reassured that we are not just another selfish arsehole. Besides, it's not as if I have made anybody homeless recently! Well, not without good reason... Anyway, I haven't called to give my £19. I'll buy another *Big Issue* instead....!

'Laters':

It would be a complete understatement to say that the last week has been a bit of a rollercoaster.

Firstly, I had the delight of returning *Daniel's* deposit in exchange for the keys to the flat, which inevitably involved more defiant arrogance... The flat still stank of them, although to be fair he had actually cleared the bags of rubbish, given it a quick once-over and any residue of body hair had vanished without a trace. However, upon closer inspection of the bathroom I noticed that mould had started to colonise. Hardly surprising as they refused to open the window, despite me politely asking them to do so on several occasions…! Anyway, the 'Key and Deposit Returning Ceremony' was, as expected, a fraught affair. To *Daniel's* visible displeasure I charged him for the oven glass that allegedly shattered of its own accord! I also somehow managed to misread the gas and electric meters, so his bill may well be a little steeper than he might have imagined. What a shame…! Well, at the end of the day they were responsible for their own demise; only nocturnal creatures could put up with their insufferable lifestyle. So a little credit on my utility bills seems like a very mild punishment for their antisocial behaviour.

I assured him that I would send him on copies of the bills, along with the £200 balance, less the relevant inflated deductions! But, firstly, I obviously needed to wait for the bills to arrive... I still do not have his forwarding address as he point-blank refused to give it to me. So, however meagre it turns out be, I'm not sure how he expects me to return it to him..! Maybe he doesn't want me knowing his new address for fear of me going around there and murdering the pair of them, though clearly not in their sleep..! Despite his condescending, self-assured appearance, I think he has finally realised that we *British* will take so much; but eventually, even our pleasant, passive nature can crack under excessive provocation. After all, he has now experienced my hot-blooded temper first-hand… I think the penny dropped when during one of our less-than-cordial exchanges I repeated my earlier protestations as he stood pierced-lipped, as dismissive as ever:

'How would you like it if one million Brits turned up and settled in Poland, and undercut the labour market because they had the benefit of sending money back home where it was worth four times as much, and behave as arrogantly as you have?'

'We see!' he smugly replied. What else!!

'Yes, we see... we see... very clever! I can tell you sir, you wouldn't like it in the slightest. And you certainly wouldn't welcome us with open arms and free access to your Benefits System either,' I barked, with a curled lip.

He replied, looking scornfully down his ugly pale nose:

'What you mean? I pay tax for English people.'

I went on, with similar disdain:

'Well that may be so. But the previous owners of this property were Polish...' I think they were actually Lithuanian, but who cares, they were from that neck of the woods. I continued, 'They were repossessed! They obviously built up huge debts as the bailiffs keep knocking on the door and I am constantly being bombarded with their unpaid credit card bills and personal loans!'

This actually got him talking, defensively:

'So... Doesn't mean all Polish people like this.'

What he said was quite true. But up to now my experiences have not been good: the one time I used a Polish plumber he cracked my sink and stole £50 from my wallet...

'No, that's right. But I'm still to meet one who hasn't been arrogant and pushy. Maybe I have had very bad luck...! I know two Czech guys, and they are positively grateful to be here. They are happy, polite, and they even understand humour!' Good job the *Do-Gooders* weren't listening in. I would have been arrested on the spot, for RACISM!!

He still had his arms folded, looking nonchalant and superior. He then grinned, smugly... I could feel myself bubbling, and before I knew it my mouth had set off again:

'You are so arrogant... You walk in here, take over, and obviously don't give a shit about keeping me awake all night!'

He replied with his usual selfishness:

'We don't want go to bed early... We watch TV... So what, is no problem.'

By now I was extremely animated. My shoulders rolling, my arms flailing all over the place and my hands gesturing, firmly, as I responded with authoritative passion in my voice:

'No... That's right... I know it's NO PROBLEM for you! You don't give a shit if I haven't slept for a month, as long as you get your lie-in in the morning. You couldn't care less... Selfish and arrogant, but we all know that... Now, if you want the balance of your deposit after the bills have arrived

I need your address...'

Another pointless conversation ensued about him not wanting to furnish me with his address, and me needing it to pass on the deposit balance and to redirect his post... After what seemed like an eternity the *'tosser'* left. I had to practically shove him out the front door, by which time it was nearly midnight. He still hadn't given me his forwarding address, although I did manage to prise out the general vicinity of his new cavernous lodgings. We parted company on an ever so sarcastic 'Goodnight!' And that was that... I hope!

I have slept like a baby for the past week. The cheque I gave him has cleared. But as far as forwarding the remainder of his deposit is concerned I am still awaiting his address! The thought had crossed my mind that his girlfriend might be an illegal immigrant. I think she could have been Russian, not Polish at all. So that could be the reason why he doesn't want me to know too much..! Not that one more *Illegal Alien* will make much difference; as it stands the press reckon there are a million here already... That's what's so great about this treacherous *Labour Government!* They really know how to kick the working man in the teeth. We can barely afford a house in our own country; if we do manage to bag one the price is so highly inflated, due to the overwhelming demand caused by their *'open-door immigration policy'*, that we are obliged to start subletting to foreigners, illegal or otherwise, in order to try and make ends meet. *'Mass Immigration = High Housing Costs and Lower Wages...'* Now that sure is an intelligent policy! More like a recipe for severe social conflict, I should say...

On that fateful day, when they moved in, I already had *Daniel's* passport details and work reference. But, until I asked him for her name to put on the 'Tenancy Agreement', her identity was kept a closely guarded secret. When he answered he only divulged her Christian name.

'*Isa,*' He said.

It was only when I asked for her full Christian name along with her surname that he hesitantly furnished me with the details, murmuring her name to me:

'*Isabella Abramowska.*'

'Is that *Abrahams*?' I asked him.

'Yes,' He replied.

Well, if it is, they certainly didn't behave in a 'Biblical' manner! They well and truly overlooked the 'Commandment' to 'Love Thy Neighbour...'! Though I suppose, with hindsight, her name does sound Polish, unless she is related to the *Russian Oligarch, Abramovich*?! But if that were so I can't imagine why she would need to live in half an ex-council house in Morden, and work as an unskilled waitress dumping gourmet burgers on tables in a themed restaurant in Wimbledon High Street!! I think being surrounded by foreigners all the time can make one a bit obsessive, always feeling suspicious and suspecting the worst. It would be a slow chug in the right direction if our *'Crappy Government'* did something about our porous borders and got us out of the CORRUPT GRAVY TRAIN OF THE EU! Maybe then we would feel a little less paranoid and insecure in our own land. But that is very unlikely to happen, for that would be a far too dangerous, retrograde step, on the 'slippery slope' to INDIGENOUS RIGHTS!!!!

Upon further reflection I think a lot of these *Eastern Europeans* still cling to old-fashioned ways, the man doing all the talking and deal-making while the woman remains in the background thinking of what to cook him for supper..!

Maybe I am just being over-analytical! It's probably my *'Mid-Life Crisis'* rearing its paranoid, ugly head again. Needless to say, being a *Highly Sensitive Person* I am predisposed to a plethora of psychological conditions... Anyway, they're gone now. I really need to get them out of my head and savour the solitude. Until the next inevitable batch of trouble..! Thankfully, that won't be until the New Year! I have changed my mind yet again! I've decided to wait until the market picks up before I consider selling the upstairs flat... I still intend to build my downstairs extension, take up the laminate in the upstairs kitchen and lay much thicker bedroom carpet, then, hopefully, coupled with a proper interrogation into the living and sleeping patterns of my next unassuming victims, this will reduce the unbearable noise to a more tolerable level!

More Shit:

My week of *malchance* continued when I arrived in town for my Tap Dancing Class, only to discover that it had finished the previous week! My friend *Mike* also blew me out on the pretext of uncontrollable diarrhoea, which was an excuse he hadn't used before..! I sometimes wonder why I am friends with him at all, as he constantly lets me down. However, if we have a proper fall-out we shan't finish our script and then we shall never, as *Mike* quite seriously proclaims, become *'Media Moguls..!'* *Mike* has a very peculiar sense of reality..! He's all talk and no action... He is the most infuriating person to work with. Without my perseverance our writing partnership would have dissolved ages ago. Underneath his self-proclaimed intellectual outer shell he is, quite simply, *lazy*; an impressionable social butterfly who flits between literary societies, acting groups and other fringe events, whilst neglecting his own endeavours every time the going gets a little too tough for him. The only way our *'Comedy Script'* will ever be produced is if I take the bull by the horns and start knocking on the doors of production companies myself. If I wait for *Mike* to get off his delusional thespian arse and be proactive the Thames will have frozen over and we shall be well on the way to a second Ice Age... Anyway, that's enough berating poor *Mike*. Everyone disappoints in the end... Maybe I'm too demanding! Although I don't think I am. I certainly don't keep letting people down. Save for exceptional circumstances, if I say I'm going to do something I damn well do it...

Seeing how I was bored and stranded in London with nothing to do I decided to text *Julie*. She was out shopping with her fragile son, in Kingston, so she texted me back to say that she would call me after nine-thirty that evening... Obviously, this was no good to me! I was having a drink in my old faithful *J.D. Wetherspoons of Holborn*, feeling a little peed-off, irritable, unwanted, in need of instant attention. So I sent her a text saying:

Don't bother, if u can't be available on demand!

She texted back, *Ok...!* Which is why I fucking hate *texting*; in the heat of the moment you can say the most stupid things, things that you probably wouldn't say face to face or on the phone. Playful sarcasm can be misconstrued, taken literally; jokiness interpreted offensively... Unfortunately this technology is now a permanent part of our shallow, superficial, faceless, unaccountable modern lives... Having been sucked into the vagaries of this world, and taken my frustrations out on *Julie*, the next day I texted an apology:

I was only joking... You know what I'm like! xx.

Admittedly, it was rather thinly veiled. But I have been on the receiving end of far worse from her... I know 'two wrongs don't make a right', but our time is coming to an end. She knows I'm desperate for a child. She says she wants to try with me, but I can tell her heart isn't in it. I know it would be difficult, considering her age, but she's not prepared to commit wholeheartedly. Besides, it's very complicated. A tall order... As she rightly says, 'What happens if we can't? You'll want to find someone who can.'

Currently, both of our lives have their fair share of turmoil! *Julie's Mum* has found a buyer for her flat, and it looks as if it will proceed quickly as the purchaser is a cash buyer with no chain. Another 'Divorce Victim', I believe! Consequently, *Julie* is, understandably, anxious about where she will live and somewhat upset about her mother buggering off to play 'Happy Families' with her sister. Naturally, she's feeling sorry for herself, abandoned, and more than a tad resentful towards her only sibling, whom she has never really got along with.

They always say you take out your frustrations on your nearest and dearest... So last Saturday morning, after sending me a curt and stroppy text to explain these developments in her personal life, she sent me one of her off-the-wall marathon diatribes. Her elephant's memory clicked into fifth gear and a tidal wave of pent-up frustration, venom and vitriol came flooding out.

I called her mobile from work on Saturday, texted another apology and asked her to return my call... Silence prevailed until Sunday afternoon...! I was at my *Mum's* house, enjoying her famously sumptuous *'Christmas Party'*; devouring her delicious home-made food, sipping Champagne and playing sophisticated butler whilst mingling with her eclectic mix of well-dressed friends. By five in the afternoon *Irish music* was in full flow, and we were jigging like mad *leprechauns* around all four corners of her stylish country house living room, in a display that wouldn't have disgraced an episode of *Strictly Come Dancing!* Consequently, I was blissfully unaware of *Julie's* latest frantic text!

Lying surrounded by woodland, my parents' house has no mobile signal. So it was only as I drove home on Monday night that text alerts started to bleep incessantly on my phone... Taking into account our irritable, somewhat fractious and less than convivial recent partnership, I knew they would be challenging and difficult in nature; so I followed my instincts, deciding to wait until I had reached the sanctity of my ex-council flat before I dared open up the messages... My assumptions proved well founded, though anger had quite clearly turned into panic. She obviously had no idea I hadn't received her messages until now so she must have, quite reasonably, thought that I was deliberately ignoring her, paying her back and all... Anyway, the first text I opened went so:

Going by your silence I suppose the answer to my question is no... I still do want you to have the Christmas present I got you, so I will send it to you... I won't bother you again, but I will miss you. x.

The text she sent one and a half hours previously had asked:

Are we still friends?

Her mind must have been racing, raging even!

Obviously I had not replied. I was blissfully unaware of her state of mind, busy indulging myself at my *Mum's* jamboree without a mobile phone mast in sight…

11.45, Monday evening, she texted me again. Not knowing how to make me respond to her essays, she sent another, you guessed it, essay:

Hi. It's going to cost a small fortune to post your Xmas present so I will come over sometime this week and leave it on your doorstep. I'll put them in a bin liner to disguise them so could you keep a look out. Hope you are well and now getting a better night's sleep now the lodgers have left. x.

She must have been quite crazy to want to leave presents in bin liners! And near a pavement on a council estate! Anyway, not wishing to engage in late night 'mobile ping pong' I decided not to respond: the prospect of a peaceful night's sleep in the comfort of my own bed being far more appealing.

But *Julie*, ever tenacious, wasn't about to give up any time soon… Bleep, bleep… First thing on Tuesday morning I was woken by the dreaded sound of yet more text alerts. To put it mildly, the regular intrusions were becoming irritating. Besides, our relationship was as much use as badly burnt toast anyhow. *'Bird food…'* Having finally rid my head of noisy lodgers, the vacuous shrill of technology was now taking over my life, creating a breeding ground for that evil virus insomnia to flourish once again… Around an hour later I decided to prepare myself. I took a long deep breath, rolled my shoulders to calm my nerves, then exhaled in as measured and even a manner as I could muster… Finally, I opened my inbox and began to read *Julie's* latest *communiqué*:

I can't keep sending these on the edge texts. Even I know when I should stop!

However, unwilling to comply with her own advice, she went on:

Are you ignoring me cos you are really pissed off, because it's fun or because you genuinely want me to fuck off now? I want to call you but have the distinct feeling you won't speak to me either. I really get that you hate me at the moment, but at least tell me to fuck off cos then you can be rid of me and this madness! I promise I won't text again if you have had enough but at the moment I am a bit unclear. Let me know, please.

Well, it would have been cowardly, and rather churlish, not to reply. She probably had 'Repetitive Strain Injury' by now and her phone memory must have been totally overloaded, to the point of meltdown..! So, after pondering long and hard, incessantly weighing up my options, changing my fragile and muddied mind on numerous occasions, repeatedly to-ing and fro-ing, and generally not knowing how to respond, I finally texted back a considered answer: *Fuck off...*

Finito

Acknowledgements

I'd like to thank my editor, Rob Matthews, for coming to terms with my incessant use of italics, and for helping me with my spelling and grammar, a proverbial problem for a self-diagnosed mild dyslexic. Many thanks are also due to my family, friends, and this amazing world we live in: a place of conflict, contrast, and wonderment. Where mood, sentiment, and reality are often pulling us in immeasurable directions, until that day when the peace we all seek becomes our paradigm. Finally, I'd like to thank my fellow countrymen and women, especially Ancient Britons, for their inordinate wit, fortitude and tolerance; such awe-inspiring qualities unrivalled anywhere in the modern world…

Ci
CLEMENT IVAN

Empires fall through complacency
nations are destroyed by
Political Correctness

Sometimes one's compelled to withdraw
to protect one's sanity

Kjvf657t8hnhj<u>bkm</u>;blfmnuey349powdkmcnhfvyghytrjfdmcbvghjrifdclc,mvnbvfc
klb vjmc, bnf;sd vbt;fld vjhewoihfvn vjvNJAIJVN BFGNDVJ CVLB,

vamoS   piku   ??JoSepHInetuesou<u>main</u>Te*nant*mAcherIe??

Colbourne Miller   ####'P-

clem*enti*van.com   /., licKylIcK*ydi*czzzzopi*tt*YdO<u>w</u>nstAIrsiGo#'

colbournemillercolbournemillercolbournemiller

Creaking Floorboards   *'Clement Ivan'*
                                      why*ce*stcoMmeca
Creaking **Floorboards**   dieuestou
li*B*e<u>rti</u>Ne##.sL*4*ghEaptRouserunzipPe*rp*Ervyluverrr/.,49rjfn

colbournemiller.com /clementivan.com

              ;'.*C*Arpe#.,'*uK*,:Ip/?#[19j..
      GISS#*#OH*#FisT#5
Wishyouwerehere   koccffo!   creak**ingfloo**rboards

'Clement Ivan Publishing'   98776gnjmkhgfxyhhccjnkljbvcgvbnknvdfghjk

colbournemiller.com

Creaking Floorboards........   <u>Colbourne Miller</u>

   CUMbYOPLopo<u>WILL</u>Upl*a*Y#/??#'[mOnpays

*cUnei*FOrmc*u*Ddle*S*##*!*   ***Clement Ivan Publishing***
                tou./Jo/.u.,r.;s"""mOn.,4 *dr*oit

Clementivan.com

<u>Creaking Floorboards by Colbourne Miller</u>

THE STORY OF IAN WILLS
CONTINUES WITH THE
SECOND INSTALLMENT
OF THE TRILOGY:

Escape to the Philippines

Anticipated early 2016
colbournemiller.com